Sexual Strategy

The train carriage began to fill up with passengers as Heleyna continued to chat with Mr Handsome – the stranger she'd admired from afar for some time. She dropped her eyes to his lap. He already had an appetite for her, because his long dick was pushing urgently against the fly of his suit trousers. As she lifted her eyes back up to his face he winked confidently at her, trying to hide the fact that he was being dominated and eaten alive by this gorgeous wench.

Now feeling incredibly hot, Heleyna removed her jacket and laid it across her knee, tantalisingly concealing her shapely thigh. The train began its jolting journey out of the station as Mr Handsome began his seduction.

Sexual Strategy
Felice de Vere

BLACK LACE

Black Lace books contain sexual fantasies.
In real life, always practise safe sex.

First published in 2003 by
Black Lace
Thames Wharf Studios
Rainville Road
London W6 9HA

Design by Smith & Gilmour, London
Printed and bound by Mackays of Chatham PLC

ISBN 0 352 33843 1

1

Heleyna sat at her desk, thinking how much she loved sex. Yet again she was lost in one of her fantasies – fantasies that would have extinguished the respectable suburban way in which she was viewed. Her nipples were painfully hard, her sex was gloriously wet, and her hands were poised over her keyboard – the magnetic attraction that draws hand to pussy gradually increasing and strengthening. To the outside world she would have appeared deep in thought, concentrating on her business report, the only visible change being the sudden indulgent flush to her cheeks and glossed lips; and, for those who were naughty enough to look, her protruding, expectant nipples poking through her crisp white shirt. A passing feeling of guilt spread over her. She should have been concentrating on her report, but she knew exactly what she would much rather be doing.

Hmmm, Troy, you naughty boy, she thought wickedly to herself. You really are the best. Just thinking about him made her wet: the tip of his dick; the texture of his buttocks; the softness and smoothness of those delicious orbs the split second before he rushed headlong into her; his soft downy hair and relaxed muscles cupped in her desperate hands.

Crash, bang! Left feeling as frustrated as hell, she was awoken from her fantasy by a loud noise that came, without warning, from further down her corridor. It was unusual to hear other people in her office at this time of night. These days she was working later, beavering away like a sad lost soul with nothing better to fill her time, and tonight was no exception. She never quite understood why she put so much into her job. She usually found herself going for promotions, because that is what you did, wasn't it? She was due to present a report to the senior management team the following day that might end in a promotion for her. On those days when she wanted a safe life this was something she believed she desired. She knew she was cut out for more than the office life, though; in fact, she was capable of achieving whatever she felt truly passionate about if she put her mind to it.

She made her way out of her executive office, heels tip-tapping across the varnished wooden floor. Not noticing the plush designs around her or the respectable photograph on her desk of her partner, Troy, dressed in designer suit and tie, she prayed she was not about to encounter something she would rather not get involved in.

Heleyna removed her three-inch-heeled shoes, then propelled herself towards the muffled sound, which had become a persistent rustle. She came to a standstill. She listened, her head cocked to one side, and tried not to breathe too deeply, for fear of being caught. As she stood, not knowing quite what to expect next, she heard low stifled groans from the darkened office just ahead of her. Heart racing, she walked forward in her stock-inged feet towards the door, her impulsive bravery receding somewhat as she neared the source. As she peered through the look-if-you-dare crack in the door-way and into the blackness of the room, she could just make out two men, silhouetted. The moon made a searchlight between the cracks in the blind and confu-sion and fear evolved into feelings of confident curios-ity, which reignited her already aroused body.

Dropping soundlessly to her knees, she watched the

two men, their embraces becoming more passionate. The smell of sex oozed through the room, reaching her in musky waves. She imagined the detail of their velvety cocks, the tightness of their big, heavy balls, and their lustful expressions. Gay sex was happening in the office! She was a naughty voyeur, and she willed the moon to be at its fullest on this wonderfully exceptional evening. The men's clothes lay randomly across the floor, and their masculine physiques were outlined in front of her. Her heart continued to race, but now for a very different and much more pleasurable reason. Aren't I a lucky bitch, she thought, pleased that hard work had brought with it such unexpected delights.

Watching intently as they touched and caressed each other, their gentleness surprised her. The taller, stockier man tenderly bit his partner's torso as he lowered himself to his knees. The other tensed his muscles and stood to attention at the nearness of the mouth, the breath, the tongue. The kneeling man stroked his own cock as he rhythmically caressed his partner with mouth and free hand. To her ever-growing delight, the clouds separated as though forced apart by the moon so that she could enjoy the same visual pleasures. Heleyna could just make out the flicking and lapping of one guy's tongue over the huge dick in front of him. She was quivering now, her skin tingling. She pounced on her waiting pussy, still hot from her previous fantasies, rubbing her suit trousers up against her protruding rigid clit and forcing her fingers harder against herself. More dry cleaning, she giggled to herself, not giving a damn. Slowly, yet eagerly, she brought herself towards the orgasm she'd been craving for what seemed an eternity. She was wetter than she could ever remember and rubbing herself firmly through her pants.

Still in their same intimate position, the men came together, both crying out uncontrollably, completely uninhibited in their pleasure. The man on his knees turned his face towards the door and slumped forward in postorgasmic bliss. Heleyna's pleasure came to yet another frustratingly premature halt, her own crescendo ceasing as the face in front of her revealed itself. She quickly got to her feet, her body still hot with lust.

Leaving the bright colours and sleek décor of the office block as quickly and quietly as she knew how, she made her way outside and hailed a cab, relishing her voyeuristic pleasure. The pleasant chill of spring night air grasped the wetness between her legs, reminding her how horny she was. How was she ever going to face her boss in the morning?

The cab ride home was a half-hour journey, and the luxury of being driven home late these days should have been costing Heleyna an arm and a leg. Actually, much of the money spent on late-night cabs came out of her boss's budget. He was invariably generous when it came to Heleyna, and, though not usually prone to acts of greed, she nearly always took advantage of it. Public transport was a real bore late at night. The frustrating journey of lights which flashed at her in the darkness through the window of the train spoke to her of happy middle-class families living their oh-so-sweet lives. The opportunity to forego that experience was too great for her to refuse. Not that she had anything against such people. But the hypocrisy of their existence was one thing that frustrated her. What was so special about being respectable? What was wrong with letting the world know what you really were – in her case, an attached woman who also had a thing for a bit of whipping and smacking and degradation on the side?

Tonight the driver was deep in his own thoughts, giving Heleyna the opportunity she needed to savour the naughtiness of her feelings. She luxuriated in fantasising about what she had just witnessed, and about men and their physiques, particularly their arses. She loved those round firm ones that seemed to call out her name, to invite her to look; the way the trousers accentuated the separateness of the warm, firm, smooth peachy spheres. She lived for fantasy, even when getting as much sex as she could manage. But to enjoy being a voyeur was more than that: it was a drug, it was intoxication, it was hedonism personified. God, I'm such a dirty little bitch, she chuckled to herself. The driver cast an insipid glance at her in his rear-view mirror before returning to his own contemplation.

At 28, Heleyna knew she had not yet reached her sexual peak. All she could do was take pleasure in the fact that things could only get better. She knew what lust was; the kind of lust that sends you into a delirious frenzy, that takes over your every thought, that turns you into a tingling, spellbound, irrational being.

Casting a disinterested glance at the outside world, she realised she was nearly home. The taxi came to a standstill, the driver looking at her as gormlessly as before. He spoke to her in his thick Yorkshire accent. She paid him, treating him with the same disinterest he had granted her, and walked towards the front door of the building in Horsforth, in which she had a first-floor flat. Her heels echoed in the darkness of the streets around her.

It was now 10.30 p.m. Heleyna chucked a ready meal in the microwave, a symbol of what her life had become, and set to work on finishing her presentation, eating as she went. Concentration was still hard as she remembered her boss, Ted Jones. Sitting at her glass-topped kitchen table, laptop open, she thought about his wife and wondered if she knew about his infidelity and his obvious desire for men.

Desperately trying to keep her mind on business and her future promotion, she was interrupted by the phone. Three rings was all she had before it clicked into answer-machine mode. She convinced herself to pick it up at the end of the third.

'Hello?'

'Hi, gorgeous!' It was Troy. 'Finally managed to get hold of you. How's it going?'

'I'm still working on this bloody report,' she complained. 'I just can't remain focused. Don't know why I bother sometimes. I'm sure there must be more to life.'

'Sounds like you need a weekend of excess, away from the city,' replied Troy. 'A weekend of good food, plenty of drink and, of course, plenty of shagging should do the trick. I'll organise something for this weekend.'

'Sounds good to me.' Heleyna loved those fuck-till-you-drop weekends with Troy, when she had nothing more complex to think about than the next meal or, more importantly, the next round of hanky-panky. The conversation was short and sweet. Troy didn't seem to mind. 'I'd better go, still got a bit more work to do.'

'Good luck for tomorrow. I'll let you know what I've organised for the weekend. See you soon. Can't wait to see that rounded arse of yours.'

Heleyna grinned. 'Bye, Troy. Can't wait to see yours either. Sleep tight.'

Heleyna worked on into the night. When she finally did go to bed, her last thought before falling into a stressful sleep of anxiety dreams was of Ted, the man she saw every day. The man who'd made her clitoris throb, her lips swell, who filled her mind with pure filth, who had restored her delight in voyeurism. The need for sleep stronger than her arousal, she disappeared into a world of wild dreams. Her face now make-up free, with her long curly dark-brown hair tied back, she looked innocent – almost respectable – as she surrendered to the void.

Beep, beep, beep, beep... 'Oh, shit!' Heleyna hit her alarm. She leaped out of bed, exhausted from the previous day's tribulations, and dressed herself quickly in a navy blazer and knee-length matching skirt. She didn't have time for a shower, just a quick wash. Too much to do, too little time. Today was to be an important day for her career, a day when she had to concentrate on her future.

Before going out the front door, she peered into the full-length hallway mirror. She looked professional in her navy suit and low court shoes, with her hair tied in a bun. Her outfit was a calculated choice. Voluptuous curves and long brown curly hair did nothing to help her to be taken seriously, and she didn't want any of those male managers, or female, for that matter, taking their minds off her proposal. She needed to look, dare she say it, respectable – a reputable businesswoman.

At school it had always concerned her that she wasn't thin, the kind of thin that girls crave at that age – all bones and sharp angles. These days she'd learnt to enjoy her body: her curvaceous arse, her rounded breasts, her small waist. She was perfectly rounded in all the right places. However, today she certainly didn't want anybody else enjoying it. Today she was Heleyna Lane, the professional careerist in search of a promotion. She was full of confidence and, she hoped, good sound innovative business advice that would show the way for SPM Ltd to exceed its already adventurous strategic goals. She loved goals, the thrill of the chase, the long-term planning and action required to achieve them.

Rummaging for her keys on the hallway table, she remembered one important aspect of her presentation – Ted Jones. How was she going to maintain her cool image in front of him after last night, after her wicked intense arousal at witnessing his infidelity?

She hopped onto the train heading for Leeds Central, for once managing to secure a seat. The train was full. People around her had their heads buried in newspapers, reports and books. A smart-looking woman in her forties read intently, a permanent wry smile across her face. Heleyna's eye flicked to the cover of the book; she couldn't quite make out the title, but, remembering the cover design immediately, she now recognised the smile as one of lust, not joy.

As her mind drifted from her usual people-watching routine, Ted appeared, the vision in her mind becoming more and more vivid. Watching, observing, peeping, her body began that breathtaking journey to arousal, a delicious ache inside her, and an increasing moistness between her legs. The handsome suited man opposite watched her changing expression and smiled knowingly. Unusually coy, Heleyna looked away, keeping her gaze firmly directed out of the window. Today no anger welled up at the suburban sprawl, the neat washing lines in back gardens, the rows upon rows of terraces with quaint hanging baskets and pansy-filled pots, and the conscientious housewives at home rammed up against their washing machines, legs apart with the postman or builder deep inside them.

She didn't even see the passing scenery. Her mind was fixed firmly on other unmentionable things, her knickers damp, her pussy hungry. How could she do a serious presentation when all she really wanted was to go home, pull out her favourite all-singing all-dancing dildo and satisfy herself? She knew she was sex-obsessed at the moment and she put it down to her mid-cycle hormones – the ones that made men turn their heads at her in the street, and that made her feel positively and incredibly sexy.

Her mobile rang as the train entered the flurry of Leeds station. It was Troy wishing her luck, reminding her of his growing excitement and anticipation of the upcoming weekend. She lied to Troy, told him she was confident about the day ahead, while in reality, and for the first time in years, there was an element of doubt. How the hell was she going to remain focused with Ted sat there watching her, when all she could think about was the way he gave head, the way he played with himself so delightfully? She was going to have to make sure her boss sat in a position where she couldn't look in his eyes or gaze at his body. It was the only way she was ever going to remain level-headed.

As she stepped off the train, the handsome suited man made eye contact one more time, flashed a wicked grin, and carried on his journey. As he walked, Heleyna glanced down at his crotch (something she loved doing) and noticed that the wickedness he had portrayed in his face was evident elsewhere too. It made her feel really good knowing that she was the cause of his bulging packet. It meant that she looked hot even when she tried not to.

Despite earlier concerns, Heleyna's presentation was as professional and innovative as ever. Fortunately, Ted had sat in the back corner away from her immediate line of vision. She talked through the aims and objectives and her short, medium and long-term strategies. She was damn good. When she offered questions at the end, she knew her hard work and dedication had paid off. The response from John, the MD, and the senior team was full of enthusiasm and delight at her vision for the future. Today, with the hero's welcome that was being bestowed upon her, she was pleased with her commitment to a middle-class existence. Tomorrow would be different, no doubt.

Ted looked at her. Obviously enjoying the prestige Heleyna had given to his department, he smiled and winked. She forced herself to look at him, managing a false clumsy smile in return. He ambled over as she packed up her laptop and data show. She'd been dreading this moment all morning.

'Well done, Heleyna. You were simply superb as usual. What would I do without you on my team? Mind you, after a performance like that I'll probably be working for you before too long.'

Looking up from under her eyelashes, Heleyna saw him in a new light. Before today he'd always been her boss and nothing more, but today he was most definitely sexual. She recalled the rugby-player physique that was now beneath his smart wool suit, his big blue eyes and cheeky grin. She remembered his solid spurting cock from the night before, the way he had created a longing in her that desperately needed releasing. Today Ted was a different person from the man she'd last said goodbye to.

'Thanks for the confidence in me, Ted,' she replied, awkwardly.

'How about a light, but very liquid lunch as a big thank you?' he suggested. 'I'll give you the afternoon off as a small token of my appreciation for all the long hours you've been doing recently.'

Heleyna thanked him profusely, but with slight paranoia rising within her over his last remark. She knew she couldn't get out of lunch. To turn him down would have been completely out of character.

As colleagues go they had a good relationship. They'd moved past the mere-working-acquaintance stage to a more relaxed yet professional friendship. She would just have to carry on as normal and hope he didn't notice her less-than-usual confidence when she spoke to him.

They headed for the Italian bistro on The Headrow

that they, along with many other colleagues, had been to many times before for working lunches and dinners. It was a sure sign that times were good for SPM Ltd. The owner, Geoff, welcomed them warmly, speaking to them in his predictably familiar way.

Heleyna was starving, her normal reaction after a big event. She ordered more than the light lunch Ted had offered.

'Glad the bill's going on expenses,' Ted teased. 'Why don't we push the boat out even further and get a celebratory bottle of champagne. I'm sure I can justify the extra expense on someone as valuable to the business as you.'

'Sounds like a great idea,' said Heleyna, the hedonist in her answering before she thought rationally. Then she thought about what would happen. 'No doubt my afternoon at home will be spent in a tipsy state on the sofa. I suppose I should stay sober and go to the gym, really ... Oh, what the hell, you have to relax sometimes, don't you!' Heleyna's hands flew avidly as she spoke.

A considerable amount of champagne was consumed ahead of the starter, and professionalism started to slip. Shoptalk diminished and intimate conversation began to flow. After a couple of glasses, Heleyna simply didn't give a damn about the night before. Leaning forward to talk to Ted she noted the twinkle in his eye and his cheeky-chappy good looks. She knew it was happening, but before too long alcohol meant she didn't really care what was going to happen. Lusting after her boss suddenly seemed a very good idea. A lightning bolt of pent-up frustration shot through her.

Excusing herself, and full of bubbling champagne, Heleyna attempted a businesslike walk to the toilet. In reality it was more like a swagger.

* * *

Ted, now left on his own, started to daydream. His mind drifted to the Huxley Club, the private club he and many of his friends and colleagues were members of. He had never considered inviting Heleyna to join before now, always deciding that perhaps she was a little fastidious. Perhaps now was the time? His idea of learning more about the usually ever-professional Heleyna had certainly been an eye-opener.

Heleyna could almost taste the musky aroma of sex emanating from her ungratified pussy as she stood in the privacy of the cubicle, surveying her reflection in the mirror. For a moment she didn't move. She was deep in thought, alcohol slowing down her brain. Staring into the mirror, she saw a glazed look appear over her face. The taste in her mouth spread softly, evolving into a sensation that made its way past her peachy lips, down her flushed neck and towards her hardening nipples. As it grasped her rounded soft stomach somewhere beneath her belly button, she opened her jacket and gazed at her breasts. Hidden beneath a layer of Lycra, they were cupped gently inside her white, lacy bra. She noticed the curve of her hips, and felt the wetness between her legs reaching her knickers once more. She was ready to explode. She needed immediate release.

She removed her panties and pushed her hand between her legs in sheer desperation, watching every move in the mirror in front of her. In her mind she was Heleyna, masturbation porn queen, playing up to the audience, to the security camera she imagined behind the glass. Almost coming in seconds, she forced herself to delay the inevitable, and explored her body: nipples alert, breasts swollen and heaving rhythmically, skirt hitched around firm thighs and resting on the curve between hip and waist. Her long, wet fingers were lost within her. Her curly dark hair masked the pinkness of her swollen lips. Her clit stood erect like a mini volcano planted in the midst of forest-covered flatlands. She caressed its visible tip with the gentlest of sweeps, and havoc hit her body. With her sex pulsating violently she slumped into a crouching position, swiftly reaching for the compact mirror she kept in her sleek leather brief-case. She flipped it open and watched the final spasms reflected between her legs – her dark secret hole pulsing in its final steps toward relaxation.

Flushed and tiddly, yet decidedly more relaxed, she returned to the table hoping that she would now feel a little less horny as she sat opposite her boss across the dinner table.

The mood appeared to have changed when she returned and Ted looked deep in contemplation. Heleyna filled their glasses with the remains of the champagne, twiddled her white paper napkin, and attempted to get the conversation flowing once more. Trying desperately not to shovel spinach and ricotta ravioli into her famished body, she asked Ted about his wife. His reply was one of disinterest.

Then, without warning, his face lifted and he leaned across the gingham-covered table towards her as though about to whisper the secret of a lifetime. After-shave wafted round her, pricking up her senses. Flashes of his naked physique whizzed through her dirty little mind, the nearness of him titillating her sensitive skin.

'Have you ever thought of joining a club? You know, one where you can socialise with like-minded people?' Ted asked, his speech ever-so-slightly slurred.

'Never really thought about it, to be honest. Why?' Disappointment, with a touch of relief, trespassed into the horny zone of her mind. In her sober condition she would never have allowed herself to get so intimate with a work colleague. She had never ever mixed the two: lust and her professional life.

'They can be such good fun, you know,' he said. His face was still poised close to Heleyna's.

'Whenever I think of clubs I always think of the WI or working men's clubs. Not really my scene,' Heleyna replied. Her right hand gave a dismissive wave as she answered.

'No, I'm talking parties, fun, people who enjoy the good times. People who get together to explore some of the more interesting things in life,' Ted corrected.

'What like?' She feigned interest. She'd never considered Ted a club man before. Perhaps a rugby club, but not one that focused on natural history, physics or outer space. That was what he was talking about, wasn't it? Anyhow, it just really wasn't her thing.

'You know, just things you wouldn't normally explore in day-to-day life.' He couldn't have been any more suggestive if he'd tried, but the tipsy Heleyna wasn't picking up on his cues.

'Obviously not your cup of tea, eh? So, tell me more about your planned weekend away.'

Conversation continued in this vein until lunch had finished and espressos arrived.

Heleyna began to yawn and tried unsuccessfully to stifle it.

Ted looked over at her. 'I think you'd better go home. I'll get a taxi ordered for you – you're in no fit state to go on the train. You'll probably fall into a drunken stupor and wake up miles from your station with dribble on your shoulder!' He laughed loudly at the suggestion of his businesslike colleague being in such a state. 'Waiter, can you phone for a taxi please?'

The waiter looked at Ted in disgust but walked off and did his job.

'No doubt you worked all night last night in preparation for today, eh?'

'I was in the office until about 10 p.m.,' Heleyna replied, unaware of what she'd just admitted. In her tipsy-yet-mellow state she didn't notice Ted stop and look across at her, satisfaction showing in his face.

The waiter approached. There was a rank of taxis outside waiting for business on the off chance, so there was no delay.

'Thanks for lunch, Ted. Look forward to seeing you tomorrow,' said Heleyna. 'When will I know if I've been successful with the promotion?'

'Definitely by the end of tomorrow. I'll let you know as soon as the final decision is made. I tell you what, though. If you don't get this, I'll eat my bloody hat!' he laughed.

'I'll hold you to that. See you, and thanks again.' Heleyna departed the restaurant, leaving Ted to pay.

Ted watched her walk out, her bottom swaying gently from side to side beneath her very sensible suit. She really is a very fine-looking woman, he thought.

As Ted ambled home his thoughts remained on Heleyna. Now he definitely knew it was her in the office last night, and this further confirmed that she was ready. But perhaps he needed to test her a couple more times. She had always seemed pretty clean-living before: committed to her job; photograph of the boyfriend on her desk; always dressed in businesslike clothes hiding her obviously desirable body. He also needed to speak with his wife in more detail and find out what she had seen and heard. How he loved this part! The anticipation of introducing her to Huxley was almost too much. Fuck, he just couldn't wait! But the time had to be right with new recruits or things could go seriously pear-shaped.

The cab reached his large Alwoodley house, and he wandered contentedly up the path. Neat velvet-like grass on either side banked up to borders full to overflowing with shrubs and flowers planted lovingly by their ever-faithful gardener. Lavender hit his nostrils as his key rattled in the front door, trying to find its way with a less-than-precise hand to guide it. He fell over the large terracotta pot as he entered the hallway, undignified, stumbling, laughing. He was lucky this time. He just missed the banister. His head was inches from the sharp edge he had hit on more than one occasion when returning home in the early hours of the morning.

'Hi, Ted! You're early.'

It was Jacinta, his wife, who worked part time just to keep her brain ticking over. The rest of her time was spent in voluntary work or being domesticated. Ted walked up to her and planted a kiss on her slender neck.

'Hello, love. I'm a bit tiddly'

'Never!' Sarcasm. She'd smelt the alcohol as he entered the kitchen, where she stood arranging freshly cut flowers from their large back garden.

'I'm going for a sleep.' Ted dragged himself through to the lounge, plonked himself on the sofa, just remembering to remove his shoes before they hit the cream covers, and was away.

Dreaming of swimming in ice-cold water he awoke, his tongue crispy dry. Jacinta had already left a glass of iced water on the coffee table, neatly placed on a china coaster. Preparing dinner, Jacinta heard his movements and came to investigate what kind of state her wonderfully excessive husband was in.

'So then, where have you been this lunchtime?' It was pleasant conversation, not accusatory.

'Took Heleyna for lunch – to say thanks for her hard work.' Now seated, his head was in his hands, his voice directed at the polished floorboards.

'Did you get any gossip? Did our little plan to assess Ms Lane work?'

He took another swig of water. 'Well, interestingly, she was at work until 10 p.m. last night.'

'I knew it. I bloody well knew it. I knew it was her trousers, her hand, her hair.'

'I thought you were watching me as you sat in the corner of the office,' he guffawed.

'I am a woman, you know. It is possible to do two things at once.'

'So then, what do you reckon? Think we should invite her along to Huxley?' Ted was keen.

'I still think it's too soon, you know. Heleyna's always been such a straight-laced businesswoman, never given any inkling before about a less conservative side. I reckon we should get to know her a bit more. Does she have a partner?'

'Yes – Troy – photo of him on her desk. Handsome chap.'

'Handsome – excellent! Well then, we'll invite them over to dinner one night.'

She returned to the kitchen, Ted following behind her. Despite his ample lunch, he was eager to taste what was causing the rich aroma emanating from the oil-fired Aga.

Heleyna was finally home, drunk and exhausted. She'd fallen asleep in the cab, not waking until the driver brought it to an abrupt standstill outside her Horsforth flat. Feeling fuzzy, but awake, she noticed the patch of dribble on her shoulder that Ted had forecast. Desperately trying to wipe it away, she paid, retrieved her receipt, and rushed inside with amazing speed for more rest.

She undressed. Leaving her clothes in a heap on the floor she clambered into bed, snuggling under her simple cream duvet, and thought about her lunchtime conversation with Ted. But before long her body began to drift, floating into the peacefulness of alcohol-induced sleep. Unannounced, and like the scene from Frankenstein when the monster sits up for the first time, Heleyna shot bolt upright and shouted, her voice reverberating round her bedroom, 'Oh, my God!' Her heart was in her mouth. 'Why the hell did I say that?' she cursed. 'What a complete and utter idiot. He's going to know I was in the office last night!' Confusion addled her thoughts. She couldn't process a good enough conclusion to this problem. In the end she decided that if she ignored it hard enough, either it would go away or Ted wouldn't put two and two together. It's amazing how wrong a bright woman, trying to rationalise an issue under the influence of alcohol, can be. Lucky really that her thought processes at work were always logical and objective or she'd still be doing the photocopying for every Tom, Dick or Harry that called upon her.

Heleyna didn't wake until the morning, raised from her much-needed rest by her ever-faithful alarm. She headed into work, butterflies attacking her in waves. She saw the handsome, suited man on the train again; he'd become Mr Handsome in her fantasies. This time she smiled and nodded, then stuck her nose in the *Yorkshire Post* to catch up on the news. She needed to keep the feelings from creeping in, the dread of seeing Ted and nerves at hearing about her promotion. The newspaper did the trick. As it turned out, Ted wasn't in the office that day, and she was able to keep her head down and get on with outstanding admin. So much for hearing about the job by the end of the day.

It was Thursday night. Heleyna headed to Troy's, a new estate home on the edges of Alwoodley. She didn't fancy going home to her lonely flat tonight. She needed companionship, someone to share her day with.

She arrived at Troy's and let herself in. Walking into the warmth of the hallway she glanced expectantly up the stairs towards the bedroom then removed her wool coat and unfeasibly high shoes. She thought about the hours of pleasure they'd had in his luxurious king-size bed: ruining his Egyptian cotton sheets with pints of strawberry-flavoured massage oil; attaching each other to the wrought-iron bed head with the furry handcuffs she'd purchased at the last sex-toy party she'd had with a group of girlfriends; and watching each other's movements in the full-length pine mirror in the corner of the room.

'Hello, anybody home?' she called. Silence. Her memories continued, and flashes of the first time she met Troy took shape.

She'd been on holiday in Gran Canaria with Chloe, one of her favourite people in the world. It was one of those last-minute bucket holiday deals that she normally took each winter. They were at a cocktail party in a smart hotel. She couldn't quite remember the name, but she recalled vividly the U-shaped drive replete with fast cars parked up for the night. She had clambered out of the cab at the ostentatious entranceway, the beefy middle-aged red-suited doorman trying desperately not to stare as she spread her legs while exiting the cab, flashing a glimpse of scrumptious upper thigh.

They had teetered into the reception area, following the other smartly dressed twenty- and thirty-some-things past the central water feature and on into the function room. Heleyna looked towards Chloe, who looked stunning with her blonde hair swept up off her face, unveiling slim neck and petite creamy shoulders. Chloe grinned, reddened lips parting to show perfect teeth. She was dressed in a straight, simple, red crushed-velvet gown that brushed the floor with each step, giving a glimpse of delicate thigh at the parting of the sweet and savoury split.

Heleyna knew she too looked her best. Her diffuser-dried locks rested on her shoulders and flowed behind her, just coating her bare upper back. Enveloped in tight emerald silk, every curve was out on display, her peachy arse pert with each step, her small waist creating a gentle sway of the hips. They meant business.

Not surprisingly, male attention was not hard to get. Troy was on the scene within minutes. Sipping marga-ritas, conversation between them was open. There was nothing shy about this man. His opening gambit was bolder than anything she'd ever known.

'Fuck, you're so sexy!' he was whispering in Heleyna's ear, the warmth of his breath hitting her ever-sensitive neck. 'I can almost taste you already.'

His eyes locked onto hers. Her body was alive, her nerve endings prepared for his large hands.

'I have to touch you, touch your pussy. I want to bury my face in you, eat you, enter you.'

She played the innocent virgin, a farcical role consid-ering her obviously and outwardly sexual nature. 'And why would I let you do that?'

'Because you know you want me. I can sense it. You're desperate to get your hands around my cock. Look, look at it, it's ready for you.'

They were oblivious to their surroundings. Heleyna cast her eyes due south. There was no way she would ever refuse such a thing, especially when it was attached to such a divine specimen.

Chloe walked towards them. She saw the mounting attraction and wanted to be part of it.

'Hello, I'm Chloe.' She offered a cool hand to Troy and smiled a cheeky grin.

He responded, noticing pearly thigh. Heleyna watched them, excitement encircling her.

'Hello, Chloe, I'm Troy. I was just explaining to your friend Heleyna here how much I'm desperate to fuck her. Perhaps you can convince her I am a man of my word.'

Chloe turned and smiled at Heleyna. 'Heleyna, he is a man of his word. You should enjoy him tonight.'

'Perhaps we can both enjoy him tonight.' It was a statement, not a question. Heleyna didn't want any more games: if release didn't come soon she feared frustration would set in. Troy turned without a word and walked away from them.

She followed the bronzed brunette, watching his delicious cheeks disappear from sight into a side room. Shuffling behind her was a glowing Chloe, her breath deeper and faster than before. As they entered the room he already stood erect. His clothes were on the floor. She had subsequently came to love that about Troy – his unswerving confidence that women wanted to fuck him.

'Come and watch.' Heleyna encouraged Chloe as she held his dick in her hand, massaging it gently, watching the end redden and swell quickly.

Chloe twittered an appreciative giggle. Heleyna could understand why. He had a huge girth. Chloe then grew in confidence. She took hold of him and they both caressed him – one hand at the base, one at the tip. Heleyna listened to his uncontrollable heartbeat, knowing they were hitting the right spot. He was close to ejaculating. She didn't want him to do it there. She wanted to feel him inside of her.

They walked over to the wooden bench at the side of the stark room, but much to her dismay he grabbed Chloe, forced up her red dress, ripped off her tiny panties and spread her legs. That was the first time Heleyna had seen pussy. Much to her delight and fear she liked it, no, craved it.

'Sit next to her and take your knickers off,' he'd ordered her cheekily.

Heleyna had readily and quickly agreed, then watched as he entered Chloe forcefully, her friend's face a mixture of delight and surprise at the sheer size of him. Heleyna enjoyed her facial responses – it drove her wild. After a few strong slow thrusts he withdrew, his exquisite frame zoning in on Heleyna. She didn't move, not even an inch. Her eyes locked on to his ever-tempting cock. Then he gave her what she craved. She enjoyed him, the sensation of his broad prick entering her slowly at first, then aggressively, animalistically. She enjoyed Chloe being there. She amused herself watching Chloe; watching Chloe watching them.

Unexpectedly, and in one swift action, he pushed Heleyna onto all fours on the carpeted floor, then guided her hand against her wetness. She looked like a porn model with her bottom in the air, cheeks apart, back arched, swollen cunt accessible to his cock. Guessing this meant he wanted her to play with herself, she readily obliged. Like a river after a storm has passed through, the addictive pleasure flowed.

Deep in self-indulgence, Heleyna felt Chloe lower herself onto her back, face down. She could feel her tender rounded breasts against her back, and they felt so good.

'Now I have four holes to choose from.' Troy laughed.

He entered Chloe again, and she gasped and grabbed Heleyna's generous tits for support as he rammed her body up and down Heleyna's back. Beneath her, Heleyna's thoughts had plummeted between her legs.

Just when Heleyna thought that was her lot, he withdrew from Chloe and nudged his way into her patient, desperate sex. She was on the precipice, so ready to take that step into oblivion. And he knew it.

'You finish yourself off, young lady.'

Unfortunately for Heleyna, that comment was directed at her.

So, that was the scene. Heleyna on all fours caressing herself as though there was no tomorrow. Chloe lying face down on Heleyna's back, her beautiful breasts rubbing her, pleasuring her. Her hands, in desperation, clamped around Heleyna's tits, painfully exciting her firm nipples. Troy, one hand on Chloe's waist and the other on her clit, his dick powerful in her pussy.

Before too long they were collapsed on the floor, hot, sweaty, pulsating. Heleyna felt Chloe against her bottom, the sensation only accentuating her concluding pleasure.

Since that frisky day, Heleyna had never looked back. As far as she was concerned, she'd met her match.

She poured herself a glass of chilled New Zealand Sauvignon Blanc from the fridge and headed for the stairs, noticing the smell of his aftershave as she passed his coat hanging from the end of the banister. Time for a relaxing bath before lover boy gets home, she thought. Normally preferring the English country cottage, when it came to modern luxuries such as a spa bath she couldn't fault a new home.

Lying back in the tub, congratulating herself on being such a star at work, she sipped her wine and cursed the fact she'd not brought the rest of the bottle with her. The warmth of the water and lavender aroma of the bath oil encased her in a world of escapism, of limitless thoughts and joyous sensations.

The door went. It was Troy. She listened to his resounding footsteps hitting every other stair on his way up to her. Opening one eye, she watched him enter the room, fighting his way through the steam like a contestant on *Stars in Their Eyes*.

'And who are you tonight, Troy?'

'Tonight, Heleyna, I am Tom Jones.'

'Tom Jones? For God's sake, you could have picked someone younger!' She was laughing, both eyes now open.

He sat on the edge of the bath, his suit jacket and tie already off, and admired her. 'So, tell me about today. Anything exciting to tell me, anything to celebrate?'

'I got it, I bloody well got it. You're now looking at the project manager leading the proclaim project for SPM Ltd. Fuck, it's brilliant.'

'I didn't doubt you for one minute, my young lady. You're a bloody star. I'll be able to retire soon, become your house slave! So, lots to celebrate this weekend then?'

'I won't be working for Ted any longer either. He's now my equal – how's that for size? Can't wait for the weekend. Tomorrow's going to drag.'

'No, it's not.'

'Eh?' She was confused.

'You're not in work tomorrow. I've organised for a long weekend. Welcome to a long weekend of indulgence. Charge those batteries. Get some action in.' He playfully stroked Heleyna's breasts, just catching her pinker-than-pink nipples. 'Feels like an age since I got hold of this,' he said, pointing at Heleyna's body, now flushed from the heat of the water.

'Hardly call last weekend an age, cheeky. I've had a busy week, you know. Don't you worry, we'll more than make up for it this weekend. I'm gagging too, you know!'

'Yes, no doubt you are, you naughty little minx. No doubt you are.'

2

Heleyna had no idea where they were heading. All she knew was that they were going northeast from Leeds, towards the coast, Troy driving like an idiot. She picked a CD, grabbed the road map with its pages hanging out, opened a bag of wine gums and started the 'eat as many sweets as you can until you feel sick' routine. Troy was more restrained.

Finding their place on the map, she started to track Troy's progress as they left the congested smoggy city and entered the fields and farmhouses surrounding the equally busy A64. The greenness of spring hit her, and she felt fortunate to be away from concrete and brick. Troy drove in silence, as was his way, responding only if spoken to. Heleyna glanced over at him in her boredom, realising how much she fancied his pants off, and stroked his knee. The hairs on his forearms stood to attention. The electricity was still well and truly prevalent between them.

'Troy, I did something stupid the other night.'

'Ya, what?'

'I mean, something which could be the end of me at work.'

'How can it be? You've just got a promotion.'

'I did something I vowed never to do – I mixed work with pleasure.'

'And who have you been shagging, you little tart?' Troy knew her well.

'Nobody.' She was defensive. 'I haven't been fucking anybody.'

He prodded her right leg as he teased her. 'Come on, now, out with it.'

Troy shut up, concentrated on his driving, and let Heleyna give him the juicy details about her now ex-boss.

'You are the biggest tart on this planet, young lady. Those hormones of yours need a bloody leash on them.' Troy was laughing so hard he nearly had to pull over onto the hard shoulder, his solid frame oscillating like a drill, tears forming at the corners of his blue eyes.

He always managed to lighten things for Heleyna. Soon she was laughing too: laughing at her hormones, the situation, the close shave, the fact she'd got away with it.

Troy made a sudden left turn and they started heading towards the North York Moors.

'We're off to the The Bear Inn, aren't we?' Heleyna asked.

'Just wait and see, nosy.'

She waited. She was right.

They woke on Friday morning, tired from the previous day's travelling through rush-hour traffic. It was 9 a.m. Heleyna looked out at the wild moors through the small leaded window and felt cosy in the warmth of their room. The restless winds battered the side of the inn, windowpanes clunking arrhythmically. It was a beautiful North York Moors day. This place always seemed to release an unlikely nesting instinct inside her.

Dressed in not a lot, she thought momentarily about work, about the promotion, about her ever-increasing desire for something more. She considered taking up a hobby – perhaps painting? Her life had become pretty soulless of late – work, Troy, work, parties, work. She didn't want to be one of those people who got to middle age or older, then looked back and regretted. Life was

27

far too precious for that. She wanted to experience different things, feel a sense of achievement, see more of life.

Her train of thought changed lines as she sensed Troy walk up behind her. The warmth emanating from his body hit her the moment before he touched her, the silky smooth skin of his limp dick brushing the peachy skin of her rounded arse just ahead of his bronzed arms encircling her. Her stomach rumbled.

'You are such a pig,' he teased. 'Let's go and get some food.'

'As long as that doesn't mean the last of that gorgeous dick of yours.'

Still behind her, he threw his head back, his chortle rattling her eardrums. 'Oh, all right then!'

They dressed quickly for breakfast, Troy lowering his head to miss the old wooden beam as they left the bedroom. They were the only people in the dimly lit breakfast room. It was Friday, after all. Sitting at the only made-up table, next to the log fireplace, they ordered the full works from the chirpy, petite waitress.

'So then, where are you guys from?' She wanted to talk.

'Just over from Leeds.' Heleyna did the responding for the two of them. Heleyna noticed how pretty this woman was even though her wayward blonde hair was scraped back in a bun, all held together with a blunt pencil. Curly strands of hair escaped, giving her that cute, slightly harassed look. 'I'm Heleyna, by the way, and this is Troy.'

'Hi, I'm Vicky.' She cast a temporary glance towards Troy then returned to Heleyna. Standing on one leg, the sweep of her hip was exaggerated by her stance. 'I should go and prepare your breakfasts.'

She turned, smiling, her head slower than her body and her eyes lowering momentarily to Heleyna's generous bosom. Vicky disappeared into the kitchen to become the chef.

'She was flirting with you.'

'No, she wasn't.'

Troy was insistent. 'Yes, she was. She looked straight at your sexy body.'

'I thought she was pretty hot myself.' Heleyna's mind entered overdrive. It'd been a while since she'd been with a woman.

Breakfast arrived and Heleyna invited Vicky to join them. She readily agreed, saying she would be back with a coffee in a few minutes and could do with a rest anyhow, as she was the only person working that morning. Troy smirked cheekily across the table at Heleyna, watching her going in for the kill. She was like a lioness on the warpath with a clear goal in sight. She always achieved her goals.

Vicky sat to the left of Heleyna, her short black Lycra skirt riding up ever so slightly to flash petite, firm thighs.

'So, how come you're on your own this morning?' Heleyna was fishing.

'It's usual for a weekday. I quite enjoy it. I can get on and do my own thing with no interruptions.' Vicky was biting. She put her head in her left hand, coffee in her right, the action giving her a delicate cleavage which just popped out from the brim of her low-cut top.

Vicky watched as Heleyna viewed, and she flashed a knowing smile.

'Does anyone ever come in at this time of day?' Yet more fishing from Heleyna.

Troy surveyed the scene from the sidelines, a linesman with no clear idea of the rules.

'Never in all the time I've worked here.'

The eye contact was now there. Both girls were on the same wavelength.

'Please, could you pass me the sugar.' It was an excuse. Vicky never took sugar in her coffee.

Heleyna obliged and hands touched as sugar passed from one woman to the other. Vicky kept her hand there and removed the sugar pot with the other. They remained in this pose for a few seconds.

Vicky wasn't scared in coming forwards. 'Do you want to touch me?'

Heleyna nodded eagerly, too horny now to converse. Vicky took Heleyna's warm hand and placed it on her knee and left it there for Heleyna to work her magic.

Heleyna moved her hand higher. No complaints. Yet higher. No complaints. Yet higher. Vicky parted her legs a little, just enough to reveal the heat that had been building up. Heleyna gently stroked her there and was feeling the wetness between her thighs before she realised the little whore wasn't wearing any panties. Brilliant.

Vicky was not shy. Before Heleyna had a chance to think, Vicky had disappeared under the table, the lit candle from the tabletop blown out and in her hand. Heleyna removed her cargo pants and spread her legs without the utterance of a conscious thought, her teeny G-string quickly pushed out of the way by Vicky's delicate cool hands.

Vicky's breath against Heleyna's sex took her breath away. Heleyna ached down to the deepest part of her clit and wished she could reach inside herself and caress every part of this most sensitive of organs. Just when she feared she might explode with anticipation, the tip of Vicky's warm, moist tongue trickled over the pinnacle of her clit before finding its way between her lips and entering her. Heleyna closed her eyes and enjoyed, her hands tightly clasped around her teacup. Troy watched, changing his line of sight from above to below the table. He coughed gently, trying to attract Heleyna's attention, and she opened her eyes leisurely, not wanting to lose sight of the joy of Vicky inside her. She looked over at the ever-stunning Troy, a smile spread across her flushed cheeks, and she nodded.

He slipped under the table next to Vicky, his tight white T-shirt riding up and giving Heleyna a quick flash of a bronzed stomach, which she instantly wanted to touch and lick and bite. Nerve endings sizzled from her toes to the end of each and every hair on her head as she relaxed into what was nothing less than ecstasy.

They took it in turns touching Heleyna – at first politely, waiting in turn, ensuring they had equal time to please her. Before long, however, civilised behaviour disappeared. Heleyna didn't know who or what was touching her, and, truthfully, she didn't care. Still gripping her teacup for support, she lifted the white linen tablecloth, glanced beneath the table, and was faced with Troy and Vicky's hands and tongues lapping at and caressing her every orifice. They were enjoying her as well as each other. Troy's veiny dick stood to attention through his open fly. Vicky's skirt was nowhere to be seen, but a candle was slipped inside her, its wetted tip just peeping out from her shaved pussy. The urge to go down there and join them intensified.

Heleyna's orgasm hit her out of nowhere like a lightning bolt, its sparks flying indiscriminately. Leaning forward over the table to control her spasming body, the teapot went flying, and warm liquid seeped over the tablecloth and dripped onto bare thigh below. When the full impact had subsided a little she lifted herself up slowly, still pulsing throughout, and watched Troy and Vicky finish each other off. Embroiled in a compelling 69 pose, they unavoidably lengthened her already indescribable orgasm.

* * *

Heleyna and Troy spent the rest of the day out in the fresh air, blowing away some of those city cobwebs, giggling about their seduction of the naughty Vicky, and creating a further appetite after a fulfilling breakfast.

They managed twelve miles, a substantial day's exercise on the peaty moors, walking through villages boasting Yorkshire stone cottages with gardens filled to overflowing with spring flowers and chimneys smoking, and pubs selling beer to die for. Stopping for the obligatory afternoon tea of scones and Earl Grey, they talked about Heleyna's current frustrations. Troy agreed that she needed something other than work to keep her occupied. They also decided that, deep down, although she loved her job, there were other things to life. Art classes it was to be. She would pick up where she had left off at school, revisit a forgotten talent. Troy was more content with his lot: work, parties, Heleyna and whoever else they chose along the way. That was him, simple to the core. Heleyna was more complex. If the truth were told, she was probably more intelligent.

Faces glowing from the cold fresh wind, they arrived at The Bear Inn. They took off their walking boots, now covered in the black mud of the moors, and entered the darkness of the wood-panelled bar. Troy was now used to lowering his head at every beam. Troy did his duty – going to the bar for two pints and a couple of packets of greasy, salty, ever-tasty pork scratchings.

Heleyna got comfy next to the lit fire and her body slowly adjusted to the warmth. She looked around the room, enjoying the informal homely feel of the pub. She took in the dim lighting, the old faded black-and-white photos of Yorkshire farmers who'd frequented the pub in days gone by, the framed old newspaper clipping above the piano. She stood up to read one. As she did, she noticed a man sitting alone, watching her. She hadn't noticed him before, sitting quietly in the corner. Supping on a pint, he had been pretending to read his newspaper. Heleyna attempted to read the newspaper clipping about a ghost who was said to have haunted the bar in the middle of the night, but her eyes kept wandering. There was something alluring about this man. He looked rugged and strong, with his dark hair and big eyes, and the stubble that covered his handsome, swarthy features. He was beautifully finished off with a dark-green turtleneck jumper, navy jeans and soft leather walking boots.

They caught each other's eye.

He smiled and said simply, 'Good morning'.

His broad Yorkshire accent suited him. She attempted to hold his gaze, but it was too powerful even for her.

'Good morning,' she replied. 'I'm just reading about the pub ghost. Good publicity, I suppose. Will draw a few more customers in if they try the old ghost story,' she commented cynically.

'Are you staying here long?' he inquired, not showing any interest in her comment.

'Until Sunday. My partner and I are here for a break from city life. Although I love it, it can get a bit claustrophobic at times.' She twiddled her curly locks with an absent-minded finger.

'I've never lived in the city. Maybe will do soon, though. Will be a bit of a shock. I love the outdoors – the wildness of the moors and the exhilaration of the hills.'

'Are you from around here, then?' she asked, not that she really cared – other thoughts were seeping into her mind, quickly blanking out rationality. Now willing and able to look into his eyes, she found herself being sucked in. Lust had truly impregnated her mind with wonderful, naughty thoughts. Why couldn't she think straight any more? Her pussy yearned for him. She tingled expectantly. Every nerve ending had woken up and made her feel alive.

'I live over near Pickering. I'm here to escape everyday life, too.'

She noticed his eyes skim over her body as he spoke to her, taking in the waviness of her long hair, her invitingly curvaceous body beneath her baggy clothes – her full breasts, small waist and rounded full feminine backside. She imagined herself on top of him, her beautiful ample breasts bouncing as she thrust herself up and down on his hardness. Heleyna knew exactly what he was thinking. The look in his eyes was enough to tell her that he wanted to ram her as much as she wanted to use him to pleasure herself. The conversation remained polite, Heleyna trying to maintain a calm persona.

'So, how are you going to cope with city living after all this?' She'd never been afraid to ask open questions.

'I'll make sure I come out here as often as I can at weekends. There're some great hiking and rambling clubs in this area. Probably join a couple of those that attract a younger bunch.' He pushed a leaflet across the table towards her. She picked it up.

'This one was recommended by the landlord. Apparently they walk by day then hit the pubs at night, savouring local beers. Sounds like my kind of thing.'

'That actually sounds pretty good. I love it out here so much. I should do something like that. It would motivate me to get away at weekends.' She could almost feel his touch, and the warmth and smell of his skin.

'Keep the leaflet. I'll get another one later from the landlord.' He flashed another of his unbearably seductive grins, revealing two deep dimples.

Troy arrived with the much-needed pints, interrupting their mounting attraction.

'Hope you're thirsty. Oh, sorry, did I interrupt your conversation?'

'Oh, no, don't worry. Troy, meet ... sorry, you never gave me your name.'

'Sam. I'm Sam Molloy. Glad to meet you, Troy.' Sam stood up from the table and shook hands with Troy.

The two men stood chatting about the local area for a few minutes, making polite conversation, Troy completely unaware of the sexual tension between Heleyna and Sam. Heleyna took the opportunity to drink her bitter and study him. He certainly was something else. The handsome Troy almost disappeared into insignificance in his presence. The scene of the two of them naked, lying next to each other, stood to attention, flitted in and out of her mind however hard she tried to remain sensible. The permanently etched memories of Ted flashed intermittently, teasing her, confirming that she truly was a dirty slut when she put her mind to it. Sam and Troy, Troy and Sam, two gorgeous specimens together. Fuck, that was sexy!

She watched them both chatting about work and laughing with each other. Looking intently from one to the other, her preference was still firmly with Sam – no, perhaps Troy – actually, the two together. A wry smile appeared on her face – what a very bad girl she was. How she loved it when her hormones gave her the ability to enjoy such treats.

Troy looked over at her. 'How about some dinner?' he inquired, then returned to Sam. 'Do you want to join us, too, Sam?'

'That would be great,' he replied. Yet Sam's tone of voice didn't display the true extent of his interest.

They headed towards the dining room and Troy

stopped off on the way to buy three more pints of bitter. Heleyna and Sam continued to the table, he following her, she very conscious of her walk.

They sat. Heleyna was short of conversation for the first time in her life. Sam grinned and leaned forwards towards her, looking very much like he was about to say something extremely naughty. He watched her response as he neared, and his grin extended, revealing two of the sauciest dimples imaginable. She inhaled deeply: she could smell his skin, feel the warmth of his body. His eyes flitted sideways towards the bar. Troy was on the return, precariously carrying the three pints, his wallet gripped firmly between his teeth. Sam hesitated, stopped, and returned to his original position. She wished she could speak openly about her and Troy – meaning Troy, her and anyone else who happened to take their fancy. Although he was a huge flirt, she hadn't yet picked up those vibes, the ones that told her bluntly that he was up for anything.

Troy plonked the pints on the table, only spilling the first millimetre from the top onto the now-damp beer mats. He sensed Heleyna's excitement and passed her a knowing look. She returned with an equally knowing expression, brazen minx written all over her face. Sam's concentration was lost in his pint.

In between mouthfuls of beef and ale stew, small talk was the order of the evening. They learnt that Sam was hoping soon to move to Leeds and was currently on the job scene trying to get back into the 'proper job market', as he called it.

'So then, Sam, are you married?' Heleyna inquired.

'No, actually, I'm single at the moment. Definitely looking though.' His eyes wandered towards Troy.

They were starting to get drunk, and Heleyna became increasingly nosy. 'What's your ideal partner like?'

'Strong physique, brunette, likes having fun.'

Heleyna thought he was talking about her.

Troy turned to face Sam. 'So then, Sam, tell me more about this job of yours.'

Heleyna was getting nowhere tonight.

After her meal and a couple more pints Heleyna was drunkenly shattered, the day's fresh air finally catching up with her. 'I'm heading off to bed. I could do with a good night's sleep.'

'Are you up for a couple more, Sam?' Troy was in a drinking mood.

'Too right!'

'See you later, gorgeous.'

Heleyna was on her way, casting a quick glance at Sam as she left. He did not return the look.

Undressing quickly down to her Mr Tickle panties and nothing else, she clambered into bed feeling an element of frustration. Sam had simply not responded. Was she losing her touch?

She awoke briefly when Troy staggered back into the room. Glimpsing her watch, she just made out the time in the light of the side lamp Troy had put on to undress by. It was 2 a.m. They must have kept the bar open late, she thought. Then she was dead to the world again, exercise, fresh air and alcohol returning her to an energising and much-needed deep sleep.

3

Heleyna wandered into work laden with the kind of despondency the end of a brilliant weekend brings, despite the thrill of a new job. She and Troy had spent the remainder of the weekend either walking, eating, drinking or shagging. They had even managed to fall upon a deserted barn on one of their afternoon walks. It had been raining heavily, but the day was warm. They ended up in there. Heleyna stood completely naked, enjoying the sharp chill of the late afternoon moors' wind between her legs, Troy teasing her behind with a piece of old rope with one hand, himself with the other.

'Morning, Heleyna. Good weekend, no doubt. Now, these are the initial concepts and draft scope for the project.'

She was straight back into work, John, the Managing Director, immersing her in the deep end of her new role, not a whiff of an induction in sight. Why would he bother? He knew she was capable, competent and always achieved whatever he threw her way.

'You will also be running the interviews for your old job. Couple of good CVs. Come by my office later to collect them. Let me know if you need any help.'

Perhaps this is what I need, she thought, more challenge at work to keep my mind from wandering towards this ever-increasing frustration with commonplace crap, the day-to-day, the mediocre. She determined that keeping her mind full to the brim would help prevent dissatisfaction – leaving not enough time to contemplate and analyse the less answerable aspects of life.

Today was fact-finding day, along with the next few days. She had to combine her vision with the views of the senior management team before she could even contemplate commencing the project she'd now been hired for. Needing to finalise and gain approval for the scope, and to get final buy-in from her seniors, was a task she was going to enjoy. It was something to get her teeth into; blotting paper soaking up the negative energy in her mind.

Heavily immersed in work, it was early afternoon before she remembered she was meant to pass by the MD's office and collect those CVs he recommended. Wandering past Ted's office on the way, she poked her head around his door to see how he was coping without her. He was deep in conversation, pacing up and down the length of his room, wearing out the Turkish carpet he'd purchased on his last vacation. He and his wife, Jacinta, always took delightfully exorbitant holidays.

Headset in place, he was talking avidly with his hands. 'Have you got us pencilled in for Huxley this weekend?'

Heleyna obviously couldn't hear the response.

'Are the rooms going to be ready on time? Uh-huh . . . yup . . . sounds good.' He walked back towards the door, noticing Heleyna's heeled boots in his doorway. 'Shall I invite new potential members? OK, perhaps next time. We could do with some fresh blood, and, you know, we've almost found it. I know, more time. Better go, love, visitor at the door.' He walked back to his desk and hit the talk button on his phone with an excessive flourish. 'How are you doing – colleague?' He was teasing her.

Confused by her thoughts and feelings, she remained in his doorway, away from his magnetic field, an attempt to remain professional, as always. 'Afternoon, Ted. You couldn't help me with an interview or two, could you? Apparently I've been tasked with replacing my old role, except this time the role reports into the project, as you already know. I could do with your expertise in this area.'

'No problem.' He changed the subject. 'But before that, any more thoughts about club membership? It's not all tank tops and anoraks, you know! Huxley really is a club with a difference.'

She felt uncomfortable, not being used to colleagues inviting her to non-work social functions. 'Well, clubs really aren't my thing at all. Maybe if you told me a little more about it you might convince me.'

'It's a deal. Dinner round at ours early next week. Bring the lovely Troy along with you too. Maybe my wife could convince you both at the same time by bribing you with one of her tasty Thai dishes.'

Ted was a cool negotiator. Heleyna couldn't escape. It would have been hard to say no when she had little else to do on weekday evenings than bore herself stupid catching up on work. He was renowned for winning people over with his boyish charm and cheeky grin. She said her goodbyes and continued on her way, the swish of her silky trousers and clunk of her boots seeming loud in the quietness of the designed and decorated corridor.

The next few days gathered pace like a storm building ever more rapidly, and soon there was a mound of paperwork on her desk. Heleyna loved every minute of it, feeling not an ounce of stress. Being busy made the days disappear in a flash. Troy left her to it. No point disturbing her too much. On the other hand, Ted would pop his head in occasionally and laugh at her, hidden behind a commotion of paperwork, her frowning face stuck permanently to her PC screen. She hardly ever responded.

Before she knew it, Tuesday had arrived. More than ready for a night of relaxation after the nine days flat she'd just worked, Heleyna could already hear the sound of the cork fighting its way out of the bottle on its journey to that ever-delightful 'pop'. She hadn't seen alcohol since The Bear Inn, let alone tasted it. Not long for most people, she knew, but a glass or two of wine was her little pre-sleep pleasure most days.

'Hi, Heleyna. Still OK for tonight?' Ted was in her doorway. He was missing the fun they had had when they worked together, the way they bounced ideas off each other – ideas that often flourished into great business plans. She was a great person to work with.

'More than OK,' she replied. 'It will be good to meet Jacinta away from a work function.' Although sounding genuine, Heleyna was still, if she'd been honest with herself, a little nervous.

'Excellent. Come by my office at five-thirty and I'll give you a lift.' His eyes dropped temporarily.

She noticed. But she pretended it had never happened. 'Thanks, Ted. I'll tell Troy to make his own way there. He only lives round the corner from you anyway.' She remembered his cock, his mouth, his groans and tried very hard to push those feelings far back into the depths of her mind.

'Any progress on the interviews? It's just that my diary is pretty full over the next few weeks and becoming increasingly fuller.'

'Shit! It'd completely slipped my mind.' Heleyna riffled through the mess on her desk until she came across the A4 envelope with the MD's scrawl on the front. 'Now, let's see what we have here … two candidates …

looks like both have pretty relevant experience in large projects ... OK, I'll sort dates, etcetera, this afternoon. Sorry, Ted, my mind is all over the place at the moment.'

'No worries. See you later.' He turned and left her office.

Her eyes glanced downwards from his broad shoulders to his solid arse. Even shocking herself, for a split second she hoped that Jacinta and he were up for more than dinner, but she knew that could be nothing more than fantasy – a fantasy that would undoubtedly give her plenty of solo satisfaction.

Heleyna was halfway through dialling the number on the front of the first CV when she finally found the name she recognised. It was in the obvious place, but in her work-engrossed state simple things were becoming so much harder, her mind overflowing with things to do. The number started ringing. Her stomach turned as the receiver at the other end rattled on the pick-up.

'Hi, could I speak with Sam Molloy please.'

'Speaking.' Voice still sexy.

'Hi Sam, my name's Heleyna Lane, project manager at SPM Ltd. I'm actually phoning you to arrange an interview time for the role of project facilitator. But I think we have met before, just a week or so ago, at the Bear Inn. Small world, eh?' She winced slightly, worried that she sounded a little foolish, and so let him speak.

'Hi, Heleyna! How are you doing? Certainly is a small world.' He sounded pleased to hear her voice.

They arranged for him to attend an interview later on in the week.

She began planning, following her normal 'breaking the barriers' routine. 'How about you stay over at Troy's after coming in here, save driving back up to Pickering? My flat doesn't have a guest room, but his does.'

Sam's voice lifted a notch. 'That would be great. Cheers.'

A bit more idle chitchat and organisation, and the conversation ended. The receiver clunked back into place and a huge grin spread over Heleyna's face. Task One was complete. She began to ponder her evening's entertainment at Troy's – a bit of executive stress relief was always far more effective than any glass of wine.

The other interview was arranged for the following day, and, whilst she was in a telephone mood, she retrieved the *Yellow Pages* and skimmed the index for local colleges. She phoned the one nearest to her home in the hope that being close meant she would need less motivation to turn up for classes each week. She was in luck: they were starting an abstract painting course in a couple of weeks' time, and to Heleyna this was a sure sign that this was meant to be. Satisfaction enveloped her, the emotion translating into a feeling of warmth in the pit of her stomach. Her life was getting back on a roll, becoming something again, gaining substance.

She scribbled down the course details on a piece of scrap paper, then shoved it into one of the many pockets in her briefcase. In the same pocket was a leaflet, a leaflet she'd forgotten about, what with work, work and more work to occupy her. Pulling it out she remembered why she'd really taken it: she'd wanted to try and draw Sam into conversation, willed him to see that she did have something interesting about her. In actual fact, she'd desperately wanted to fuck him senseless: up against the wall, sprawled across the beer table, across the bar – she hadn't really cared, as long as he fucked her.

She opened it and began reading, her initial cynicism turning into a hesitant interest. 'We cater for all fitness levels ... most members are in their twenties and thirties ... focused on introducing our members to the outdoors ... we also have kayaking and mountain-biking trips ... North York Moors, Dales, Lake District,

Scotland and beyond.' She actually found herself liking what she read, despite the fact it was a club. She could do with learning new things, activities that were not work-related. Art and the outdoors – the two seemed disparate, yet synonymous. Uncrossing and recrossing her legs, she wondered if the club was full of painfully boring nerds. There was only one way to find out. Heleyna logged onto their website and filled in the online membership form before she could change her mind. This was something she was going to do on her own. She was booked onto a weekend in the Lake District in one month's time. Two-day walks with accommodation in a bunk house near the base of Blencathra. Just enough time to buy the recommended gear: boots, sleeping bag, rucksack and a seriously waterproof jacket.

Heleyna was about to embark upon a change of lifestyle, a lifestyle that so many other career-focused people missed out on in their obsession with the rat race. She was satisfied for once, pleased to have made at least the first small step towards a more fulfilling existence.

Ted drove out to Alwoodley via Headingley, chattering to Heleyna all the way, nipping in and out of the traffic in his silver Audi TT. He had the horrible habit of turning to face Heleyna every time he spoke to her. Deep red marks appeared on her left hand, created by the French-polished nails on her right.

Today when she looked at him he was just Ted Jones, her ex-boss. She was relieved.

'You know, I really miss having you around at work. We were a great team.' He patted her trouser-covered thigh with his large, square hand as he spoke. 'Beginning to feel a tad bored these days. We were a great team.' He repeated himself.

They hit the ring-road roundabout just up from the hotel-and-leisure-club complex that many of Heleyna's friends were members of. On the occasions when she could be bothered to go to the gym, she would hit an unobtrusive one not far from her flat. Mirror preening in all-in-one Lycra was just not her cup of tea – unless, of course, it was her little black dress, Troy's favourite.

'I know what you mean. We do work well together. The temporary team assigned to the project is just not the same. We just don't gel that well. Maybe we will with time.'

'Perhaps.' Ted knew, after more working years than Heleyna, that good working relationships were hard to find. They'd been truly lucky.

They drove past the Yorkshire-stone six-foot wall surrounding Ted's house. The automatic garage door lifted as they approached.

'You're such a poser, Ted, a real gadget man.'

'What else is a man supposed to do with his money?'

'Dunno, I suppose. Would rather spend it on doing things than on having things.' This was a new train of thought for Heleyna. She surprised herself.

'Well, that's where we differ. As many material possessions as I can get my hands on, that's what makes me happy. Along with Jacinta, of course!' He pulled the key out of the ignition with a swift clean action, as if trying to make a point.

Jacinta opened the door that led from the house to the garage, all smiles and welcoming-hostess mode. 'Troy's already here,' she called in her ever-so-middle-class accent.

Heleyna could smell spicy food – that wonderful mix of coconut, fresh coriander, chillies, garlic and lemon grass with a hint of lime. Thai green curry, she reckoned. It could be nothing else. Heleyna followed her into their elegant old house, Ted behind her. A prim-looking Jacinta was dressed in a long, deep-red ankle-length skirt, high strappy black shoes and cream see-through blouse, a lacy teddy underneath just maintaining her dignity. Despite her own height, Heleyna felt positively dumpy in her presence. Jacinta towered over her: elegant, slender, ladylike, a true clotheshorse.

Troy was in the kitchen holding up the marble-topped breakfast bar, a glass of Pinot Noir in hand, the bottle half-empty beside him. His cheeks already had a red-wine-induced glow about them. He looked like a man at peace with the world.

'Hi, gorgeous!' Heleyna walked towards him and smiled at his cuteness. She planted a meaningful, smoochy kiss firmly on his lips then spoke again. 'See you're already knocking them back,' she teased.

'Let me get you some. Make yourself at home.' Ted reached for a large bowl-shaped red-wine goblet and poured her a quarter of the bottle. It only half-filled the black hole of a glass.

Jacinta busied herself in the kitchen.

'Can I do anything to help?' Heleyna was being polite.

'Don't you worry about me. I love cooking. Just get yourself sat at the bar and relax. Dinner will probably be a while, though. So, if you don't mind we'll stay in here for a bit.' She inspected Heleyna as she levered herself up onto the stool, noticing her rounded bottom caressing the seat.

Two hours of non-stop conversation later they were sat in the dining room, three empty bottles of wine left on the kitchen-counter top, a fourth finding its way into the dining room, care of Ted.

'So, tell me a little about Huxley.' Heleyna's request was pointed at Jacinta, this action purposeful, as Ted had done little to tempt her so far.

Jacinta placed her slender elbows onto the table.

'Well, there are about one hundred and fifty members or so. All professionals from the Leeds area. We tend to meet here at ours. Normally fifty or so turn up each time we meet, so as you can imagine it's pretty busy in here. It's really more of a social gathering than a club – food, wine, laughter and the like. Really, it's an excuse for a big party, a time to let your hair down and forget about the mundane suburban existence!' She smiled. 'I find it pretty ... hmm ... relaxing, a chance to be yourself once in a while. How about you, Ted?'

'Same, same.' The wine had numbed his brain, the usually complex mass of electrical impulses now reduced to a mere one or two, and even they were slothful.

'So, if Troy and I wanted to join, what would we have to do?' She was leaning forwards, her upper body supported by her elbows, an unconscious stance she took whenever she felt interest or enthusiasm.

Jacinta looked over at Ted then returned her line of sight towards Heleyna. 'You have to be invited along by a member, and the rest of the members have to vote you in after your first party. It's a kind of vetting – bit like an interview, I suppose.'

Heleyna still didn't feel she had a good grasp of this club. 'So, I suppose we need to convince you to invite us along if we are to find out more!' she chortled, activating her incredibly full bladder. 'Oh, too much wine. Where's the toilet, please?'

Ted showed her the way and returned to his dinner.

As she passed the telephone on her return to the dining room Heleyna caught sight of a folded piece of paper. It was next to the cordless phone on the small antique oak table that stood on beautifully ornate curvaceous legs. She stopped. Curiosity had grabbed her and she didn't try to stop it. She enjoyed her overinquisitive mind, which gave her all sorts of insight into things and made her so, so good at her job. She picked it up. It was blank, other than the letterhead. Damn, she thought. She read the letterhead. 'The Huxley Club: Chastity – the most unnatural of all the sexual perversions (Aldous Huxley)'. Now she was hungry for facts, her thoughts immediately turning to Ted and his escapades with another man. This could be very, very interesting, she thought.

When she re-entered the dining room, neither Ted nor Jacinta was there. The delicious aroma of fresh coffee and sound of pots clunking told her they were in the kitchen. She gave Troy the gory details of what she'd seen, yet he didn't seem as convinced as she was that there was anything untoward about the letterhead.

'Look at Jacinta,' he hissed. 'She's a goddamn domestic goddess, as clean-living as the best of them around these parts. You probably misread it, anyway, after all the wine you've drunk.'

Heleyna had to agree. Thoughts of Jacinta doing anything that involved sex other than with Ted and in the missionary position just did not seem to fit.

Jacinta and Ted rattled the pots loudly in the kitchen in the hope of masking their conversation.

Even Ted managed to keep his voice low for a change. 'Do you think they're twigging?'

'Not quite sure. They're quite gorgeous, though, aren't they?' She patted Ted's arse as he bent forward to put plates in the dishwasher. 'I don't know how you've managed to resist inviting Heleyna to Huxley for all this time.'

He swung round and grabbed her by the waist. 'You, my dear, need your little bottom smacking. I do think about other things sometimes, you know. I know it's hard to believe, and the other thoughts are rare, but it does happen. Plus, she's never flirted with me before, never given me a sign that she finds me the least bit attractive. We've spoken about this before.'

Jacinta's hand rested on his stomach. 'How could she possibly resist?' She dropped it down to his groin, stroked him gently then cupped his balls in her manicured hand.

He responded to her touch. She teased him some more before grabbing the coffee plunger and walking back to the dining room, grinning at him over her shoulder as she went, wiggling her hips at him provocatively.

'Bring the coffee cups and milk with you.' She was gone, leaving Ted in an unfit state to return to his guests.

Heleyna jumped as Jacinta returned to the room. She too had been getting friendly with her man. She sensed Jacinta trying not to notice as she returned her hand to the tabletop. There was tension in the air for a brief, uncomfortable second.

Troy lightened the atmosphere. 'Thanks for the feed, Jacinta. You're a fine cook. Your husband's a very lucky man, that's for sure.'

Jacinta blushed. 'Thanks. I know the wine didn't really fit the food, but then again we drank most of it before we ate!' She had become the domestic goddess once again.

Ted ambled back into the dining room with the milk and sugar for the coffees. 'Stop apologising. Don't put yourself down, woman. She's always finding fault with herself, you know.' Ted looked at his wife. 'You're bloody brilliant at everything you turn your hand to.' He turned to his guests. 'You wouldn't believe how good she is when the Huxley Club is here. A true maître d'. Runs the show like a real pro. Makes sure the guests have everything they need, but still manages to have fun herself. Don't know how she does it, don't know how she does it . . .' His sentence tailed off.

True to form, Jacinta had poured coffees for everyone, leaving them to help themselves to milk and sugar while Ted continued to wax lyrical about his wife's prowess as a hostess. Heleyna could tell by the direction Ted's eyes were looking in that he was visualising her in her role. Picking up on other people's body language was a skill she'd learnt on a business course, which touched on NLP. Though, for the life of her, she still couldn't remember what on earth NLP actually meant. 'So then, when do we get to see you on duty?' Heleyna was keen to be invited along.

Ted grinned at his wife. 'Well, the next event isn't actually for a few months. We're having a bit of a break, possibly a holiday somewhere exotic thrown in. Can get exhausting always organising, you know.'

Jacinta nodded. 'Yes, but don't worry, we'll make sure you get a formal invite.'

Jacinta and Ted nodded at each other as if confirming they were both in agreement.

Troy piped up at last, 'Sounds excellent, Jacinta. Thanks. How about we return the favour and have you two round for dinner in the next few weeks, then you can tell us some more about this club.'

Jacinta replied, obviously the diary keeper in the relationship. 'Sounds wonderful.'

'If you don't mind, I'm getting pretty tired.' Heleyna's hard work was catching up with her; that mixed with a bottle of fine wine. 'Thanks for a lovely evening, you two.'

Heleyna and Troy got to their feet and Jacinta showed them to the door.

'Watch yourselves on that pot of lavender. Must ask the gardener to move it. Ted's forever falling over it, you know.'

They pottered down the path, saying good night on their way, and headed towards home on foot. It was only a twenty-minute walk, but it was much needed by Heleyna after days cooped up inside, hardly seeing the light of day.

'There's definitely something about this club thing.' Heleyna was trying to establish Troy's feelings on the subject.

'You're not fretting are you?'

'A bit, but I'm also pretty curious. I mean, what happens if it is a club where the Jacintas and Teds of this world come together and get up to all sorts of sexual exploits?' Heleyna's old concerns about the work/pleasure mix were haunting her.

'Look. Stop worrying. Jacinta is as prim as they come. You work with Ted and have known him for some time. You would have picked up before now if he was up to that kind of thing. I know what your bloody hormones are like – they can pick out a needle in a haystack when it comes to opportunities of a sexual nature.'

'But, I saw him the other night ...'

Troy interrupted, some annoyance showing in his voice. 'So? Doesn't mean he's running orgies from his home, does it.' Troy put his arm round her shoulders. 'Come here, you. You're one strange cookie. You're always gagging for a bit, but as soon as it's work you shy away. Bloody Church-of-England upbringing has a lot to answer for!'

She giggled. 'I know. Repression, guilt, they've all got me and made me into the truly bizarre person I am today! Oh, by the way, I forgot to tell you. Guess who's coming for an interview at SPM on Thursday?'

'Go on, tell me. Who?'

'Sam. You know, the Sam from the Bear Inn? Hope you don't mind, but I've suggested he stays Thursday night at yours, seeing as you got on so well. It'll save him the drive back to Pickering. Small world, eh?'

Troy's reaction was typically affable. 'Bloody hell. Excellent. Great bloke he was, too. It'll be good to see him again.'

They walked on in silence for a few minutes, the kind of comfortable silence which comes from contentment in a relationship, Troy's grasp still firmly and protectively round her shoulders. She could feel him watching her, studying her features in the orange glow of the street lamps. She shivered slightly, a mixture of tiredness and desire.

They entered the alleyway that led to Troy's house and the light disappeared. Darkness set in. The sprinkling of hornyness, which remained from the earlier superlative sensation of solid cock beneath the dinner table, overcame her. She was still on heat. Turning to face him, she spoke, her voice low and husky in its attempt to remain quiet as they stood amidst the tight-knit houses.

'God, I want to fuck you. Want to screw you outside, here in the cold air. Up against this wall, right here and now.' She began undoing his belt.

'Fuck, I love it when you're like this.' He was already prepared for her. He had been ready after her first sentence, springing into action at the first utterance of sexual dialogue between them.

His trousers and boxers were now round his ankles, and she lowered herself to her knees. 'Your cock makes me so bloody horny.' Her lips touched him and conversation from Heleyna ceased as she tasted his pleasure-giving juices.

'That's right, just there. Oh, yes. That's so good. Please don't stop, please don't stop.' Troy was disappearing, oblivious to the outside world, his world now just Heleyna and him, him and Heleyna. He was begging her. His voice carried down the passageway, resounding as it hit the solid stone walls of terraced houses.

Neither of them even thought to care.

Delicate as can be, she caressed every part of him with lips, tongue and warm moist breath: his dick, his balls, the base of his shaft deep between his legs. He spread his legs further. She buried herself in there, her face covered with the wetness of her own saliva. She was lost. Thoughts, and not just conversation, had now ceased.

Serious self-control coming into play, Troy lifted Heleyna to her feet and away from his overwhelming cock, ordering her to remove her trousers. He wanked himself inches from her face, as she willingly obliged his order and bent to step out of her burgundy suit trousers. It was now her turn. Heels still firmly in place, she stood with her back against the wall for support, her nails desperately grabbing on to the cement grooves between the moss-covered neat brickwork of the alley wall.

Without kissing her he bent to his knees, his hands sliding with ease over her rounded hips. His fingers found their way to her moist slit and he touched her, nudging his fingers within her fleshy lips. He could feel her wetness through her knickers and he groaned, grabbed her hips firmly and pushed his face into her crotch, taking in her smell.

Violent in his desire to have her, he vigorously removed her black lace knickers to reveal her hungry muff. Stroking her pubic hair, he teased her cruelly.

'Please, just fuck me,' she moaned. 'Do it to me as hard as you can'. Her request emanated from her sub-conscious, a reflex response.

He didn't obey. His thoughts were focused on her clit, protruding and swollen and desperate for his tongue. As he parted her lips gently with cool hands,

53

his tongue swept over the length of her bud, finding its resting place on the pinnacle of this most sensitive of organs. He didn't move for a split second, and she nearly exploded with anticipation. He continued, his tongue now finding other hot, moist places to explore, his fingertips continuing to push her to the brink. She grasped the wall harder, her legs spread as far as they possibly could. Chilly air swept past her stomach, up and under her shirt, finding its way to her rock-solid nipples. She groaned, uncontrollable in her desire and desperate for more icy blasts to heighten her already craving, sensitive skin.

'Shit, I'm coming. I'm coming.'

Troy stopped abruptly. However much he was enjoying teasing and pleasing her, he wanted this one to last a while longer.

Getting to his feet he swung her round, pulling her backwards towards his generous purple cock. Her heels echoed with each step in the darkness. She bent forwards, the palms of her hands against the roughness of the brick wall, her arse and pussy on display. Expert at her cunt, he rammed her with one majestic action, his largeness filling her to the brim. She sighed as one of his hands rested against her, taking her on a journey she never tired of.

Solid in her stance, Troy began his violent thrusts, his balls slapping against her as he reached her depths. They were desperate for each other, grunting and groaning, animalistic in their desire. Troy rammed, pumped and caressed, and she rubbed herself frantically, heading towards the delectable orgasm they both craved. They reached their priceless goals: Troy shuddered, Heleyna exploded, the orgasm taking over her entirely, filling her to the brim with intense, extraordinary gratification.

4

Heleyna couldn't settle all Thursday morning. She was completely unable to concentrate on her work, actually feeling a little bored by the task at hand. Developing the project plan for SPM's latest product just wasn't giving her the fulfilment she had envisaged. Yes, the job was much busier than her last position. Yes, she had more responsibility, was more accountable due to her increased seniority. Yes, she was earning a lot more money. Content with her lot? No.

A reminder flashed up on her PC. 'Interview with Sam Molloy', it read. She glanced at the time. It wasn't for an hour. She'd put the reminder on to give her time to prepare herself, ensure she looked the part, and to put herself in the right frame of mind. Uncharacteristic butterflies hit her stomach. This man was something to be reckoned with. He had a demeanour she couldn't penetrate, and that was surprising for her.

Phoebe, the new and incredibly irritating project administrator, popped her head round Heleyna's door. The managing director had appointed her prior to Heleyna's promotion. 'Interview with Sam Molloy at one p.m.,' she reminded Heleyna.

'Thanks, Phoebe.' Heleyna gritted her teeth. Phoebe had irritated her the moment she set eyes on her. She was so annoyingly happy and chirpy all the time. She was bubbly to the extreme, twenty-one years old, five foot two, with bleach-blonde bobbed hair, and she was always dressed in bright colours with huge sparkly earrings dangling from her lobes. Rather overdone, in Heleyna's estimation.

'Anything I can do to help?' Forever and annoyingly helpful.

'Please could you print off the interview questions – the ones the HR department sent by email yesterday fo the first interview.'

'No problem. How did that interview go?' A high pitched squeak.

'Not overly exciting. She would be OK, but wouldn' set the world on fire. Could you also grab me anothe chair – and set them up round my coffee table, please along with water and glasses.' Heleyna enjoyed getting her to do the menial tasks: it took away some of the irritation of having to work with her.

'Whatever you say – boss.'

Heleyna was a little unsure if there was sarcasm in the last statement, but to be honest she couldn't give a damn what Phoebe thought. For some reason Phoebe annoyed Heleyna more than anyone she had ever worked with, expect, perhaps, a couple of men she'd eaten alive at university. At the time she'd often described them as flies round a fresh cowpat, until a friend pointed out that she was likening herself to the cowpat.

It was the overweening helpfulness above and beyond the call of duty that set Heleyna's teeth on edge when, underneath, she suspected it was to cover up a deep-seated loathing of being told what to do – of being an underling. She played the game herself, giving as good as she got in the insincerity stakes.

'You're such a sweetie, Phoebe. Sometimes I just don't know how I coped before you came along.' Definite sarcasm.

Phoebe didn't seem to notice. She left to get on with her chores, her pumps squeaking down the corridor with each step. Heleyna grimaced. It was a sound that reminded her of school – of teenagers running their nails down the blackboard, turning the classroom into a state of panic, with childish hands clamped firmly over ears.

Heleyna was relieved. Now she'd palmed off all the crap jobs, she had time to go and check herself out in the ladies and make sure she looked professional, though with a definite hint of sexiness. 'Oops!' Heleyna giggled to herself. She'd just realised what she was doing. She was attempting to go down a path that had previously had a large barrier across with a flashing luminescent NO ENTRY sign attached, preventing her from taking even one step.

Standing alone in the ladies she looked down at herself. She was wearing the obligatory suit, the skirt a couple of inches shorter than her usual work choice. Beneath her skirt she wore hold-ups. These had never been an item she'd picked out for work before today. High heels and a lacy see-through blouse were also the order of the day, a camisole beneath, just allowing a glimpse of generous cleavage as she bent forwards. She carefully reapplied her make-up, adding just a hint of lipstick to titivate already plump lips.

In order to compose herself, and re-enter a world where she was boss rather than servant, she sat in a cubicle for a few minutes: she was meant to chair the interview and lead the discussion, not giggle and flirt and think naughty thoughts. She'd almost reached a meditative state when she heard two sets of footsteps entering the toilets: one set squeaking, and the other clunking. Phoebe spoke first.

'That fucking Heleyna thinks she's so important. I know she's senior and all that, but I just can't stand her attitude. Treats me like dirt.'

Heleyna sat still in the cubicle. She could see Phoebe

in her mind, her head all over the place, earrings flying in all directions.

'Really?' It was Sue, John the MD's personal assistant. She was always neutral and professional, never passing an opinion on personalities – far too risky in her role.

'She's such a bitch. Gets me running around after her. She thinks she's God's gift at work and to men. She's not really anything special in my opinion. Needs to lose a couple of pounds, if you ask me.'

'Now, now, Phoebe. She is a senior manager here. You need to show her some respect, whatever your personal feelings. If it was a man asking you to do those things, you know as well as I that you would be as happy as could be.'

Heleyna liked that voice of reason from Sue.

Sue continued. 'She is also an attractive woman with a handsome boyfriend. I think you're just jealous, really.'

Heleyna could hear Phoebe huff, then enter the cubicle next to hers, her pumps making that annoying grating noise on the lino floor. Heleyna chose this time to exit hers, making sure she spent a good couple of minutes talking with Sue as she washed her hands and took one final look in the mirror. She sincerely hoped she'd taught the little cow a lesson or two. She couldn't wait to see her again before the interview.

Heleyna entered her office. Ted was sitting in one of the comfy chairs that had already been set up round the coffee table by Phoebe. She was always efficient. Heleyna couldn't fault that. She scanned her room, her domain. It looked tidy – some paperwork shoved into a spare drawer, the remainder shared between her 'in' and 'out' trays, and in no particular order. She vowed to bring Phoebe in to do some filing, help sort her life out for her. Maybe having an assistant wasn't so bad after all, she thought.

Ted looked up at her. He was reading a glossy car magazine. 'Hi there. So let's have a look at this CV, then.' He put the magazine away in his black leather folder. Heleyna's hands were sweaty. As she handed Ted his copy, her fingers stuck to the paper, leaving a light greasy mark across the tops of the front and back pages. Her feelings were reminiscent of the first public-speaking contest she'd entered at school – and won. She still remembered what she'd presented – a very naïve argument on the importance of marriage. Boy, how she'd changed since leaving the protective nest of her parents!

'There we go. Just need to give you a bit of back-ground on this one. I have met this candidate before. Troy and I spent an evening with him once in a pub on the North York Moors. So, I need you to retain complete objectivity in any decision-making here, Ted. Whatever my personal feelings, we need to get the right person for the job or the project will fail easily.'

'OK.' Ted cast her a sideways glance. 'You all right there? You look a bit tense. Not like you.'

'I'm fine, fine. Let's move on. Now, I would like you to lead the interview for that very reason.' She was forcing the professional woman mode upon herself, hoping it would stick.

As Ted read the CV and Heleyna scribbled notes in the margin of her copy, Phoebe walked in, water jug in one hand, papers in the other.

'Just put those down there, please.' Heleyna didn't condescend a glance. She couldn't bear to look at the queen of bad taste.

'Sam Molloy's here, Heleyna. He's in reception.' Phoebe kept her head down, her voice lower than usual.

'Bring him in in five minutes, please. We need time to reread the questions. Then I would like you to sit in the corner of the room and take notes, please, save us having to do it. We need to concentrate on the task at hand.' Heleyna knew she was being a bitch and was actually quite enjoying it for once in her life. Actually, she wanted to spend the next hour or so ogling, and didn't want to have to take her eyes off him even for one moment to write down his comments and answers.

Phoebe walked out of the room without a word, her usual skiplike steps not to be heard.

Ted was always fair with his staff. 'What's all that about?'

Heleyna was adamant. 'Oooh, she really irritates me, that's all.'

Ted turned and looked at her straight on. His face reddened, the early warning signs of very rarely displayed anger. 'Look, Heleyna, a piece of advice. Don't let personality clashes effect your judgement. You can't always love everyone who works for you, but it's up to you to make that relationship work. You are the one in control, after all, higher up the pecking order, so to speak.'

'I'll do it my own way, thanks, Ted.' Heleyna dismissed him.

The confrontation, if anything, had made her forget that Sam was about to enter her office and mess with her mind.

They spent the next couple of minutes assigning questions and were deep in conversation when Heleyna sensed him at the door. He was standing behind Phoebe, though his presence was firmly in front of her. Heleyna jumped to her feet, ignoring Phoebe, virtually pushing her out of her way, and firmly shook his hand.

'Welcome, Sam, welcome. This is Ted Jones, project manager. He's managing the Gateway project – the other key project at SPM Ltd. Please, take a seat.'

As requested by Heleyna, Ted led the interview. Not only did she feel incapable of lengthy and intelligent conversation, she also wanted time to study him in detail without the beer goggles she'd had on in the Bear Inn to dull the senses. Smiling sweetly, she poured him a glass of water and indicated to Phoebe to sit in the corner. Phoebe obeyed. Sitting in the low chair, Heleyna's skirt rode up just enough to parade her hold-ups. She knew she looked pretty damn hot – she certainly felt it.

Heleyna's mind wandered unashamedly throughout the meeting. Almost dribbling with desire and forgetting her role on more than one occasion she just managed to regain composure when and as needed, relying more on the reflexes learnt in business than on any rational thought processes. He was still well and truly delicious, bringing the first tinglings of lust to her lightly lipsticked mouth. She could feel herself moistening at the thought of slowly removing his tie and white shirt, unzipping his suit trousers and watching them disappear to the floor, and then taking out his cock in readiness for . . .

The interview ended and disappointment hit Heleyna as a knot in the base of her abdomen. He was gone. He was professional and didn't even bat an eyelid at her, his eyes remaining perfectly poised towards hers whenever he spoke to her. She took it out on Phoebe.

'Please go and type up the notes, and as quickly as possible so that Ted and I can collate our case for John at the earliest.'

Phoebe ran. If she'd been a puppy, her tail would have been tightly curled between her hind legs. She knew she was being punished and didn't even bother to fight against it, hoping subservience would win the day.

Ted spoke, clearly sensing Heleyna's unusual demeanour. There was humour in his voice. 'What *is* going on with you? Come on, out with it.'

'Nothing.' Heleyna couldn't bring herself to look into his eyes as she gave her one-word answer. Ted knew her too well to know exactly when she was lying, or 'twisting the truth', as he called it.

'Come on, Heleyna, you're not your usual business-like self.' There was a grin across his face, which he'd planted there to try and stop the remark he really wanted to make: Heleyna Lane, you dirty little tart, sat there in your short skirt, pushing your tits out, goggling like a schoolgirl. This was the first time Ted had seen Heleyna being openly sexual in the day-to-day work environment and he was enjoying it. He felt like he was beginning to get inside the real Heleyna, the Heleyna that he wanted her to be, the Heleyna that he and Jacinta wanted to see again.

Still no eye contact. 'I'm truly fine, Ted. OK, then, let's put forward our recommendations to John. Might as well get it out of the way while the memory is still fresh. Tell me, what is your opinion?'

Ted switched back into the mode that Heleyna obviously wanted them to be in – her safe zone. Within a matter of an hour they had the business case ready, with interview notes already completed and attached by the compliant and nervous Phoebe. Sam Molloy was to be the new project facilitator, working directly for Heleyna as her right-hand man – once John had signed on the dotted line, as per SPM protocol. He would, of course, never have questioned the professional judgement of either of these members of his management team.

It was 6.30 p.m. and Heleyna picked up the phone and dialled Troy's. She was well and truly pissed off. When she'd delivered the business case to John he'd loaded her with a deadline she had to meet the following day. It was going to be another late night and she was going to miss the fun of spending an evening with Mr Sex-on-Legs times two: titillating Troy and sensual Sam. The answer machine clicked in. She hung up – actually she threw the receiver down, creating a huge clatter.

7.30 p.m., she dialled again. Answer machine. She hung up and this time the phone nearly jumped off the hook. She continued working, eager to finish as early as possible. 8.30 p.m., she picked up the phone more abruptly this time. She was hungry, and it made her angry that Troy hadn't even bothered to call to say he and Sam were off out. What made her even more irritable was the fact she was sat in an office, dolled up like the office slut, and she had no party to go to. She'd turned into a boring 28-year-old. This time it was picked up, and the phone didn't need to be submitted to the same hostile treatment.

'Hullo.'

'Hi Troy, it's me.' She was certainly not her friendly self.

Troy hesitated for a second, knowing he had to choose his words ever so carefully. 'Hi darling. I hope you're coming home soon. Sam and I are cooking dinner.'

'Look, I'm sorry. I just can't. John's dropped a real whopper on me this afternoon. Nothing I can do. Fuck, why do I do this to myself? I'm not even enjoying this.' Her right hand flew around aggressively as she spoke, her left only kept in check by its position on the receiver.

'I'm sure once you get into the painting lessons and start to enjoy something other than work again, things will improve.'

'Yeah, whatever.' God, she could be an icy cow. 'Bloody Phoebe has been winding me up again today too. She's so annoying. I can't put my finger on it, but she winds me up. Bloody John and his recruitment decisions. Why he just couldn't wait until I took the job so I could get someone I liked, I really don't know. It's like he's done her a favour for some reason. She's not our usual type of employee at all.'

Troy couldn't be bothered any more, knowing that if he responded to her negativity he would only fuel it. 'Can we talk about this tomorrow night? You need to do your work so you can get home at reasonable hour, and I need to entertain my guest.'

His approach worked. She softened.

'Oh God, sorry. How is Sam?' She didn't let him answer the question. 'I'll let you get back to him. Enjoy dinner. I'll come over to yours tomorrow night after work. That OK?'

'Excellent. See you then, sexy. And remember, don't take life so seriously. You only get one chance.'

'Bye.' She hung up.

She was shattered. Being a bitch certainly took it out of her. Daydreaming for a moment, her stare passing straight through the screen of her laptop into no-man's-land, she tried to understand what was making her so mad. Light bulbs began to appear, Sam's fantastic face glowing out of each one. Never before had she met a man she craved who she hadn't managed to tease and flirt into the bedroom. It was more than that, though: this combined with her desire for a man who was probably going to end up working for her was driving her insane. Even if he did want to eat her alive, even if she could be successful with her teasing and flirting, she didn't have that option any more. Those were the rules of life and the ethics of the workplace: no hanky-panky with work colleagues. This rule, her rule, was even stricter when it came to people who worked directly for her. It could never ever be broken.

She worked on until 1 a.m., her frustrations slowing down her thought processes at every turn. She had no choice, though, but to work on and meet the demands of her job. If she'd bothered to ask John for an extension she would have got it, but she was a perfectionist and achieved everything that was asked, which was usually why she was asked in the first place.

Heleyna had never been so grateful it was Friday night. On the traffic-jam-filled journey to Troy's she was already envisaging herself curled up on the sofa in her tracksters, takeaway on her knee, half-empty beer sat in front of her on the coffee table, video player running with her favourite chick flick. More run-ins with Phoebe along with a later night the day before had left her shattered. One good thing had come of the day, though. The sign-off for Sam's appointment had come swiftly, thanks to her relationship with Sue. And she'd earlier had the verbal offer accepted by Sam. The written offer was already on its way, thanks to the HR team, and that meant the end of any slim chance she might have had with Mr Molloy.

She entered Troy's bachelor pad, removed her boots and wandered into the living room, plonking her palmtop in her briefcase as she walked. She'd been updating her task list on the way from the car to the front door. She often thought on the run.

Troy was laid on the floor, face down, away from her, putting in the last of the CDs he'd set up for the night in his sound system, a system with so many buttons and flashing lights, and so much digital text, that Heleyna had still not dared touch it.

Before she knew it, she had involuntarily walked across the room towards him, any thoughts of a relaxing evening now far from her mind. Not a word was said between them; these days they didn't always need conversation to know what the other was thinking. She rested her briefcase on the floor.

His jeans enticingly showed the round firmness of each buttock, separated in their glory, his narrow waist and broad shoulders enhanced by his slim-fitting T-shirt. Unknowingly he had seduced her – drawn her to him, giving her exactly what she needed – though she hadn't known this until confronted with the rear view of her gorgeous man.

She straddled his waist and pulled up his T-shirt to reveal his muscular back, and began to move her body up and down his, rubbing her demanding crotch and rigid nipples up against his butt whilst firmly stroking his bareness above.

'You could do this to me all night,' he whispered.

How could she fail but feel the same with a backside like that to delight her? Not willing or able to wait any longer to see him, she reached round and undid his jeans. As she unwrapped her prize, her hot pussy spasmed in anticipation and a sense of urgency overcame her. Gaining enjoyment out of still being clothed herself, she quickly removed his remaining garments. He was submissive, putty in her hands. She felt like she was in control. In reality, she knew she was putty in his.

She stroked her fingers up and down his backside, feeling the separateness of the curves, then firmly pulled his cheeks apart, revealing his puckered paradise. Hoping to hurt, she spread his cheeks still further, and he groaned. She knew he wanted her to touch him, to lick it, to penetrate it. He would have to wait.

She bent her face close to him and the urge to bite him overcame her. He cried out in ecstasy beneath her as she bit every part of each mound in front of her. Hot and sweaty with lust, her mind focused on the man in front of her, on ravishing his body, on bringing them both to a delicious, delirious orgasm. Spanking his smooth solid buttocks in between each bite, she devoured the irresistible sound that echoed around her ears, around her muff, disappearing into her infinite black hole. Her clitoris throbbed, desperate for contact. She wanted to throw her clothes off and ride him, but knew that if she did their pleasure would be over too soon. She wanted this feeling of horny anticipation to last forever.

Heleyna lay down over the length of his body, leg to leg, arm to arm, hand to hand, and began to thrust her groin into his buttocks, the seam of her trousers roughly exciting her moist, wanton clit. She was in heaven. Afraid of the orgasm that was building within her, she quickly withdrew herself from him and focused her attention on his pleasure once more.

Her fingers found their way to his secret orifice, which he willingly presented to her. She stroked it gently, desperately wanting to enter him, to find his magic spot, to make him come violently. He thrust his groin in a reflex response to her enchantingly wicked ways, rubbing his cock against the thick deep carpet beneath him. Heleyna moved her hands slowly round his pelvis, her touch moving closer to his weeping solidity. When she found it she knew why she lusted for this man. His dick was one she classed as beautiful, perfection personified. As a teenager she would have called it a 'tear-jerker'. Today she called it her saviour. Bending over, she brought her face close to his body and nibbled his side, just managing to catch a peek of what was to come.

Needing to get up close, she lay down on her back. He lifted his body in response and she eased her face beneath his hot, slender stomach. Taking in deep breaths, she gulped down his sweet, salty smell before losing herself in the delights of mouth, tongue, balls and cock. His dick was so ready. She could feel the fullness of it, the way it quivered in the depths of her throat. God, how she wanted him to spurt now as he drilled into her, irrational, wild, lost in sensuality. She knew he wouldn't, though. He would want to see her unclothed, to watch her bouncing breasts, her wobbling arse, in front of him.

She watched him closely as he lifted himself off her, his eyes giving away his thoughts as he began to undress her. He was truly mesmerised by her melon-like rounded boobs, adorned with exquisitely ripened nipples. He pushed his raging penis into her Wonder-bra-designed cleavage and pounded, allowing his tip to touch her peachy lips with each thrust. He tasted and smelt sublime. His swollen cock twitched aggressively, its purple end angry and desperate.

Again his attention returned to undressing her. She watched him carefully, his glistening penis hypnotising her into submission. He could ask anything of her now and she would willingly and eagerly obey.

Leaving her G-string in place he began to thrust into her, the material accentuating the movement between them. He raised himself onto his hands, allowing both of them to watch as he moved in and out of her, pushing her G-string harshly into her, the abrasive nature of the material taking her breath away.

Heleyna was ready now, her cheeks and neck flushed, her mind focused on her goal, her body tingling with the anticipation of the oneness that was to come. She never tired of this instinctive journey, a welcome release from the objective, rational thinking she was expected to produce in her career.

Troy led her to the soft down-filled sofa and sat. She removed her soaking string, her oozing pussy straddled his cock and, slowly, she lowered herself onto him, enjoying every movement of the first touch inside her, of him reaching the end of her chasm and touching her spot. Holding firmly on to the back of the sofa to control her movements, she rubbed herself up and down his swollen dick.

Looking her in the eyes for the first time that night, his own expression filled with wonderful wickedness, he spoke in a deep, lust-filled voice. 'I want to put my dick everywhere, to feel it everywhere.'

He moistened his finger with his warm, smooth tongue and inserted it slowly, gently, into her exposed, vulnerable anus. As she pumped him more aggressively, so too did his actions become more violent, his one finger becoming three, his gentle movements becoming powerful.

Knowing that he enjoyed watching her caress and pleasure herself, she felt for the spot that would push her over the edge. Both her holes filled to the brim, her fingers pushed between her slit, Heleyna was in paradise. On the precipice of desire, her enjoyment became increasingly audible. He knew where she was heading. He withdrew himself from her, stood up and bent her over the sofa, and, taking his cock in his hand, he pushed it alternately in and out of her cunt and then rubbed it against her arsehole, all the while scrabbling at her clit. She loved the feel of her swollen firmness against his fingertips. She wanted more and more and more. Every inch of her body spasmed as she went over and into the abyss, screaming out in ecstasy. Every muscle, every hair, every nerve was alive. Her pulsating cunt gripped his cock, milking it of its life as it spurted deep within her.

When a starving-hungry Heleyna woke an hour later she lay there for a moment examining Troy's beautiful face. As she contemplated each feature, she realised, with satisfaction, that the anger had disappeared. It still amazed her how chemicals could alter her very being so dramatically.

5

Heleyna walked into her first art class, apprehension written all over her face. She was dressed sensibly for the occasion – old bootleg jeans, skateboard shoes and fleecy top – with her long hair piled up randomly on the back of her head. She was carrying cheap pre-stretched canvas and a plastic bag filled with goodies. Everything was new, no tube of acrylic or pencil yet touched. The familiar smell hit her nostrils, an odour she had smelt many times before in what felt like a previous life: the aroma of industrial cleaning fluid mixed with paint and thinners and clay gave her an uncanny feeling of being back at school.

She sat herself at the bench, her plastic bag still clutched in her hands, and acknowledged the other students with a smile and a nod as they entered the room. It looked like it was going to be a small class with a real mixture of students. People-watching, Heleyna began to feel more comfortable: many of the others were taking out materials that looked as fresh as her own. She was quietly relieved that she wasn't the only one who was there to learn from scratch.

A scatty-looking woman entered the room. She was quite clearly the tutor; she had artist written all over her, in her dress sense and demeanour. She was a large woman with heavily made-up features, her deep purple-dyed hair rebellious and wild. It suited who she was – not many people could have got away with it. Introducing herself as Bet, she dumped a huge box on the front desk, and asked the class to do the obligatory round-the-room introductions. 'So then, who would like to speak first?'

Eyes looked everywhere apart from at Bet, even Heleyna's.

'OK then, we'll start with you, then move clockwise round the room.' She was pointing at a young man with mousy floppy hair and large blue eyes with eyelashes most women would kill for.

'Hi, I'm, er, Ben.' His face flushed a glorious rich red. He stuttered a little then continued, mumbling all the way, his mouth hidden behind his hand. 'I'm 21, used to paint at school, but never abstract painting. I'm pretty busy with the final year of my degree, so thought I should do something as a release from that.'

'Thanks Ben. Good to meet you.' Bet smiled a warm, friendly smile.

The introductions continued.

'I'm June and this is my husband, Fred.' June pointed to the grey-haired man next to her, who smiled at the group, 'The last of our children has just left home – at the age of 23, I might add – and we finally have some time for hobbies. So, here we are.'

Fred felt he had nothing more to add and so Heleyna took her turn, unusually nervous even though she was used to public speaking. 'Hi, everyone. I'm Heleyna, I'm 28. I currently work as a project manager in the centre of Leeds. I've decided I need to achieve more with my life than just work. Um ... used to paint at school, but done nothing since.'

'Thanks Heleyna. Nice to have you here.' Bet nodded at the young slim blonde woman next to Heleyna.

'Yes, I'm Jemma. I teach yoga and want to be able to express the spirituality I experience in my yoga on paper. I've never painted or drawn before, and don't know if I can do it yet. But something inside of me is craving a creative outlet.' Her voice was soft and girlish, and light.

'Oh, it's my turn. I'm Todd.' He peered at the rest of the class over his small round glasses, which looked comical on his podgy face, teetering on the edge of his small pug nose. 'I'm an accountant. No opportunity to be creative in my role. I have painted before, but could do with some help to develop my skills further. You know, get the creativity flowing.'

The final person, a horsy-looking woman, spoke next. 'I'm Bernadette. I don't work officially. I do a lot of community work and work for the Church. I have two children, Sarah and Timothy, and four dogs. I normally do fine watercolour landscape painting so was looking to do something a little different – extend the repertoire, so to speak.'

'Thanks, team. Good to meet you all and learn a little about you. I'm sure I can do something for all of you over the coming weeks, help you all achieve and give you the confidence to go it alone. Right then, let's get to business.'

They spent the two-hour class learning about abstract painting, and what made a painting abstract. Bet also stimulated discussion on pieces by a wide variety of famous and not-so-famous artists, asking them to voice their likes and dislikes to assist them in drawing out their own personal style.

Heleyna felt her hackles rise whenever Bernadette, the horsy woman, spoke. She had a strong opinion on everything Bet showed to them in her numerous art-history books, and she made sure everyone around her knew exactly what that opinion was. The others all seemed pretty easy-going. In fact, June gave Heleyna 'that look' whenever Bernadette spoke, obviously annoyed by her as much as Heleyna.

When 8.30 p.m. arrived, Heleyna couldn't quite

believe it. The session had flown by and given her exactly what she'd been craving for some time: an escape; a knowledge of something other than the intricacies of project management; new people with different attitudes to life; and a creative outlet. It had filled at least one of the little gaps in her life that had been niggling away at her for some time.

June invited everyone down to the local pub on the way out. 'Give us a chance to get to know each other, seeing as we're going to be painting together for the next ten weeks.'

June passed Heleyna another of her looks when Bernadette made her apologies. At the beginning of the evening Heleyna would never have imagined that June would be one of her allies; people never ceased to amaze her.

Sat in the Rose and Crown, a half of bitter in her hand, a sense of happiness seeped into her, a contentment that began at the tips of her fingers and toes and worked its way through her body until it reached her core. She felt glowingly satisfied, a slight grin evident as she perched on the end of the bench next to Ben. For fear of frightening him, she kept her very obvious feminine charms at a distance and spoke more softly than normal. 'So then, Ben, where do you live?'

He jumped slightly, surprised that she'd spoken to him. 'Oh, oh I live in Kirkstall – the town end. Got the bus up here tonight. You?'

'Just round the corner, actually, so this is pretty handy.' She studied him carefully, her eyes flickering over his features and body the way that humans inspect each other on first meeting. He was cute but not particularly masculine. Nor was he a great conversationalist, so Heleyna gave him something easy to talk about. 'Tell me about your degree.'

'I'm studying history – single honours.'

Heleyna wanted to grab his hand and move it out of the way of his mouth; she'd never had much tolerance of self-consciousness. But, instead, she kept up the small talk. 'Good choice. I did English and politics. Not quite sure how I ended up in project management.'

He moved his hand temporarily, giving her the opportunity to have a good look at his face in totality. He was fetching, in a public schoolboy kind of a way. Not Heleyna's type, though – far too shy. She always seemed to go for the confident unsubtle ones who flirted outrageously and fucked her brains out. Sam and Troy, together at once, she thought, her grin extending even further.

Ben looked at his watch. 'Must remember not to leave after ten; no buses running after then.'

'I'll give you a lift home if you like. My car's just back at the college. That's why I'm sticking to the one half. Save you having to worry about the time.' She was unsure where her generosity stemmed from.

'Oh, thanks, that would be really helpful. Not that pleasant walking the streets in the dark round here anyway.'

Heleyna couldn't quite believe it – shy *and* afraid of the dark. What a wimp!

She spent the next hour or so speaking with June and Fred about walking. They were keen ramblers and knew quite a few of the good walks in the dales and moors. They were fit, too, making Heleyna feel very lazy despite her recent moors visit. She took out her filofax, made a note of the recommended walks, and vowed to get herself on the trip list should any of their recommendations be advertised at the hiking club. Still unsure of her motivation for joining the club, she guessed it was one of two possible options: a moment of madness or discovering a snippet of who she really was.

She saw Ben yawning out of the corner of her eye. She was pretty shattered herself. 'OK, Ben. Let's get you home.'

They said their goodbyes and were on their way.

Heleyna initiated the conversation as she'd expected she would have to. 'So, are you going to get the chance to practise some painting at home?'

'Well, our student flat is pretty poky. But I live with a guy – Jez – he's studying fine art and said I could use his studio if I liked. He's a brilliant artist. You should come and see his work. It's certainly inspired me.' Ben was warming up, conversation now coming more easily to him in this one-on-one situation. 'His studio is down near the university.'

'Actually, I would like that.' Heleyna wanted to exploit her new-found interest and not lose the momentum that was rapidly building. 'I've got a good idea – why don't I come and pick you up from the uni on the way out of town next week, then we could go then and head out for the class. I don't usually take my car in, but it's the only way I'll get home on time for class each week.' Enthusiasm flowed, and for once it wasn't rooted in work or men. She was pleasantly surprised.

Looking up at the sky through the windscreen she noticed, for the first time in many, many months, how beautiful the night sky was, the larger stars and planets looking down at her as they penetrated the glow of light which surrounded the city.

'Great idea. You want to take the next left. There, that's my flat on the left under the second street lamp.' He pointed his effeminate index finger at a particularly squalid-looking building.

Heleyna pulled over and scanned the street. It reminded her of the grotty places she'd lived in as a student: rubbish adorning the streets along with old furniture, and houses with bars across the windows to keep out the teenage petty thieves who invariably broke in on Saturday nights, leaving with the TV under their arm, and not much else. 'I'll see you next week, then: I'll pick you up at five-fifteen at the uni steps. That OK?'

'Thanks, yes. Thanks for the lift, particularly as it's out of your way.'

'No worries and see you soon.'

She spun off up the street in her Beetle, not bothering to indicate in the deserted road.

The following week disappeared, and Wednesday came upon her frighteningly quickly. Work was manic as usual; now even more so than before, as she had Sam's induction programme to arrange along with his work-station. Boring, tedious tasks, the easiest of which she'd dished out to Phoebe to keep her busy and out of her way as much as possible. Heleyna was still taking advantage of the fact that Phoebe couldn't do enough to please her. Heleyna never mentioned the conversation she'd overheard, and Phoebe certainly wasn't about to. Heleyna was overjoyed that she'd finally got Phoebe where she wanted her – subservient and quiet.

On her way out of work she took a trip via John's office to drop off what she hoped was the final version of the project plan for approval. She was shattered – it had been backwards and forwards so many times, in and out of meetings with her as she attempted to get stakeholder agreement to timescales. She hoped and prayed that this time it was acceptable and would get John's illegible signature across the bottom of the cover-ing memo. She just couldn't be arsed with any of it any more: the politics, the hidden agendas, the personalities to please. Her drive had receded into oblivion, leaving behind only traces of what it had once been.

Neither John nor his PA, Sue, were to be seen. She

entered his office, with its personal coffee machine and comfy sofas, and moved towards the large mahogany desk. Negotiating its rounded corners to place the plan across his keyboard so that he couldn't miss it, she caught sight of a pile of papers in his in-tray. A bolt of surprise hit her, her heart missing a beat. She'd just seen something she'd only seen on one occasion before – the Huxley Club letterhead. The intrigue that had become apparent at Ted and Jacinta's was reawoken. Her mind went into overdrive. About to nosy her way through the pile of papers and retrieve it, she was halted in her quest by the sound of Sue's efficient, clicking footsteps coming towards the room. Sue was a woman every senior manager needed on his or her side. Heleyna stalled herself with amazing and unusual self-control.

'Hi Sue, I've just left the project plan on John's desk for approval. Hope that's OK.' Her voice was on edge, higher and quicker than usual.

'No problem. I'll make sure he reads it quickly. You're off home early, for you.'

'I'm on the way to art classes. I started them last week. If nothing else it will force me to leave the office at a decent hour at least once a week.'

'You really shouldn't work so hard, you know. Enjoy the class.' Sue was trying to hurry Heleyna out of the office.

Heleyna took the hint. 'Good night.'

She drove the short journey thinking about the Huxley Club. 'What the hell is this club about?' She was talking to herself, and it didn't go unnoticed by the carful of lads next to her. They honked their horn and whooped at her. She gave them the V, just masking the patronising look she bestowed from the comfort and security of her loveable little car.

As she approached the steps of the university building, she saw Ben sitting, his floppy hair blowing round his face in the light breeze. He was chatting to another man. She pulled up and put on her hazards, blocking the road temporarily. He noticed and walked towards her, grinning, his arms full with folders and books, the other young man not far behind. Couldn't be much older than 25, she thought.

Heleyna exited the car and walked over to the boot so that Ben could dispense with his load. 'Hi Ben. How are you doing?' She didn't let him answer. 'I assume this is Jez?'

'Hi Heleyna. Thanks for the lift. Hope you don't mind, but I suggested that Jez come along too, then he can tell you all about his work. Then perhaps you could drop him off at ours on the way through to class?' Ben was different today, masculinity and confidence seeping out of him.

'No problem, you guys,' she said, then added, a grin across her face, 'Bloody cheeky students.'

Both men laughed.

They hopped into the car, Ben in the back, Jez next to her in the passenger seat. He chatted nonstop as they made their way to his studio in Hessle Road. Ben was silent in the back, just sitting and listening to his pal, his gaze staring down at his hands. Checking he was OK, Heleyna passed the odd look at him in her rear-view mirror.

As they talked Heleyna began to realise that Jez was eyeing her up. She could see him from the corner of her eye gazing semi-discreetly at her breasts, her rounded hips and legs, which were almost hidden beneath the straight cut of her work attire. Although at first taken aback, she soon started to enjoy being the object of desire. To her it was a game, a game she had played many times before but usually with the most experienced of men. She arched her back, just a little. She wanted to be the older woman teasing these two young bucks into submission, into wanting her so much they hurt. Then she would be free to eat them up, chew them around for a short time until they bored her, then spit them out – two shattered, battered, but more worldly wise young men.

Jez responded. He seemed to know and understand that the referee had blown the whistle to start play. Now he watched her more intently, taking her clothes off with each glance. Pretending that comfort was on her mind, she wiggled her bottom in the seat and her skirt rode up, displaying a magnificent thigh. Not once did she look over at him. Her actions were mainly intuitive. She did, however, cast a peek at Ben's reflection. His eyes no longer inspected his hands; his line of sight was now firmly placed on the driver's seat and the display taking place within it. Heleyna was on a roll.

They arrived at the studio. Jez walked round the bonnet of her Beetle and opened the door for her, a real showman, strutting his stuff all the way. Heleyna took the opportunity to have a look at him properly, and for the first time since they'd met. He was tidy, for an artist, his style mainstream. He isn't model material, she thought, but he's young and nubile and very keen to please me. On that day, and at that moment in time, that was enough for her, just what she needed: a takeaway burger rather than a gourmet delicacy.

She showed him what he wanted, opening her legs as she exited her seat. Once he'd taken in the transparent opportunity to see her dampening crotch he smiled and looked her in the eyes for the first time. She smiled back, viewing him from beneath her thick lashes. Ben was now standing next to his friend and he gazed at her nipples, nipples that were just on display beneath the slim-fitting twinset. Standing together, the two men made her very glad she was such an incorrigible tart. It amazed her how her blatant naughtiness always seemed to reap such rewards.

Ben led them into the studio, his walk now seemingly unfearing; she was suitably impressed that testosterone could have such a powerful impact on a man. The room was surprisingly orderly, the walls covered in amazing oils, acrylics, charcoals and watercolours, and there was a part-finished textural work sitting on a large wooden easel. Heleyna loved that smell of drying gloss varnish and paint.

She wandered round, pretending to look at the work around her, frantically focused on pouncing on one of these men and the mouthwatering thought of one of their dicks entering her and of her showing them the way. She didn't care which one: either would plug the gap she needed filling. Though more than aware that the two men had planned this little excursion, she felt in total control.

Surprisingly, Ben made the first move. He came up behind her and ran his hand down her spine and over her arse, pulling her hair roughly on the way. Her breath left her for a second. She turned, tormenting him with her tightly enclosed breasts as she removed the outer layer of her twinset. The look in his eye told her he was one-track-minded, focused on shagging, lost in lust. Brilliant, she thought. It's my lucky day. She didn't know quite what she'd done to deserve such a treat.

He took a step towards her and ran his hands over her breasts, making an impression on her nipples. She was desperate for him. In fast forward she removed first Ben's clothes, then her own, and ordered him onto the central table, where they were surrounded by artists' tools. In their lust for each other they scattered pots of paint, brushes and pallets across the tabletop, some toppling onto the lino floor below. Paint was everywhere, rich red acrylic seeping out of one pot pooled near to his right shoulder. Her skin was on fire, craving sensations that would drive her wild. She touched the red thick silky fluid as she straddled his groin. He was shoved firmly between her legs, rubbing himself up and down her, touching her greedy clit.

At first she was unusually coy, only covered one finger with the luxurious liquid, then smeared it over his smooth hairless chest. It felt good. The false modesty dissipated. The second time she grabbed a handful, covered his torso, the paint squishing and squelching between her warm fingers.

She fully opened the lid, took hold of the pot, and poured the thick, silken-feeling material over her receptive breasts. Large droplets left her nipples and sploshed onto her lover below, like heavy raindrops in a thunderstorm. This time it was Ben's turn. He massaged it into her, taking care of her nipples and sensitive convex stomach, exhibiting the modest muscles in his arms as they fought against gravity. He wanted to be in control now. He removed her from him, laying her face down on the now red, slimy table. She slipped over the surface, her tits drinking in the smooth greasy oil slick as yet more paint was smeared over her thrusting wobbling arse.

Both of them covered head to foot in acrylics, he pulled her to her feet, and together they created their first abstract masterpiece. A beautiful clean ready-stretched canvas board became their bed. Before long it was covered in prints from every aspect of their bodies – smeared into one awesome image of fucking. God, he felt good. His dick found every nook and cranny of her demanding cunt. His arse was as firm as a pumped-up air mattress, his shoulders broad and arms lean and strong – all accentuated by the astounding effects of a pot of moist cool silky red paint. The two of them disappeared, lost in fucking.

A noise brought Heleyna back to consciousness and she suddenly became aware of a presence – she'd forgotten about Jez, who'd been enjoying the scene from the doorway. He was leant up against the wall, his flies undone, cock in his hand. Too aroused to give a damn about consequence, Heleyna beckoned him. Ben smiled knowingly as Jez approached. Heleyna manoeuvred onto her side from her favourite doggy-style position as Jez undressed and climbed onto their canvas. He created footprints on the way down, his long slender dick rigid and ready. His body was also long and lean, his long hair falling over his shoulders.

Ben opened her legs wide from behind and eased his prick into her arse, an oily jelly of some kind easing the way. The initial tears it brought to her eyes soon disappeared as Jez lay in front of her and entered her cunt, his eyes staring over her shoulder towards his mate. To him she was an anonymous tight warm hole, and his desire was obviously meant more for Ben than for her. She enjoyed the selfishness of their acts, all three of them in this for their own gain.

So full that she feared her insides would spill out, she eased her position a little as they collided into her, using their cocks as battering rams, their movements in sync. She was powerless as these two amoral beasts pleasured themselves within her, the pain Ben created pushing her closer to orgasm as she buffed her clit like an agitated Aladdin. Simultaneous shuddering and groaning ensued, the three orgasms creating an incredible energy, adding more texture to the masterpiece beneath them.

* * *

Heleyna and Ben did get to their class that night. They were a little late, the shower and change of clothing taking care of that. Heleyna never did get to wear that skirt and twinset ever again, a glorious memory of a stunning hour of her life.

When she finally got home after two hours of experimenting with brush techniques, she phoned Troy.

'Hi, Troy. You'll never guess what happened to me this evening.'

'I know that phrase and tone, my dear. Who was it this time? Which poor man was seduced into the spider's web?' He was laughing.

'It wasn't a man at all.' Heleyna couldn't accept that she was so predictable, the tone of disbelief showing in her voice.

'Hey, you've not been after a woman again, have you? You could have asked me along!' He was still laughing.

She was delighted he wasn't able to guess – not that predictable after all. 'No, it was men – plural – or, rather, boys – two together mixed with paint and canvas. God, it was good.'

'Looks like you're back on form again. These art classes must be doing you the world of good. So then, when do I get my turn?'

'I'll see you at the weekend, you gorgeous beast.' She still craved him. 'I also need you to help me pick up some hiking gear for next weekend. New adventure part two.'

'Not that I know anything about hiking, but, sure, I'll come along. Not sure if I'll be any help though. At least it'll mean seeing you for an hour or two. Oh, by the way, Sam's coming to stay at mine from that weekend until he finds himself a house. Hope you don't mind one of your underlings being pals with me.'

'No, why should I?' She was a little defensive. Although she'd never openly expressed her infatuation with Sam, she thought Troy must know. He did know her well, after all. 'Of course, he starts a week on Monday. Excellent. I need someone on board, so then I can start working more reasonable hours and spend more time with you. Then you'll wish you hadn't complained about never seeing me!' She was teasing him. She was also still feeling defeatist about the whole Sam situation, at not getting her wicked way with him, especially tonight, after such a horny experience. She was fired up and raring to go.

'See you at the weekend then. Give me a ring on Saturday morning. Let me know what time. Actually, better thought. Come and stay at mine on Friday night so I can have a taste of what you had on offer this evening.'

'I'll look forward to that, you tart.' Heleyna enjoyed their badgering.

'Takes one to know one!'

They hung up. Heleyna walked to the fridge and pulled out a cold beer, then found her favourite spot on her sofa and watched half an hour of TV, a rare treat.

Art class the following week gave her as much of a thrill as the previous weeks, the two hours never seeming long enough. Ben, his stutter no longer in evidence, was now making a play for Jemma, his stance almost cocky. Heleyna left him to it. She'd had her wicked way with him and now he bored her. He was not the kind of man who would ever interest her again. He was too young for a start. She needed men with more experience and more oomph; men who oozed testosterone and lusted after every ounce of her body; men who could dominate her but also had enough self-confidence to allow her to dominate them.

6

It was the day before her first weekend away with the hiking club, her favourite day of the week, Friday. Heleyna's Beetle was filled with things it had never seen before, goods that wholesome people have, not dirty tarts who know nothing about life other than work and sex. She had to be ready to leave swiftly at 5 p.m. to meet the bus for the trip over the A65 to the Lakes.

She'd been hanging out for this day ever since she'd spied the letterhead in John's office. She knew John was away on conference and that Sue had accompanied him, and not only had Heleyna stolen his reserved parking space in the car park beneath the offices, but she'd also been plotting to enter his office and retrieve the information she just had to see. This information wasn't the approved project plan which John had personally returned to her, congratulating her on her efficiency in achieving the first key goal; this was the Huxley Club letter which she hoped would reveal a little more to her about what went on at this elusive, exclusive club.

She waited until morning teatime, when the smokers were hanging around outside on the road and the rest were hanging around the coffee machine having the usual Friday wind-down gossip – both activities she'd never bothered to take part in.

Walking into John's office, she was ever confident; she needed to look self-assured, like she was up to good as opposed to no good in case a colleague saw her. Not wanting her footsteps to be heard once her foraging began, after closing the solid door behind her she removed her heels. She was back to her old self at work – sensible clothes, sensible shoes. Her hussy-for-the-day dress strategy to impress Sam was nowhere in sight. It was a plan that had defeated her and, irritatingly, she no longer had the option to achieve it; this was a rare failure for a usually infallible woman.

The light in the office was dim; it was an overcast day outside and the blinds were closed to half-mast. As she tiptoed round John's desk and past the video monitor, annoyingly, her toe managed to find the sharp corner, the last corner before she had access to his tray. She went into comedy-sketch mode: her face purple and in full grimace, her stubbed foot in one hand and hopping on the other, her mouth closed tight and her teeth clenched. She remained in this bouncing stance for a couple of minutes until the subsiding pain allowed her to relax. For the first time in her life she'd managed not to verbalise her pain. This was something she was usually extremely good at, always wanting to share agony with whoever was willing to listen to her moans.

She grabbed the pile of papers from his in-tray and hobbled towards one of the comfy leather sofas, her toe throbbing and hot, a frown still evident across her forehead. Despite her pain, she took in the surroundings. One day I'll have an office as impressive as this, she thought.

Sunk into the black luxury, her legs curled under her and with her skirt up round her thighs, she waded through the impressive pile of papers. Her inquisitive mind ensured she read a few of the more interesting pieces in the pile, giving her a bit of background information on profits and a potential buy-out from a competitor. None of it concerned her. SPM had always been financially viable, a competitive force in the market even though it was a small entity. Large global organisations were always making a play for them. It was flattering.

It wasn't long before she saw the letterhead she wanted, just peeping out, only a handful of pages beneath the letter she was reading. She discarded the rest of the papers, no longer caring about the corporate world, and held the golden ticket in her hand. With her heart in her mouth in anticipation of what she was about to discover, she began to read.

Dear John,

Please find enclosed the videotapes you requested at our last meeting. I trust you will find them as enjoyable as we have. I will invoice you on the next payment run on 20th of the month.

We would also like to take this opportunity to thank you for recommending we introduce Phoebe to the Huxley Club. She appeared to enjoy the first night immensely and interacted well with the other members. The club committee is now more than happy to accept her as a full member to the Huxley Club. We will be writing to Phoebe separately with this news.

For your information, the committee has also agreed to invite both Heleyna Lane and her partner Troy to the next meeting of the Huxley Club for an introductory night.

We look forward to seeing you at our next gathering and to gaining your feedback on the potential new members.

Yours truly,
Jacinta Jones
Social Secretary

She had signed it simply 'Jacinta'.

Heleyna continued rummaging through the letters to see if there was anything more pertaining to the club. She was out of luck. She took the single A4 page to John's personal photocopier and made herself a copy, then returned the papers, which she'd carefully kept in the order she'd found them, and replaced her shoes. She'd been twenty minutes.

Her toe now less painful, she re-entered confident mode. She opened the office door and strode out, closing the door behind her. There was no one in the corridor. She returned to her office, her low heels loud on the polished floor and her bottom moving flawlessly in her knee-length skirt.

Sat now at her own desk she re-read the letter slowly, attempting to read between the lines and determine the facts about Huxley. Nothing jumped out at her other than Phoebe's involvement. There was one thing that did make her wonder, though – the fact that the letter seemed guarded, giving the information needed without giving anything away. But then Heleyna thought about Troy and how he would react. He would probably laugh at her and tell her that her imagination was in overdrive. He was a great leveller for her.

The day's detective work apparently futile, Heleyna filed the letter away in her personal files and continued with her duties. She vowed to continue her search, especially now Phoebe's name was mentioned – the sly little minx had got in before her.

Changed into hiking gear, Heleyna made her way in her Beetle, which she loved to death, to the school in Skipton where the hiking club's bus was to depart. She loved early summer, especially once out of the city and amongst the fields and greenery and villages.

She felt weird: a dash of nerves shaken up with a splash of the unknown. Troy had laughed cruelly when she'd first told him what she was about to do. Firstly, it was a club, and, secondly, she'd never before shown an inkling of interest in anything outdoorsy. He had asked her if she was entering a premature midlife crisis. Unable to voice her reasons, she'd just hit him playfully round the back of the head, then ignored him. What was the point? There was nothing to explain. It was simply something she'd had an urge to do, so why not? She was always being told that life was too short, so she wasn't about to let Troy's criticism stop her.

She pulled up and the bus was already there, people milling around outside, talking and filling the bus's boot with rucksacks. She turned off the ignition and sat for a moment before getting out of her car. She looked down at herself and across at the others. At least I look the part, she thought. She was dressed in lightweight quick-dry walking trousers and dri-fit slim-fitting T-shirt, a fleecy jacket on the seat beside her ready for when the sun dropped and the coolness of evening set in. On her feet were new thick wool socks surrounded by clean new walking boots, which were bloody hot. The others looked the same, only their gear wasn't quite as box-fresh.

She was ready now. She jumped quickly out of her car, as if trying to convince herself it was the right thing to do. A forced smile on her face, she walked towards the group.

Within a few seconds her fears had dissipated. The trip leader, Meg, had recognised her face as new and sought her out.

'Hi there, are you Heleyna or Mandy?' This woman certainly knew how to speak quickly.

'Hi, I'm Heleyna.'

'Hi Heleyna. We've got two new people tonight – you and another woman called Mandy. What tends to happen on the Friday evening is we all head up, usually in quiet mode, to our camp for the night. Then we do formal introductions in the morning. Saturday night is usually the social evening. So don't worry too much if people don't appear friendly. It's hard to do too much socialising in a moving bus. Right then, bring your bag over and we'll get it on board.'

'OK.' Heleyna wandered back to her car, wondering if Meg ever came up for air. She hadn't even noticed her taking a breath between sentences.

Heleyna took her seat on the bus, wishing desperately that she'd brought something with her to eat; Meg hadn't mentioned a dinner stop. Meg had been right though, the group were pretty quiet, just talking in their pairs on the seats around her. She was beginning to feel like an outsider when a friendly woman in her thirties sat next to her.

'Wow, I was almost late. Bloody children. Hi, I'm Mandy.' She turned and shook hands with Heleyna.

'Hello Mandy, I'm Heleyna. You're the other new girl on the block then?'

'Oh, great, you're new too. Makes me feel a little less nervous.'

Heleyna was relieved. Mandy looked like an amiable woman with kind eyes and a pretty smile. The two chatted along for a while before Meg stood up to do her bit.

'Hello gang. Right, we now have a full posse. It's about three hours from here to the bunkhouse near the base of Blencathra, with a short stop for food, so we should arrive about 9 p.m. When we get there we have a twenty-minute walk to the bunkhouse. Enjoy the journey. I'll give you a full briefing in the morning at breakfast – 7 a.m. sharp. We intend to commence our walk over Sharp Edge at 8.30 a.m., weather permitting, of course.'

'Come on, Meg, let the driver do his job.' A lanky-looking guy near the back of the bus was shouting good-naturedly, obviously used to her ramblings.

'Thanks, Tom. OK, we're off.'

Meg sat herself down in the front seat. Heleyna could still hear her talking from five rows back, and she looked over at Mandy and they both laughed.

'I hope they're not all like guide leaders,' Mandy was whispering under her breath like a naughty schoolgirl, a cheeky grin spreading across her freckled face.

'What a laugh.' Heleyna's voice was also low.

'Imagine if we have to spend tomorrow evening round the campfire, Meg leading a wholesome singsong. I think I'd piss my pants.'

Heleyna's tone became more excited. 'Fuck, that would be hysterical. I'd spend the whole evening snorting with laughter, then probably have to go and stand in the corner with a dunce's hat on my head until I learned how to behave properly. I remember doing that in assembly at school once. I was laughing so hard, my hand tight over my mouth, my face as red as a strawberry. My mate at the time kept catching my eye, and that could keep us laughing for another five minutes. I remember this occasion above all others because I was desperate for the loo, and before I knew it I'd peed my pants. There was a pool of wee all over the school-hall floor and more running down my legs.'

The two continued in this vein for the rest of the journey, telling stories, laughing, and learning snippets from each other's lives. Heleyna couldn't remember laughing this much in quite some time. She knew that Mandy and her were going to be great friends. It reminded her of the chats she'd had at school, gossiping and giggling with a group of girls. She'd also forgotten how great it was just to chat about nonsense – no work, no business proposals, no bullshit, just plain good fun.

They arrived at the bunkhouse after the brief walk and headed straight to bed. They were all shattered from a week at work topped up with travel. Mandy and

Heleyna managed to get on bunks in the same room and next to each other. There were eight people to each room. The dorm was simple: no frills, basic mattresses on wooden bunks, a wooden floor and windows straight to the outside. It was a world away from corporate business trips! Heleyna lay looking out into the pitch darkness, listening to the breathing bodies around her. A hint of sadness seeped into her at how small her life had become for the last couple of years. She'd turned into a dreary workcentric person with little depth to both her life and the experiences within that life. At least I'm doing something about it, she thought, comforting herself, and she drifted off to sleep.

She was awoken in the morning by the raucous sound of Meg's voice.

'Come on, campers. Time for breakfast and the morning briefing.'

It was 6.30 a.m. Heleyna couldn't remember the last time she'd woken up at this time on a weekend morning. She lay there for a moment with her head inside her sleeping bag, remembering the glorious dream she'd been having about Sam. He'd been shagging her senseless in John's office across his huge desk. Her skirt was hitched up around her waist, her panties still attached to her left ankle and her heels hanging off the big toe of each foot. He was thrusting into her, his beautiful frame outlined clearly in front of her. Her black shoes, which smacked against her soles with each thrust, threatened to jump off her big toes and hit the floor, alerting colleagues in neighbouring offices. She was mesmerised by his face, his expression, his dimples that lit up with each stifled groan.

'Come on, Heleyna, twenty-five minutes to get up and dressed.'

'OK, I'm up, Meg.' In her mind she was shouting loudly for Meg to fuck off and leave her to her fantasy.

She guessed Meg had never encountered a fantasy in her life. It was always the prim outdoors girls who could probably do with a good fuck from a very real man to put them straight!

The walk up Blencathra was something else. Heleyna was challenged by the ascent over Sharp Ridge. They were not something she'd ever tackled before – heights and steep drop-offs. But she knew she was a fighter and could put her mind to anything thrown in her direction. Mind over matter, she said over and over again in her head as she peered over the edge and saw where she was heading if she put one foot out of line. Mandy wasn't quite as confident as Heleyna, so she'd taken up the rear in a slower group.

Heleyna's group reached the top and sat looking out over the view. She felt contentedly tired, her legs noticing the climb more than they should have done at her age. The peacefulness hit her as she took the time to recover and enjoy the great sense of achievement; it was so quiet the silence rang in her ears. It was a still cool early summer's day with a few wispy clouds visible in the distance. She could see for miles, the deep green of England clear even from that height.

They all sat for a few minutes in total silence, taking in the atmosphere. Heleyna was stunned by the sensation of being at one with nature, of how small she felt, of how she was just part of the large universal mechanism. This, for her, was going to be a life-changing experience. She realised then that life was too important to throw away: it wasn't just words that people threw at her when she voiced her discontentment. Her cogs began turning – she was going to go home from this weekend and make sure she turned her life in the direction she wanted it to go, rather than sitting there waiting for something to come along and find *her*. She would make it happen because she was the only one that could.

She arrived home on Sunday evening and phoned Troy as soon as she walked in the door. She'd missed him. She was shattered but happy from two days of exercise. It'd been a shock to her system after hardly even entering a gym for the last few months: her legs were stiff, her face had signs of windburn, she was still recovering from a hangover and she smelt of sour sweat.

'Hello.'

'Hi Troy. It's me.'

'Hello you. I've missed you this weekend, you know,' he replied.

'I've had such an excellent time, Troy. I've met a woman called Mandy who I got on with from the first minute we met. She's just gorgeous. We laughed the whole time like a couple of schoolgirls. She's married with two children and joining the club was her way of doing something for herself. She lives out in Shipley. The trip leader was a scream – a real wholesome jolly-hockey-sticks type. She would have driven you insane. You should see me. You'd hardly recognise me. I'm sat here with no make-up on, unwashed and sweaty, red-faced and with the stiffest legs. The people were great, the walks out of this world. Can't believe I even thought twice about doing this. I've been missing out on so much.'

Troy hadn't been given the chance to respond until now. 'Bloody brilliant. I'm so pleased for you. It's good to hear you so excited about something other than work. Want to hear about my boring suburban weekend?'

'Go on then.'

'Sam's here. We've eaten, drunk down the local pub, done some clothes shopping for Sam's start tomorrow, drunk some more and slept. Still had a great time, though. I managed to spend some money too – bought myself a bread maker to try and tempt you to move in with me. When do I get to see you again?'

'I'll come over Tuesday night if that's OK. Need to unpack and do boring things like washing tomorrow night.' She remembered her naughty dream about Sam and instantly felt pissed off.

'Excellent!' he replied. 'We also need to plan a time for Ted and Jacinta to come over for dinner in the next couple of weeks. I bumped into Ted down at the supermarket and it reminded me. Bring your diary with you.'

'I can't wait to see you. I'm feeling so horny, you know. That's the first weekend in a long time I've not had the pleasure of some nooky with my favourite man.'

'I'm glad you mentioned that,' Troy whispered quietly into the receiver, obviously not wanting Sam to hear. 'I've been dreaming about you. Last night you gave me a wet dream to die for. All I want to do is take you up to my bedroom, rip your clothes off and get at that divine body of yours. You know what? In my dream there were three of us. We haven't done that for a while either. Perhaps we're getting old!'

If Heleyna had had more energy and felt sexier she would have responded differently to this conversation. She and Troy were great at phone sex, talking dirty, bringing each other to orgasm over the wire. Their lust for each other was truly and tangibly tempestuous.

'Actually, that would be pretty damn good. Perhaps we should go out hunting for a partner on Tuesday night?' She was testing Troy, who hadn't shown or discussed any of his sexual exploits for some time. In fact, thinking back, the only time Heleyna could remember him showing interest in someone other than her recently was at the Bear Inn, when she'd been there.

Normally, at least once every few weeks, he would become embroiled in some dirty game and tease Heleyna with the erotic intricate details.

'You're on. See you then, my dirty little wench. And wear some sexy underwear.' He sounded keen.

'As long as you wear your tight boxers, it's a deal.'

The alarm went off far too early for Heleyna. She needed about fifteen hours of sleep after the weekend she'd just had. She hit it, groaned and then curled over, drifting back to sleep. It went again. She hit it again. On the third reminder that it was unfortunately still morning and time to get up, she suddenly remembered Sam and swore at herself for being such a lazy bitch. She had lots to prepare before he arrived at 9.30 a.m. that morning.

She dressed herself as quickly as her sore legs would allow, trying hard not to put on her ever-so-slightly see-through blouse or her tight trousers which paraded her arse so magnificently. She was going to find this one hard: pretending not to want to get into someone's pants was not a game she was used to. She put on her Chinese-style straight-cut black jacket and swishy baggy silk trousers, then walked into the bathroom to do her make-up. She couldn't face shoes yet, her calves screaming at her even with bare feet.

Horror hit her as she looked in the mirror. Her face was pink and blotchy with skin peeling in places, and she had the biggest bags in the world nestling under both of her usually beautiful big eyes. She hadn't wanted to look too sexy for her new team member or too much like she was trying to tempt him into some steamy shagging across John's desk, but she at least wanted to look loosely attractive. What a day this was going to be.

The train journey was relatively painless, despite her

usual pondering about the goings-on in the terraced houses that embraced the railway line. She saw Mr Handsome, who had now become a regular feature of her journey, but today she kept her head down, embarrassed by her less than wonderful appearance. What she wasn't aware of was the fact that her bags had now diminished to small coin carriers only visible from close range, and her moisturiser and foundation had done the trick she had hoped for. If she'd bothered to get out her compact from her briefcase, she would have realised she looked as hot as ever.

She arrived at work later than she'd hoped. It was 8.45 a.m., only giving her a short time to prepare herself for the entrance of Mr Sex-on-Legs Molloy. She hobbled round her office, clearing away her mess, ordering Phoebe to get a copy of the business plan, project plan and any other documentation on similar subjects she could chuck at Sam to read on his first day. She knew it would bore him, but it was necessary. She was flustered beyond belief, her stomach turning circles, her head trying to pull her hormones into line.

Heleyna had just about forgiven Phoebe for her comments, especially now she'd discovered she was a member of Huxley and, furthermore, had been introduced by the big boss. She knew she should be a bit more careful with this one. And that if she played her cards right, she might even get a bit of inside information from her. Phoebe was, after all, the infamous SPM gossip.

Sam walked into her office, led by Phoebe, as Heleyna was just in the process of bending down, bum in the air, putting rubbish into her bin. She hadn't been prepared for his entrance. He was early. Startled, she stood up quickly when she heard his delicious deep voice wishing her a good morning. Her hair was all over the place and her face a foundation-submerged pink, the effect of having just been upside down. She looked like a neurotic, harassed businesswoman: this was not the impression she wanted to give this man, this demigod in front of her, who had to be a product of Zeus's dirty dealings with a mere mortal.

Heleyna ruffled her hair into a more aesthetically pleasing style and spoke. 'Hello, hello. Welcome, Sam. Good to see you again. Hope the accommodation was acceptable at the weekend!' She couldn't help noticing how damn good he looked tarted up in business attire, unlike herself.

'Hello, Heleyna. Yes, Troy's a great host. Very generous of him to let me stay.' He walked forwards, his arm stretched towards her, inviting a handshake, an invitation she readily accepted. Any excuse to come into even minimal physical contact was welcome.

'Good to hear it.' His aftershave wafted gently under her nose, tempting her to keep hold of his hand and pull him towards her, to feel his groin against her stomach. 'Phoebe, can you grab us two coffees, please. How would you like yours, Sam?' Please say 'up against the filing cabinet', she wished, wickedly.

'Black, no sugar, please, Phoebe.' He winked at her. 'And thanks for bringing me up here and making me feel so welcome.'

Phoebe scuttled off and left them to themselves.

Heleyna invited Sam to take a seat in the chairs they'd used for the interview only a couple of weeks earlier. He sat directly next to her. She wished he hadn't, as now he would get a close-up view of the mess she was in today.

Blinkers on, she handed him a paper with his induction programme set out on it. She explained that this would mean little project-based work or, in fact, little working with her for his first month or so at SPM. She'd scheduled his time: time with each of the main project stakeholders; time for a company and health and safety tour; time to meet with suppliers; and a day to be spent in each of the departments learning how the organisation functioned as a whole. It was important to her that he didn't see the project in isolation and that she kept focused on her work and didn't notice how very sexual he was. There was not one bit of him she could fault, that she couldn't envisage nibbling or biting or coating in chocolate spread and removing with her hot ready tongue.

Phoebe entered the room with two steaming cups of fresh filter coffee. Heleyna thanked her and smiled in her attempt to play the fair boss. Phoebe didn't see her smile. Heleyna noticed this, and also saw that Phoebe was as taken with Sam as she was. She attempted to distract her from her lustful curiosity.

'Thanks for the coffee, Phoebes,' she repeated. 'By the way, do you fancy going out for lunch tomorrow – just the two of us?'

Phoebe replied almost absent-mindedly. 'Oh, yeah, OK.'

Her smitten brain would have said anything at that moment, and Heleyna knew that. She'd taken the opportunity to trap Phoebe into time out of the office on their own together – time for Heleyna to ask some subtle questions about Huxley and hope the little chatterbox would feed her the information she wanted.

Heleyna and Sam were now on their own in her office, chatting about work. Heleyna was sat with her legs crossed tightly, her mind saturated by hormones. Sam appeared unconcerned about anything other than the information Heleyna was feeding him. Even though she hadn't expected an enthusiastic response to her less than gorgeous self, to Heleyna he appeared overly disinterested. He had flirted quietly when she'd first met him, but since that time he had been totally unresponsive to her charms. She'd never come across such a substantial brick wall in her life before; she normally demolished the brick wall within minutes or, at the most, hours.

Rage, which was fuelled by frustration, began to well up inside yet again. It started as a small seed and flourished into a very obvious tree over a short space of time. Needing to get out of his sight, she led him to his office next door to hers and left him to start reading through the mounds of background paperwork, promising to take him on an office tour later that day. She needed space to get her feelings under control and let her anger disperse – anger that had blossomed out of lust and had not been turned into action. She was suffocating in his presence, losing respect for herself, because of her inability to take on this man – he was only another human being, after all. She wondered what was wrong with her. Was she regressing into a much younger and more insecure self, a teenage Heleyna?

She returned to her office, closed the door and sat at her desk for a few moments. The prickling sensation of fury was present in her face, neck and lips, and her hands were clasped so tightly that when she finally did relax deep indentations were left in the palms from her neat nails. Fuck that man, fuck him, fuck him, fuck him. She paced up and down, hobbling all the way and whispering to herself quietly, her line of vision firmly on the varnished wooden floor. Calm down, calm down, calm down – she was mumbling like a mad woman. Her sensible work shoes clumped across the floor surface. She kept pacing, her long hair bouncing with each step. A few more minutes of marching, with her face full of frown lines, seemed to bring her back to her senses. She sat back down in her chair, closed her eyes and tried her favourite relaxation technique: tightening then relaxing every muscle in her body. When she'd completed her sequence she attempted rational thought. It was then that she realised there was a warm dampness between her legs, a dampness placed there unknowingly by a man who refused to show any interest in her bewitching womanly assets.

At 3 p.m. she returned to Sam's office, this time with her feelings wrapped up with industrial tape. Considering her earlier state and the dampness that had reappeared between her thighs, she managed a spectacularly professional tour of SPM, including an introduction to Ted, whom she hadn't seen much of recently. Ted appeared suitably impressed with Sam, as had John and most of her colleagues. She knew he would make a great ambassador for the Proclaim project, helping her to get everybody on board. If she couldn't convince people to achieve what was necessary, he certainly was going to prove an exceptional backup.

They returned to his office. It was already 4.30 p.m.

'Well, Sam, I hope you've enjoyed your first day, got a bit more of a feel for us as an organisation.' Don't look him in the eye, don't look him in the eye.

'Thanks Heleyna. I certainly have. After taking time out of the business world for the last twelve months it certainly is good to be back in the driving seat. There's just one thing I think I need to get off my chest. Is it OK if I ask you an open question?'

Her heart was thumping now. Had he noticed how much she wanted him? Was he going to ask her to leave him alone? Was he going to tell her that he really didn't find her attractive at all? Was he about to declare undying lust for his new boss? 'No, no problem, Sam. Fire away. Always best to have things out in the open, I always say.'

'I just hope that my friendship with Troy won't cause us problems at work, that's all. It just feels a bit odd with you being my boss and also his partner. I suppose I would like to gauge your feelings on it, really, so that I can understand your expectations of the situation.'

Some relief hit her. More relief would have been evident if he had asked her to fuck him there and then, though. That was what she really wanted from this man. 'Sam, firstly let me tell you that the situation does not feel the slightest bit uncomfortable to me –' except for the fact that if you didn't work for me I would rip your suit off right now, '– and secondly, although mixing work and home life are not usually on my agenda, I will have to behave differently with you in the workplace. Also, you need to understand that, just because there is a personal connection, I cannot do you any favours or treat you any differently from anyone else. However, I do hope we can build a good friendship out of work and that you and Troy continue to enjoy your friendship.' She knew she was rambling.

'No problem. I too hope we can become friends out of work, but I will completely respect the professionalism needed in the workplace.'

'Well, you might as well head off for the day. Make the most of it being your first day. See you tomorrow, and perhaps even briefly tomorrow evening. I'm heading over to Troy's then. I think we're going out for the evening.'

'Cheers Heleyna. I'm going to enjoy working here. See you tomorrow.'

She walked out of his office, embarrassed by her dreary work clothes. She also felt disgusted by the state of her skin and puffy eyes, which, if she had bothered to take time to look, actually looked almost as ravishing as always. What she didn't see was him watching her as she left, eyeing the bottom that Troy loved so much and Ted had admired on more than one occasion.

7

Heleyna sent an email invite to Phoebe for their lunch date: she didn't want her to make pathetic excuses, in her usual aggravating overfriendly tones, about forgetting the agreement. Phoebe accepted within a few minutes. Although confused by Heleyna's sudden desire to be friends, she was not going to turn down a free lunch opportunity.

At 12.30 p.m., Heleyna wandered round to the open-plan office where most of the administrative staff were based. Phoebe had made no exception to her usual bright clothes rule. Today it was orange and yellow with a touch of purple, and adorning her ears were a pair of the largest and most vulgar fake gold earrings Heleyna had ever seen. Phoebe caught sight of Heleyna and jumped out of her seat in her incessantly enthusiastic manner, a smile across her petite face, her earrings flying randomly. Heleyna thought how pretty she would be if she made an effort to present herself in an even vaguely more subtle way and hadn't masked her fine facial features with the excessive bleaching of her bobbed hair.

'Hi Phoebes. Ready for a good feed somewhere?' Heleyna was trying very hard to be an amicable boss.

'Too right. I'm looking forward to it.' Her earrings were now almost at a standstill.

'Where do you fancy going? You choose.'

'How about that place you all go to? You know, the place where all the managers go on the Headrow?'

'*Ciao?* OK then. Let's go.'

Heleyna walked out quickly, Phoebe scuttling behind her like an ever-faithful puppy.

As they walked in the door of *Ciao* she remembered the last time she'd been there. She took comfort in the fact that there'd been no questions from Ted about her late-night working – that he hadn't seemed to twig that she'd watched him at his most intimate with a rather well-endowed man. She smiled to herself at how lucky she always seemed to be when she was at her most curious. It gave her the confidence she needed to probe and investigate and nosy around to find out more about Huxley.

They ordered and Heleyna began her attack. 'So then, Phoebe, what keeps you busy when you're not at work?'

'Not too much, really. I make jewellery sometimes, but mainly I just hang out with my friends. We like to go out clubbing once or twice a week.'

'You know what, I've recently started art classes. I suddenly realised I needed to do something more exciting with my life than work.' Heleyna's style was open. She hoped that this would induce an equally open response from Phoebe. 'You know what I also did? I surprised myself and did something I've never done before. I joined a club, a hiking club. We went up to the Lakes last weekend and, believe it or not, I actually enjoyed myself. Are you a club person?'

'Apart from nightclubs, no, not really.' Phoebe's hand hid her face as she answered Heleyna, a sure sign she was hiding something.

Heleyna, impatient for answers, decided it was time to come out and ask her straight. 'Really? I assumed you were also a member of the Huxley Club? Hopefully, I'm coming along to the next meeting, thanks to Ted and Jacinta.'

'Oh, oh that club. Sorry, I never really think of that

as a club. It's more of a … social gathering, really, than a club. Anyway, I've only been to it once.'

'Is it good fun?'

'Well, I loved it.'

'What do you get up to there then?' Heleyna had now more than given up on the subtle approach.

'Oh, you know, just lots of socialising really. Chance to get dressed up and go to a party and meet lots of people like me. It's great fun. I can't really tell you any more, you know. I'm not meant to talk about Huxley at all. The only reason I have done is because, as you said, you're coming along to the next meeting.'

Heleyna didn't want to push her luck so she changed the conversation in the hope she might get another snippet of information later on over lunch.

Wanting to give her body a healthy treat, Heleyna ordered a basil and tomato salad with crusty French bread, and Phoebe a rather extravagant seafood delicacy with scallops and mussels and crayfish. Heleyna didn't blame her; she would have done the same in her situation. A second thought, and Heleyna called back the waiter and ordered two glasses of the finest Sauvignon Blanc on the wine list.

Heleyna was bored by the conversation Phoebe threw in her direction. She talked endlessly about inane absurdities like fashion and the intimate details of tedious conversations she'd had with friends, giving more information than Heleyna could be bothered to listen to. Heleyna remained polite, though if Phoebe had had even an ounce of intuition she would have noticed the glazed look, a clear indication of thinking going on behind the scenes. In fact, Heleyna's mind was drumming up ideas for more detective work. Phoebe was too busy explaining what he said and what she'd said in return in the unrelenting way that all office gossips do. Whoever 'he' and 'she' were was of no interest to Heleyna – she simply couldn't have given a damn about a single word of it.

Not having the opportunity to contribute to the conversation to any great extent, Heleyna was close to sleep with boredom. She'd also finished her lunch way ahead of Phoebe and was watching her tackle the delicious looking crayfish.

Heleyna jump-started herself. 'So then, are any of these friends of yours members of Huxley?'

'Oh no, not those friends. I don't think any of them would really fit in.'

'So how did you get to go in the first place, then?'

'John, of course, he introduced me.' Phoebe's hand flew across her reddening face and she covered her mouth, realising she'd said more than she should have.

Although Heleyna had not learnt anything further about Huxley, Phoebe had confirmed two facts for her: that John the MD was a member and that Phoebe obviously knew him outside of the work environment. Heleyna guessed their relationship must also have been fairly close, as Heleyna had worked alongside Ted for some time and only recently been invited. She couldn't quite believe the lack of professionalism from her new boss: recruiting his shag piece rather than the best person for the job. Heleyna filed those thoughts in the back of her mind, then allowed Phoebe to overcome her embarrassment by excessive waffling.

Fuelled by sexual frustration, Heleyna spent the rest of Tuesday smouldering with acrimony. On returning from lunch she'd checked through her voicemail. Troy had left one of the six messages. He explained long-windedly that he wouldn't be able to make their night out on the pull that evening. He hadn't bothered to grace her with even a simple explanation, not that an explanation would have done anything to calm a horny-as-hell Heleyna. She'd been looking forward to Troy, whether they found a third person or not. Sam had put her well and truly in the mood for lots of naughtiness. Instead, tonight would have to be a night of self-indulgence: a hot bath, a glass of Chardonnay and her favourite supersonic vibrator.

She stomped out of the office at five o'clock, not bothering to consider extra work in her current state of mind. Walking swiftly to the station, her gaze locked on to the pavement, she realised that in recent weeks anger had become a recurring emotion, despite her extracurricular interests. How volatile she was, swinging from anger to joy like an overexcited pendulum. She already knew that some of it was down to Sam, as well as knowing she needed to change her purpose in life, her career, if she was ever to be fulfilled.

Arriving for her train unusually early, she had a choice of seats. Relaxing into hers, her mobile rang loudly in her briefcase. She'd picked a more traditional, old-fashioned telephone ring tone for her phone. She couldn't tolerate those hideous, grating fanfares so many people chose. It was Mandy.

'Hi Mands, good to hear from you. How are your legs doing?'

'A bit stiff. Great weekend though. Just phoning to see if you're definitely doing the weekend away next month – the trip to Snowdonia we talked about?'

'If you're going then I'm definitely up for it. You know what, I can't believe I've never considered walking before. Being up there on those hilltops is something else, isn't it?' Heleyna's enthusiasm was evident.

'It bloody well is. I used to do a lot with my parents when I was younger. So pleased to finally get back in the driving seat. Excellent. Glad you're coming. I'm just about to phone and book myself on, so I'll book you on too. Fancy a coffee next week? I'm heading into town one day to do a bit of shopping. I could do with another girlie session.'

'Yes, please. Give me a ring when you're heading in and I'll make sure I'm free.'

They said their goodbyes and Heleyna smiled to herself, pleased she'd found someone like Mandy, someone solid and reliable and genuine. Hearing from Mandy lifted her anger, like the sudden dispersal of morning cloud as the heat of the sun makes its mark. She was now in a much more relaxing and pleasing place.

Closing her eyes, she began drifting into that space between sleep and consciousness when she felt someone sit next to her, their relaxation into the seat heavy and obvious. The person, a man, spoke.

'Well, hello, I finally get to sit next to you.'

Heleyna really wasn't in the mood to converse; she felt peaceful and content in her own personal space. She forced open her eyes and turned to the man next to her. 'Hi. Yes, indeed.' It was Mr Handsome. She held out her hand in her usual businesslike way.

'So then, what does a rather beautiful girl like you do for a living?' He was forward, but not slimy with his approach.

She explained and he reciprocated.

The train began to fill up with passengers and the two of them continued talking. Heleyna slowly warmed to this man she'd admired from afar for some time now, and who'd certainly admired her on more than one occasion. She remembered the view he'd given her of his crotch the first time they'd flirted, firstly across the carriage and then later continued briefly, yet delightfully, on the platform. Her evolving sexual thought patterns changed shape as their idle chatter unfurled, and she began to wake up very quickly. At that moment she was very glad she was a woman with the instinctive ability to do two things at once. She was using this precious skill to continue pleasant conversation at the same time as imagining this man's cock deep inside her, her bare bottom up against the cool wall of the train toilet. She was on a roll.

'So then, do you normally chat to young women on trains?' She took in his athletic physique and strawberry-blond purposefully tousled hair, his eyes a mesmerising pale blue.

His gorgeous face lit up with the opportunity she'd presented him: the opportunity to begin the joyous journey of shameful flirting with a fuckable stranger. 'Only the extraordinarily pretty ones.'

'Why, then, are you speaking to me?'

He whispered. 'Because you are the sexiest woman I've ever seen on this train. I've been watching you closely for a while now. You have the most beautiful feminine body, the kind of body so many women strive to ruin with excessive exercise and dieting. Your bouncing brown locks draw me to you every time you wiggle your pretty round arse onto this train. What I would do to spend an evening with you.' He turned and faced her directly, one arm against the high back of the seat.

Heleyna let him finish his compliments. Not wanting to boost his already incredible ego, she didn't reciprocate his flattery, but instead chose to answer his final statement. 'That would be no problem. In fact, I could give you just that this evening.' She uncrossed her legs and recrossed them in his direction, her functional work skirt now up higher than the usual knee length. 'We could get off this train in Horsforth, go round to my flat and have an incredible evening.'

Her face was now rosy, her voice low, her eyes locked straight on to his. This man could be exactly what she needed to drive Sam out of her system.

Handsome man could do nothing more than smile and nod his answer. Heleyna dropped her eyes to his lap: he already had an appetite for her. His long dick was pushing urgently against the fly of his suit trousers. As she lifted her eyes back to his face, he winked at her confidently, trying to hide the fact that he was being dominated and eaten alive by this gorgeous wench.

Now feeling incredibly hot, Heleyna removed her jacket and laid it across her knee, tantalisingly concealing her shapely thigh, and the train began its jolting journey out of the station as handsome man began his seduction. His hand disappeared under her linen jacket onto her thigh and eagerly upwards between her legs. She uncrossed them, willingly granting him the access he so obviously demanded. As his hand neared her wanting, frustrated pussy she burned for his touch, the sensation reaching the depths of her clit and finding its way along the length of her nervous system to the sensitive skin of her neck, ear lobes and lips.

Sitting very still, she enjoyed every inch of movement, watching his face closely as he observed the progress of his hand beneath her skirt. He finally reached his goal and with one swift movement tore open the crotch of her gossamer-thin expensive black tights. If the other passengers had bothered her, she would have noted that those across the aisle had their heads stuck in newspapers, engrossed in the day's events. She was free to enjoy this man's delicious touch, a touch that was now inside her tights and working its way beneath her lacy panties.

He moved his head towards hers and her nostrils detected his flagrant masculinity – masculinity that was oozing from every pore of a body she couldn't wait to see.

He whispered in her ear, the warmth of his breath

sending goosebumps tumbling down her neck and shoulder and on towards her lower back and thigh. 'Take them off,' he growled.

She obeyed, and his expression took on a mixture of surprise and pleasure. With her hair falling over her left shoulder she grinned at him cheekily as she took her final step to freedom from her very sexy red panties.

He eagerly regained his position, as she did hers, and his fingers soon found her wet curly brown locks. Warm fingers encased her and he pressed gently, the base of his palm against the base of her clit. The pressure grew rhythmic and his fingers spread her lips and entered her slowly, purposefully, expertly. Still she sat unmoving, her mind oblivious to the people or movement of the train: she'd disappeared into a horny haven.

Frustratingly the train reached her station and Heleyna and handsome man made their way off the train. Heleyna was both pant- and tightless by then, and he was trying to hide his evident pleasure. Both were oblivious to anyone or anything as they made the ten-minute walk to Heleyna's flat, absorbed in their desire, walking without a word. With each step Heleyna could feel the nakedness between her legs, the delicious wetness spreading over the tops of her inner thighs.

They entered her flat, a flustered Heleyna only just managing to make her key work in the lock. He, her fancy piece, walked in behind her and slammed the door shut, the sound echoing throughout her modern minimalist apartment. She turned quickly to look at him, her curly hair coming to rest across each shoulder. Animalistic, he grabbed her and began pushing her roughly towards the kitchen, all the time scanning his lust-filled eyes over her delicious body. He wanted action and he wanted it now.

They reached the kitchen and Heleyna lifted herself up onto her granite worktop, wiggling her bottom suggestively in her attempt to reach the high surface. By now her skirt was round her waist and her legs wide, revealing her excited pantless state.

Handsome man dropped his trousers eagerly and removed his silk tie with a quick expert tug, using just one hand. 'You're so sexy, do you know that?'

She did.

He continued. 'I've wanted to fuck you for so long. I've been waiting and dreaming about this moment, the moment when I would smell and taste your hot sweet pussy.'

'Come and get me then, Mr Handsome. I'm all yours.'

Heleyna watched intently as he moved towards her, his long thick penis bouncing gently with each step, teasing her into submission. His athletic body was revealed as his shirt hit the kitchen floor, his long toned muscles and creamy smooth skin on display. As he neared, he bent his head and neck and disappeared into her swollen mass of sensitivity.

He came up for air. 'You taste as good as I hoped you would, you naughty, naughty woman.'

She didn't respond. His head lowered again to give her the pleasure she'd been seeking for the last few days. There he remained for a while until suddenly he stood and walked away. She sat there flustered and confused, her face glowing, and a gentle sheen of perspiration across her brow.

She watched his pert bottom pitching provocatively with each step as he walked towards her large stainless-steel fridge, which was adorned with a flashy ice maker. Disappearing behind the door, his feet were the only part of him still exposed to her licentious gaze. She listened to him rummaging through her salad drawer, then stand and close the door, exposing his nakedness once more. In his hand he now held a cucumber, the size of which Heleyna had giggled at the day she'd purchased it in the local supermarket. She hoped she knew the purpose of this ice-cold phallus.

He returned between her legs, which he pushed forcibly apart, teasing and exposing her impatient pussy, then nudged the large cold cucumber slowly inside her, allowing her to enjoy every inch of its wonder. She watched it disappear inside her. Her breath did not come, but was smothered by the intensity. Eventually a small gasp escaped her lips and he looked up at her, his handsomeness bowling her over.

'Please, do it harder,' she whispered.

Her wish was his command. He twisted and pushed and pulled and twisted some more, then inserted the phallus as deeply as she could allow. He stood back and watched, attentive, as it slowly left her body and landed with a thump on the black-and-white-tiled floor.

Beside herself with lust, Heleyna lowered herself onto her feet, removed the remainder of her clothes and pushed him back towards her glass-topped table. Her seething body touched his with each step, the seemingly trivial touch of receptive skin against receptive skin tingling almost painfully.

She turned him so that he faced the table and guided him onto the chilly glass surface. He knew exactly what she wanted from him: he began thrusting his groin, rubbing his sensitive tip against the coolness of the glass. This time it was Heleyna's turn to attack the fridge. Returning to him with her hands full of ice, she dropped it, piece by piece, into his crack and watched it melt over him, causing him to shudder and groan and moan and thrust harder and faster.

The ice now a pool on the table that was dripping onto the tiles, Heleyna disappeared below him. She lay sprawled on the hard floor with her legs wide, her head in line with his cock, her pussy with his face. Her hands began pleasuring her tits, thighs, stomach and cunt. She watched every inch of his lean body as she caressed herself: the firmness of his chest and stomach, his long arm muscles evident with each thrust, his cock spreading wetness above her head, his face pink with exertion.

Desperate for him to come quickly so she could watch his dick furiously exploding through the see-through table top, she spoke dirty to him. 'You're so fucking sexy. I can see every inch of your gorgeous body and solid cock. Look at my cunt, at how hot it is for you. I'm so wet. I'm so ready. Push harder, go on, I want to see that wonderful prick of yours erupting all over my table.'

She didn't need to say any more. His body entered the heavenly convulsions of orgasm, coating the glass with the creamy essence of sensual pleasure.

Heleyna had not finished with him yet: she wanted more from him, to feel him inside her, for him to entertain her with his solidity. She dragged him off the table and into her bedroom. His exhausted body collapsed onto the bed and Heleyna began the game of rearousing this man, the man who was allowing her to vent days of sexual tension. She opened her wardrobe door and found what she wanted: her double pronged vibrator and box of strawberry-flavoured ribbed condoms.

She clambered onto the end of her double bed, all the time smiling at Mr Handsome, who lay with his head lightly propped on her mass of pillows and cushions. She chucked the box at him so that he knew exactly what she expected of him, then turned her back and subscribed to her favourite doggy-style pose, exposing her full glory to him. Her vibrator was now buzzing and firmly in her right hand. Still in her exquisite position she rammed it into her waiting warm holes until it reached her depths. There it remained. Deeply con-

...u all to bring in one piece of work you've com-
...outside of the classes so we can all see how styles
...veloping. Any questions?'

... and Jemma passed knowing looks to each other
...mma giggled in response.

...r class, Heleyna caught up with Ben as he walked
...m in arm with his new sweetheart. 'Exactly what
...are you playing with me?'

...game. The painting truly is great. Friends who've
...by the studio always comment on it. You should
...ud, not angry. Remember what Bet taught us –
...t is as much about the process as the finished
...He winked at Heleyna. She didn't respond.

...what the hell is she giggling about, then?'
...a was pointing aggressively at Jemma.

...ma is giggling because she too has created a
...piece very like yours, except hers is a very appro-
...pink with a light splash of purple. We're bringing
...next week, too.'

...the purple was an accident. I got a bit carried
...t one point, one of my yoga positions knocking
...colour we hadn't planned on.' Jemma giggled
...her hand as she spoke.

...yna realised they were innocent in their actions.
...o lust birds enjoying each other and the game
...cidentally introduced to a now very horny Ben.

tented and unable to hold back her pleasure, she slowly circled its vibrating rubber prong over her swollen clit.

She kept up the entertainment for some time, her actions quickening and becoming increasingly agitated, and her breath deep and audible. She stopped and, looking over her right shoulder through the long hair that was now plastered across her reddened forehead and cheeks, she looked at him. He was sat, propped up by pillows, his eyes locked on to her pussy and his dick solid in his hand. Heleyna removed the humming device and backed up slowly towards him. She reached him and lowered herself onto him, the ribbed sensation tickling her sensitive walls on its journey. He gasped loudly as Heleyna began her slow rhythmic movements over the entire length of his manhood. She ensured she reached the sensitive tip with each outward thrust so that he could watch the full penetration with each ecstatic plunge.

His hands found their way round the curve of her hips to her pulsing clit. Between each of her movements he tormented the ever-sensitive end with the gentlest of touches. As she craved more of his touch so she had to increase the speed of her rhythm. She screamed for him to caress her more readily, but he refused, forcing her to thrust faster and harder than she could ever remember doing before. Just when she thought she couldn't take any more, her body pierced the fine line between almost there and well and truly there and, exhausted, she dropped the few inches to the bed onto her cheek as her sex spasmed its way through the incredible journey of orgasm.

Fuelled by an orgasm that threatened to suck the life out of his rock-solid cock, he lifted his pelvis and pushed into her wet warmth until he too lay shattered and happy, every nerve ending alight and intoxicated.

Heleyna dozed off into a postorgasmic haven. She was exhausted and relieved to have finally had an opportunity to disperse at least some of the Sam-related excess hormones that had been threatening to overflow and change her into a very unpleasant woman to be around.

When she awoke Mr Handsome was gone. The only evidence that he'd not been just a very explicit and wonderfully naughty dream was the remains of their pleasure on her dining table.

Another week was lost in overwork. Heleyna hadn't had the pleasure of Sam's company for the remainder of the week. Much of his time had been spent on his induction programme, keeping him a very necessary arm's length from Heleyna's lust. She had caught sight of him briefly as he walked down the corridor towards her, deep in conversation. He was with boring Bernard from accounts. He'd flashed her a gorgeous smile, displaying those sumptuous dimples that Heleyna had craved to touch since the first time she'd set eyes on them. She had smiled in response then looked down at her dowdy attire. She knew she shouldn't worry about what he thought of her: she was his boss, after all, and bosses should never ever lust after their subordinates, should they?

However, she'd managed to speak to Troy each day, though she had not had the opportunity to see him. He'd been overly apologetic for standing her up and then they'd made up with a wicked session of phone sex, a side effect of the details she'd given him of her evening with Mr Handsome. They both got a lot of fun out of these phone sessions, which usually kept them from getting too frustrated between the times they saw each other.

Heleyna still hadn't told Troy abo
and she knew exactly why: by not
it she was hiding something not o
also herself. Sam was well and truly

At art class that week Heleyna pa
acrylic on hardboard made up of
strokes and swirls. Bet, the teacher,
she did her round of the room, he
shirt billowing out behind her very
know, strokes like that are normall
up frustration. I've seen it many tir
out, girl. Often it's the only way to
ling. Can't beat a good painting ses

Ben, who'd become increasingly
chirped up in response. 'It's alway
put your feelings and emotions i
know, Heleyna. I've seen some of t
when you put everything into it, a

He'd certainly become very cock
Heleyna guessed that his new
increase in testosterone were play
developing arrogance. Heleyna blu

Bet continued. 'You've been doi
of class, have you, Heleyna? Ho
you could bring some in for us all

Heleyna faltered slightly. 'Ac
But Ben's got it. I went to h
evening and I painted it then.'

She flashed an angry glance a
in return, his floppy hair, which
smothered with red acrylic,
immensely.

'Perhaps Ben could bring it i
all share our work. In fact, tha

like
plete
are d
Be
and J
Af
out a
game
'N
come
be pr
that
piece.
'So
Heley
'Jer
maste
priate
that i
'Yes
away
over a
behind
Hel
Just tw
she'd a

8

As always, Friday night was a relief. Troy had mentioned in passing that she should drop by his and spend an evening with him and Sam, but they hadn't firmed up their plans. She decided to drop in anyway. She was eager to see her man after not seeing him either the weekend before or during the week. That was unusual for them, but Heleyna knew that the extra activities she was doing meant she would be much better company when they were together.

As she left work, Ted, who was ever the joker, had come up behind her and pounced on her, nearly causing her to wet herself.

'You arsehole, Ted.' She was laughing. She missed seeing him and working with him every day.

'That's no way to talk to your ex-boss! So then, how's my favourite Heleyna doing?' His cheeky grin worked a charm.

'I'm good, good. Quite a lot on at work, but I'm getting there. How about you?' Her eyes flashed subconsciously to his chest and shoulders.

'Oh, you know, miss working with you, but apart from that everything's great. Jacinta's busy with the club, getting ideas together for the next event. You two still interested?' He inquired.

'Yes, absolutely. I'm a little confused as to what it's all about, though.'

He was not about to give anything away. 'You'll see, you'll see.'

'So then, when do we get to see you two again?'

Heleyna realised where she was focusing her gaze, and forced it back up to his face.

'Oh, yes, dinner. Troy spoke with Jacinta the other day and they made arrangements. No idea when for – Jacinta is the organiser in our relationship. You'll need to ask her or Troy. I'm sure it's reasonably soon.'

Heleyna was genuine in her response. 'Excellent, I look forward to it. Doing anything fun for the weekend?'

'Just spending time with Jacinta, pottering around. You?'

She realised how close together they were standing; she took a small slightly startled step back. 'No plans yet. Went hiking last weekend with a club, though. It was brilliant. I'm not so unsure about clubs any more! In fact, I'm going away with them again soon.'

'Good for you. Me, I'd rather be sat at home or spending my money. Anyhow, I'm off now. Ready for a glass of vino or two, that's for sure. We should do lunch one day next week.'

'That would be great. I'll let you know when I'm free. I've got a friend coming over one day, so that's the only day when I can't do it.'

They kissed cheeks like old friends, Ted grasping her shoulders as he did so, and went their separate ways.

In the taxi on the way to Troy's she giggled to herself again as she recollected Ted with the other man. In some ways it relieved her to know that other people got up to no good behind closed doors, too. Two factors made her uncomfortable, however: she just hoped that Jacinta was in on the fun; and she truly hoped he had not twigged it was her who had spied on them – the thought of a work colleague finding out what a dirty little tart she was made her cringe excruciatingly. It was enough for her that she'd come close to flirting with Sam, but to actually put on a sexual display and be caught by a colleague was almost more than she could bear.

The taxi pulled up in front of Troy's toytown-neat modern home, a true bachelor pad. There were two cars in the driveway along with Sam's second vehicle, a very sexy looking Ducati motorbike. Feeling flustered, she exited the cab, made her way to the front door and let herself in. Downstairs was empty, so she climbed up the stairs to the bathroom hoping to find Troy lolling in the bath with his tanned physique exposed. She couldn't hear Sam either, which relieved her – she couldn't cope with the thought of bumping into him walking from the shower with a towel round his waist revealing a body which until now she'd only ever fantasised about. She was afraid she would be incapable of self-control.

Silence infiltrated the upstairs corridor; even her stockinged feet were quiet against the thick carpet. Excited at the thought of seeing Troy, she pushed open his bedroom door with enthusiasm. She was on her way to his en-suite. As the door opened, revealing the expanse of his fashionably designed bedroom, her heart flew rapidly into her mouth: there, under the duvet in Troy's bed, were two writhing bodies obviously enjoying each other's company. Initial shock subsided as one of the bodies unveiled its identity.

Troy stuck his head out from the duvet, the sound of the door opening highlighting the presence of a third person. Hair all over the place, his face flushed and breath quick, he spoke in between his panting. 'Hi sexy. I was hoping you might come over this evening. Why don't you come and join us?'

Heleyna began undressing immediately. 'First I have to know what kind of beast you've got under there!'

'Male, incredibly sexy, dark hair, big blue eyes, stubble to die for. I'll let you join us, but only if you promise to wear the velvet blindfold. I don't want to spoil the surprise.'

Troy disappeared again and the excitable movement and gentle groans continued. Heleyna rushed to the drawer where she knew Troy kept his sexy accessories and put the blindfold on. She then removed the last of her clothes and found her way under the duvet towards the mass of limbs encased in darkness. It was uncomfortably hot but, once she found the bodies, the sensation of heat vanished into her subconscious. Lust had taken over as it nearly always does.

She could feel the two men were wrapped tightly around each other, face to face, their penises rubbing and touching and teasing. Heleyna grasped a pair of balls in each hand and fondled them lovingly, not wanting to damage the source of her own pleasure. Both cried out. As she caressed them she could feel the firm masculine bodies finding pleasure in each other. Not caring who either one was, she peeled the two men apart and her mouth found the dick of one. She took it up, realising immediately that this wasn't Troy in her mouth. This man was even longer and wider.

Troy moved up behind her as she took the entire length of this stranger inside her. The groans of this guest worker she was enjoying became stifled. Troy was lost inside his mouth, his short thrusting movements kneading her back with his strong quads. All that's missing is a fourth person, she thought, someone to lose their head between my legs.

Heleyna was now eager to discover exactly who she'd been tasting – and what a divine flavour he was, too. Leaving his cock for one minute, she made her way up his large frame until her groin was level with his, Troy moving out of the way to let her through. At that point the stranger held her firmly where she was, evidently welcoming the sensation of pussy against his hot rigid penis. His grip became harder, his fingers digging into her upper arms, and she groaned in delight. His grip became harsher and, suddenly, with what felt like real aggression, he pushed her onto her back. Not caring that he'd knocked the wind out of her, he shoved open her legs and thrust into her. He didn't appear concerned with what she needed, but it was something she welcomed – he penetrated as hard as his muscles would allow, gripping her tightly with each thrust.

'This is so good!' she was whispering under her breath.

Troy lay close, his head resting in the space between her head and shoulder, his left hand all over the bottom of this very manly man, shoving him into her harder and harder. At every available opportunity he rubbed his very excited penis up and down her thigh, moistening her with each substantial movement.

Heleyna could barely contain herself. Eager for him to remain within her, her pelvis followed the withdrawal of this man. He was unbelievably strong, his unceasing movements forceful beyond her wildest dreams. She knew she was going to be tender the next day, but at that moment in time she really didn't give a damn. This man made Troy seem positively effeminate, not a word she would ever have used to describe Troy until today.

She was pinned so tightly to the mattress she had no option but to lie there and enjoy it, the occasional movement of her groin towards him the only action he would allow. She was tantalised, trapped and tamed.

He spoke to her, 'You feel so good, you dirty little whore. I'm going to fuck you until you beg me to stop.'

Heleyna knew that voice well. Her responses paused momentarily as her mind went into overload. It was a voice that belonged to a man she had craved for so long – the out-of-bounds Sam Molloy. Thoughts ran wild:

was she to continue on this path, the unforgivable path of sex with a subordinate at work, let lust rule her head, or should she keep to her rules? Stupid, stupid rules, she thought angrily.

He was insulted by her sudden standstill and again he addressed her with a real sense of fury. 'What's wrong with you? Am I not good enough for you? You, my dear, need a good telling off.' And, with that, he withdrew, suddenly removing any decision-making from her.

She was left feeling dejected, confused and ready to burst with lust. Now was the time to stop this game before her head lost the last remnants of rational thought. She had to obey her self-imposed standards. She ripped the blindfold from her eyes.

'I can't do this. Not with you, Sam. This isn't right at all.' She was finding it hard to speak in her breathless state.

'Shut up, slut. I know you want me. Stop playing the holier-than-thou role. It doesn't suit you.' He lifted the duvet, then Heleyna, and plonked her over his shoulder. This man was incredibly strong.

She was so shocked that, initially, she just didn't know how to respond. Troy just laughed, not knowing the complexity of the dynamic between Sam and his lover. Sam held her tightly and then, much to her surprise, began spanking her plump cheeks as he carried her across the room. It stung, yet it felt great, and his wicked, wicked ways began to overpower her.

'Stop it, stop it, stop it!' She thumped his back with her fists, the view of his arse fantastic, even from upside down. Tears filled her eyes.

'Shut up, will you, and stop whingeing,' he said, 'or I'll give you more next time.' And he most certainly did when her wailing continued. He administered one almighty spank that left a burning hand-shaped feeling right across her right butt cheek. It was delightful.

He reached the rocking chair at the other side of the bed and secured a struggling Heleyna with a pair of very real-looking handcuffs. Her bottom stung painfully, even against the soft cushion. Troy could sense this and was laughing from the comfort of the bed. Her mind was filled with confusion: one minute it brought rage, the next lust for this sexually awesome man.

She looked over at Troy on the duvet-free bed, her hair falling wildly over her shoulders and face, her arms tightly secured through the open back of the chair. She was flushed, furious and fucking horny. Troy read her emotions and returned her glance with one of his smouldering lust-filled gazes that scrutinised her heavy breasts and scrumptious thighs, then focused his desire on the returning Sam.

'Troy, unite me now,' she was shouting, her voice shaking and high and pathetic.

Troy didn't answer. He already had both his hands round the extraordinarily large cock Sam bestowed upon him. The lucky, lucky bastard, Heleyna thought as she battled to free herself.

Sam spoke with authority and unbelievable concentration. 'This is your punishment for ignoring my pleasure. You can sit there and watch me giving Troy exactly what he deserves – the opportunity to pleasure me. And you, you naughty whore, can get frustrated. You're not coming out until you have learned your lesson.'

Heleyna wiggled in the hope of an escape, although she knew her actions were futile. 'Sam, let me out. I thought we spoke about the need for professionalism between us. Sam, listen to me, will you. This is wrong. Sam...'

She gave up. She'd resigned herself to his desire to humiliate her, his boss. She dealt with his game the only way she knew how: she closed her eyes, a measure she'd used often as a child when she wanted to pretend she was in a wonderful place, not sat in school learning her ABC. That way she could tell him later that she'd not actually seen him, and she would be back in control. Her breath deep and heavy and her wrists now sore behind her, she attempted to relax into the chair, rocking it gently, striving to comfort herself.

The two men were audible as they moved rapidly against the Egyptian cotton sheets. She could hear their breathing, their groans, their gratification, which tempted her to take just one sneaky peek. Keeping her eyes tight shut, her face locked in a grimace, she tried to focus on something other than her anger and the noise that filled every corner of the bedroom. The rocking motion of the chair brought with it some comfort to her chaotic mind. She was so unbelievably mad with this arrogant man. Her only option was to sack him, dismiss him during his probationary period for poor performance. She vowed to go and see the human resources department on Monday to get some advice and make sure he was gone within twenty-four hours.

Wanton feelings kept rearing their ugly heads between her thoughts, the rocking motion suddenly feeling incredibly erotic. The pressure against her swollen pussy teased her with each downward movement of the rocking chair. Her body began to relax, anger-filled thoughts lessened and the rocking quickened.

'You dirty cow. Are you playing with yourself over there?' It was Sam.

Heleyna felt herself blush and her already pink cheeks turned a bright fluorescent red. 'No, I was just ... just trying to ignore you.'

'Don't lie to me, Heleyna. Admit it, you want me.

Always have done, since you first clapped eyes on me. And now you have the opportunity to, you become all sweet and innocent. Just open your eyes and enjoy the show.'

'Stop it, just stop it!' She was humiliated by his comments, the truth hurting more than she liked to admit.

'No worries. But just think what you're missing out on. Might as well enjoy. Who's going to know, after all? And, don't think I'm undoing those cuffs. You're there for the long haul. You need to be taught exactly who's boss.'

Much to her relief there were no more words from Sam, and the noises recommenced their teasing. Unconsciously, she began rocking herself once more. Her eyes were still closed but in a more refined manner. She looked her beautiful self. Heleyna felt in some ways like she was watching a horror movie, with the contradiction a good one brings: viewing with a cushion clasped to your face with one eye peeking over the top. The only difference was that so far she hadn't even taken one indecent peek at the display. But, God, she was so desperate to.

She rocked and listened, the burning between her legs frustrating the hell out of her. Just one little look won't harm, she thought. One look and only at Troy. She decided she could do it and ignore Sam, pretend he wasn't there. That way she would feel like she'd maintained her rule. She counted to three and opened her right eye just a fraction. The little look turned into a big look. Her left eye joined in the fun. Now both eyes were back to their usual gorgeous size and both moved from Troy to Sam and back again. She rocked harder and harder and harder.

Heleyna had forgotten everything she'd ever learned about the protocol of relationships. Troy and Sam now absorbed every cell of her brain. She watched intently as she rocked herself into a frustrated frenzy, a frenzy that she knew would never get release thanks to the wicked Sam.

Sam had Troy bent over in front of him, his hands tied to the bed head, and was enjoying every part of Troy he could: he moved readily and swiftly from mouth to butt. Troy was silent but, judging by the look on his face and the state of his dick, he was in total ecstasy.

Thrusting into Troy's mouth, his cock coated in a chocolate-flavoured condom, Sam spanked him hard and Troy lifted his bottom, keen for it to continue. Heleyna kept rocking. Sam spanked again, leaving pink finger marks across Troy's delicious cheeks that were bronzed from his weekly sunbed sessions at the local leisure club. Heleyna kept watching. Sam spanked again then moved his hand between Troy's cheeks, and his fingers entered a very willing Troy. This time Troy groaned and his wet cock spasmed uncontrollably. Heleyna rubbed herself with each movement of the chair, unashamedly marking the linen cushion cover, and desperate for her clit to receive the attention it desired.

Sam followed his fingers into the well-oiled hole, his hands tight round Troy's toned waist. He turned his head towards Heleyna and opened his eyes. 'Look at yourself now, you dirty tart. Trying to fuck yourself against a cushion. Broken our little standards now, haven't we? Do you like what you see?' His voice was breathless, but still he managed to maintain his patronising yet very arousing tone.

Heleyna felt shamed, yet her pussy knew the response and it was her pussy that spoke. 'Yes, I do, I like what I see. Please, fuck me too. I need you. Please.' She was almost whining.

Sam laughed. 'Not a chance. You can sit there like a good little girl and watch. It was your stupidity that got you there in the first place, and now you'll pay for it.'

Heleyna didn't respond. She understood that her whingeing was pointless.

Preoccupied and seemingly unaware of the conversation, Troy pushed back hard against Sam and his breath quickened. Sam was feeling kind. He bent over Troy, his crescendo still building, and his hand found its way round Troy's slim hips and onto his weeping cock. Heleyna had never heard Troy shout with such relief in all the time she had played with him. Sam had taught her a good lesson – tease them, make them wait.

Heleyna's wrists were burning now in her desperation as the handcuffs dug deep. Her writhing body was exhausted, her hair wild. The divine picture of a very naked Sam pleasuring himself in her gorgeous man frustrated her to hell. She just wanted to scream out for Sam to fuck her too. She'd wanted him for so long.

Both men came: Troy first, followed by Sam. Heleyna writhed and rocked. They both fell to the bed, Sam on top of Troy. Heleyna rocked some more. She was so completely turned on and ready to be filled and touched. She watched as the two men relaxed, twitching gently every once in a while. Animosity returned. Sam and Troy dozed off into a postorgasmic slumber, looking like two divine Greek gods. Heleyna was left strapped to the chair, her wrists sore from her hopeless struggling, her pussy unwanted and desperately frustrated. Though her anger remained, she grew cold.

Two hours later, Sam and Troy awoke. Sam looked over at her, smiled, dressed and left the room. Troy, in his attempt to remain her man, took the keys and set Heleyna free – a Heleyna he had never seen before, a

Heleyna who had not got her wicked way for once in her life.

'How long has this been going on between you and Sam?' She was unbearably jealous of the fun Troy had been having with him.

'Since the Bear Inn.'

'Why didn't you tell me?' She was still full of fury, her voice higher than usual.

'Why didn't you tell me you had been lusting after him too?' He turned and left the room, knowing that anything they said to each other tonight would result in a fight.

Heleyna needed time to calm down and realise how much fun this whole thing could be, if only she would allow herself to let go and join in.

Heleyna had been dreading Monday all weekend. She'd disappeared secretly from Troy's and not spoken to him for the rest of the weekend. Troy had phoned her a number of times, but she'd refused to pick up the phone. She wanted to talk to him, she wanted to see him, but the shame she'd had imposed upon her by Sam still stung – shame that Troy could very easily have halted, but didn't. Even a call from Chloe inviting her out for a pint or two hadn't tempted her to leave her own private space.

She'd filled her time painting and walking, taking in the countryside of north Leeds. She'd treated herself to a map with all the paths of the area and decided she would knock them off one at a time, get out into the outdoors whatever the weather was throwing her way. It was on her walk over Otley Chevin, and whilst taking in the awe-inspiring view from the ridge, that she remembered the promise she'd made to herself on top of Blencathra the weekend before: she had to make her life her work and not her work her life. Ted had always been a good listener with great ideas and she vowed to bring up the subject when she saw him for a coffee in the week.

Monday morning she was a bag of nerves. Even applying her make-up had proved a trial, her liquid liner refusing to take on a straight line above her upper lashes. She knew she couldn't escape the arrogant Mr Molloy: his induction programme called for him to attend her project meeting along with other senior associates and stakeholders from SPM.

The meeting was due to take place at ten-thirty, giving her adequate time to prepare her work, her agenda, and finalise her brief presentation on the latest and approved project plan. She was relieved she had Phoebe to help her today, someone to check and filter her emails, photocopy documents and set up the room. Though she still annoyed Heleyna with her sweet chirpy ways, Heleyna had been forced to respect her now she understood the connection between her and John, the MD.

By nine o'clock she'd still managed to avoid Sam. She wandered into the general office to find Phoebe and assign her her tasks for the day; she was looking forward to it. Phoebe was nowhere in sight. Lucy, one of Phoebe's colleagues, informed Heleyna that she was off sick with an attack of fever. Now she was stuck: she needed access to Phoebe's system in order to get at her work for today's meeting. She decided she had no option but to go and sweet-talk Phil the IT guy, a twenty-something weedy-looking dweeb with black hair and bottle-end glasses.

Wandering into the IT offices she wondered what kind of creatures these people were. All she knew was that they were very different from her: they the badgers, she the lioness. She walked into Phil's office. 'Hello there, Phil, long time no see.'

Phil had his face stuck to his monitor, black rings evident round his dark eyes from the hours of computer work. 'Yeah, what do you want?'

As charming as ever, Heleyna thought, the usual customer-service level I would expect from this department. She didn't display her thoughts. She needed something out of him. 'Any chance of a favour, Phil?' She smiled sweetly, explained the saga, and even managed the occasional bout of gentle flirting. Not that she expected him to read the signals: as far as sex went he was as dead as a very dead dodo.

He agreed to reset Phoebe's password 'just this once' and Heleyna returned to her own office and logged on as Phoebe. She found the document she needed and went about putting the finishing touches to her slides. It was all considerably quicker work than she'd anticipated, so she used the spare twenty minutes to scan Phoebe's email headings to check there was nothing important there for her to action. Most of them were pretty mundane, or the compulsory not-very-funny jokes that do the rounds in every organisation. About to log off, her eyes caught sight of an email from John with no subject heading. It'd been sent soon before eight o'clock that morning. She double-clicked and opened it, her overcurious, prying mind directing her thoughts.

Phoebes
As always you were spectacular, my naughty little filly. I've been thinking about you nonstop since Friday night. I can't wait to get inside those magnificent knickers again and taste your divine little pussy. How about this Friday? We could take a run out in my Jag

onto the moors again. I want to make the most of having you to myself before the next Huxley Club meeting, when all and sundry will be keen to enjoy your company.

'Good morning!'

Heleyna nearly jumped out of her skin. She quickly exited the message and looked round at Sam, her skin on fire at the sound of his voice, her mind a stew of confused thoughts. 'Hi.'

He walked towards her, a smug look across his dimpled stubbled face. 'So how are you this morning ... boss? Have a nice weekend? Get up to anything exciting?'

She flushed. He had her where he wanted her, pushed into submission. She didn't know how to respond. 'Fine, thanks. The weekend was fine.'

'Excellent. Mine was good too. Managed to do something I've wanted to do for a while now. I'm planning on doing it again soon, except next time it will be even better, a chance for all to get involved.' He was now standing next to her chair within inches of her shivering body.

'Oh.' Still speechless.

'My, you are nervous today, aren't you? Anything wrong? Anything I can do to help?'

He took a final step towards her and, lowering himself, brushed her right nipple with his fingers through her blouse. She was already pert; she had been since she first heard the sound of his Yorkshire accent fill the room.

Heleyna jumped at his touch and her eyes lowered away from his gaze. 'Don't do that. Just don't, OK?'

'And why ever not? Remember, I know what you're like. You might have been able to hide the true Heleyna from your colleagues, but I know what you're really wanting. You're just a little tart desperate for a quick fuck whenever you get the chance. How is your gorgeous pussy, by the way? Still frustrated at not getting what it craves – my very horny cock?' He was staring at her very obvious nipples that peeped up to the ceiling and screamed to be looked at.

She was drowning, losing herself in him. 'You're despicable. You are going to ruin my position in this organisation with games like this. Leave me alone and remember who is boss.' Heleyna stood, still shaking uncontrollably, collected her papers and left the room for her meeting.

He called after her as she departed. 'I'm going to eat you alive before the month is out.'

She turned, all the while attempting to regain her composure. 'In your dreams, you arrogant, obnoxious bastard. In your dreams.'

She chaired her meeting respectably well under the circumstances. Sam stared at her throughout, attempting to provoke her. She ignored him as best she could, only catching his eye on one or two occasions. His look was domineering: he was trying to keep her in the place he wanted. He was successful.

Even more interesting for Heleyna was the presence of John. She'd invited him out of courtesy, not expecting him to attend. She took the opportunity to request him to introduce the meeting and purpose of the Proclaim project for the strategic direction of SPM. He accepted and then rattled on for fifteen minutes, demonstrating the enthusiasm of an extremely committed businessman. Throughout his speech Heleyna studied him and her mind wandered to him and Phoebe, imagining him on the moors, his head up one of Phoebe's grotesque skirts, disappointed at discovering she was really a mousy brunette and not the bleach-blonde bombshell he had fantasised about. She tried to restrain her smile.

John would have been handsome when he was younger. Now he was a tad overweight, with the features of a man who was highly stressed: his face red and podgy with predictable bags under his eyes. He was single, a divorcee, Heleyna believed. She guessed he was about fifty-five, perhaps late fifties, judging by the lines round his eyes. She couldn't envisage him getting sexed up about anything or, even more ridiculous, Phoebe getting sexed up over him. She wondered what on earth he had that Phoebe could possibly want. Two possible attractions sprung to her ever-naughty mind: either he had a huge cock that worked ever so hard after months if not years without use, or a bloody massive bank balance. If she'd been a betting woman, she would have put her money on the size of his wallet.

The meeting closed and she thanked everyone present for demonstrating their commitment to the project by attending the inaugural meeting. As she spoke her pearls of business wisdom, a feeling of desperate sadness hit the base of her gut; all of this corporate talk now seemed like the biggest load of bullshit she could imagine. Frustration with her work had quickly evolved into a sense of apathy and cynicism. All these eager people sat round the table listening intently, watching a woman who'd previously been a pillar of SPM, ready to put in long hours at the expense of family and friends. And for what? For larger profits, and bigger bonuses in the pay cheques of the senior executives. She had no choice now: she had to move on from this into something that would be meaningful to her, something she could put her heart and soul into.

Heleyna was feeling angry about most things these days: Troy, Sam, work, Ben. Her only saviours were the thought of another weekend away in the not-too-distant future and spending time with Mandy. She was a rock, Heleyna's grounding. Painting classes were now going to be a trial, with Ben and his cocky comments, but she was determined to continue and not let an immature boy get in her way.

Mandy contacted her on Tuesday to let her know she was coming into town for some serious clothes shopping. They arranged to meet for lunch in The Calls, Heleyna deciding to have a longer-than-usual lunch break, a sign of both her apathy for work and her fondness for this very special woman.

A very attractive woman flapping her hands in Heleyna's direction caught her attention as she wandered into the little café they'd picked. It was a very different-looking Mandy from the one she'd spent two days with in the Lakes: her auburn hair was tied back in a French pleat, her lipstick a deep red and her clothes sophisticated – classic. Heleyna felt incredibly unfashionable in her usual and seriously boring work garb.

'Heleyna, Heleyna, over here!'

'Hiya Mands, how's it going? You look absolutely gorgeous, no, stunning.'

The two women embraced in a warm hug and sat.

'I'm great, and thanks for the compliment. Already managed to spend four hundred pounds. Paul's going to go mad!'

Heleyna realised how little she knew about this woman. 'I take it Paul's the hubby?'

'Yup, and a very cute one too.'

'So, what have you done with the kids today?' Heleyna asked.

'Josh is at preschool and Jack at primary school, so I've arranged for some of the other mums to take care of them for a couple of hours after they've finished there. Great group of mums – we all help each other out once in a while, so everyone keeps their sanity!'

'You seem such a happy woman, Mands. How do you do it?'

'Took the bull by the horns one day and decided to do what I wanted with my life. It was pretty scary, I can tell you.'

Their conversation was interrupted by the waitress taking their order. Heleyna decided to go for the devilish-looking croissant filled with everything naughty under the sun, Mandy for the French onion soup and a not-so-healthy salad. Both made the excuse that they needed to build themselves up in readiness for another weekend of walking; both knew they would more than make up for any exercise they did at the weekend with beer and pub food and daytime chocolate snacks – to keep their energy up – of course.

In her current frame of mind, Heleyna was more than keen to discover exactly which bull Mandy had taken the horns of. 'Tell me more about this life-changing decision you made.'

'It's kind of boring, you know, but if you insist!' Mandy's cheeky grin appeared. She looked stunning.

'I am very keen to hear your story. I think I'm about to approach that bull myself soon, and hearing what you have to say might just give me that kick up the backside I need.'

'OK, you've twisted my arm. I'm not a great storyteller by the way.'

'Look, stop making excuses before you've even started and just tell me the bloody story, will you!'

They both giggled.

Mandy continued. 'Ever since I was in my teens I always knew I wanted to be a mum. But school and parents pushed the whole career thing on me so I blindly took that path. I studied law and commerce at uni, then joined one of the big corporations in London.

Worked my arse off for a good five years, fighting my way upwards in a short space of time – earned lots of money too. I even managed to break through the old boys' network – that glass ceiling we all know still exists, even today.'

'Why the hell did you drop all of that?' Heleyna was listening intently, in awe of both Mandy's success and her strength of character in abandoning what most would consider a successful existence.

'I got to my late twenties and one day remembered my dream. It was probably combined with meeting this gorgeous solicitor who swept me off my feet. Paul brought out the best in me, made me realise a lot about myself I had forgotten. We were married pretty quickly, followed by a pregnancy. Actually, it happened the other way round, but we didn't tell our parents that! I was so completely happy with our baby, Jack, that I just thought "Sod it all!" and didn't go back to work after maternity leave. My parents thought I was mad leaving such a good job.' Mandy's hands flew all over the place as she spoke, nearly knocking the waitress who was carrying her soup as she swore.

'Didn't you get bored at home after all that mental stimulation?' Heleyna asked.

'Absolutely! That's why I decided to set up my own business. I still run it now – I contract out my services on an ad-hoc basis to lots of the big names in Leeds. Initially, I used my old business networks to get the enterprise off the ground. Now it seems to just come to me. So I have the best of both worlds.'

Heleyna frowned. 'How did you manage to make that jump? I'm just finding it so daunting.'

'It is and always will be. But you know, sometimes you just have to jump and take a risk to get what you've always wanted. Just bloody well do it. As the old saying goes, this is the real thing, not a dress rehearsal.'

'Thanks.' Heleyna was addressing the waiter.

The pair continued gassing for another hour, the conversation now on the shops Mandy was still to go to to spend hideous amounts of money.

Heleyna returned from lunch full of enthusiasm and motivation. She was finally going to get off her frightened backside and do something different. She knew she had the brains and the brawn for business, just not somebody else's. She promised herself she would talk with Ted and offer a proposition – hopefully, one he wouldn't be able to refuse.

Her excitement was short-lived. No sooner had she sat at her desk than in walked the domineering, predatory Sam. Heleyna forced herself to look into his eyes. Her immediate sexual response constrained her into submission. 'Afternoon, Sam. How's the induction going?'

He closed the door behind him. 'Very good. I just need to talk to you.'

Heleyna felt a little more comfortable and a little less aggressive: he had his professional voice on. 'How can I help?'

'Do you mind if we sit over here?' He was pointing at the comfy chairs in the corner of her office.

'No problem, Sam. Is everything OK?' He was so uncharacteristically serious, she actually began to feel a little concerned for this aesthetically pleasing beauty.

Sitting next to him, every hair on her body came alive, the inevitable response she'd feared. She was mad at herself for still wanting to shag such a bastard of a man. However seductive his physical charms, he'd still treated her brutally, taken advantage of her obvious lust for him; watched her at her most desperate and left her to smoulder with a frustrated, eager pussy.

They were sat relatively close. He turned to face her, his expression serious. She could already feel him touching her, imagined his lips on her neck, his hand up her skirt, his fingers touching her expertly, sensuously, purposefully. She blushed slightly. He spoke. She had already melted into his arms.

'Heleyna, I need to talk to you.'

'Whatever it is, Sam, that's what I'm here for. Fire away with whatever's concerning you.' She was being the caring, attentive boss, her eyes now focused away from his strong gaze.

He leaned forward as though about to whisper his darkest secret, his mouth now close to her neck and ear. 'I so want to fuck you. You are the hottest woman I could ever hope to touch. I want to feel your curvaceous body surrounding my cock.'

Heleyna jumped slightly. She was so hot for him, yet incensed that he'd tricked her. It was so wrong for her to get even close to this situation. 'Oh!' She was speechless.

He took her hand in his and pressed it against his rigid crotch. 'See how much I want you?'

Heleyna felt like a rabbit at night, startled by oncoming car headlights. She knew she was in danger, but the dazzle of the lights had blinded her, kept her stationary. She didn't pull her hand away. He began stroking himself with her hand. She began perspiring. The stroke increased in strength. She responded. He let go of her hand. She continued.

Knock, knock, knock ... 'Shit!' Sam stood quickly and moved one seat away before relaxing into an 'I've done nothing wrong' pose, which by definition always looks decidedly shifty.

'Come in.' Heleyna attempted to recompose herself. Inside she was a quivering hormone-saturated mess.

'Sorry to disturb you.' It was John. 'I was wondering if you've seen Phoebe around today?'

'No problem, John, we were just talking induction.

Phoebe is still off sick, hasn't been in since Friday. A fever apparently. Is there anything I can help you with?'

'No, no worries. I was simply ensuring she was OK. I did recruit her into SPM, so I need to make sure she's settling in OK.'

Heleyna was privately amused by the lies he presented to her, fabrications that emanated out of his podgy little face whilst he was thinking about whatever it was they'd been up to in his Jag.

'That's very kind of you, John.' She could feel Sam staring at her, probably eyeing up the thigh that was now showing as she twisted her body to talk with John.

'And how are you doing, Sam? Hope she's treating you well. Hard worker, Heleyna is, and bloody good at her job. You couldn't ask for a better mentor.'

Heleyna couldn't believe what a smooth-talking charmer he could be when he put his mind to it. Great businessman, though – she couldn't fault him there.

'Thanks, John. I'm settling in well. Enjoying the induction. Great organisation you have, and some very impressive people, too. You must be incredibly proud. Heleyna and I are going to get on just fine.'

Heleyna squirmed at his last comment as the realisation of what she'd just confirmed to Sam set in. She'd just dug herself an even bigger hole. In fact, the hole appeared to be so large she guessed she was stuck in there for eternity: not even the world's best rock climbers could find their way out of this one, she thought. The arrogant bastard.

9

Heleyna tracked a still-sick Phoebe's emails again on Wednesday, but found nothing exciting. Becoming a little disillusioned with her detective skills she began to think about ways she could find out more about Huxley. John, Ted and Phoebe were all members. Her imagination began to flow and, before too long, she had tagged every SPM employee but herself as a member of the club. She still couldn't decipher its purpose, although a flash of something slightly seedy kept rearing its head. Troy's rational words came back to her; he had to be right – she couldn't comprehend Jacinta having done anything naughty in her life.

The phone rang. She answered it in her usual efficient way after three rings, no more, as she'd had drummed into her in her earlier career. 'Heleyna Lane speaking, how may I help you?'

'Hello, gorgeous. I miss you. When am I going to see you again?' It was Troy.

'Oh, it's you.' There was still an ounce of anger left inside her. The anger had been subsiding, though: when she thought long and hard about it, she imagined she would have done the same if Sam had handcuffed Troy, and enjoyed every single little last bit of it.

'You're not still mad at me, are you? Come on, Heleyna, it was only a game. You're normally up for that kind of stuff. Why should this be any different?'

'Because, Troy, I happen to be Sam's boss. That's why.'

Troy's voice was assertive. 'Why does anyone other

than us have to know? You could have your cake and eat it, then. I know you fancy him as much as I do. I saw what he did to you in the rocking chair, and I know how very voluntary those actions were. Just chill out, Heleyna, and live a little. Enjoy your life, you only get one chance.'

'Don't lecture me, Troy. I live my life my way, you live your life yours. Anyway, I promise not to be mad any more, as long as you come round to my house for a change. Perhaps you could come for the weekend?'

'Great. I'll be there, and with bells on.'

Ted was bored. He was playing a game of 'twirl in your office chair as fast as you can whilst juggling three pieces of scrunched-up paper'. He was not being overly successful. It wasn't that he hadn't enough workload to keep him occupied for a good fifty hours a week, it was simply a matter of motivation – he no longer had any. Realisation had set in that it was working with Heleyna that had made work so interesting, and now that source of enjoyment was no longer around to make work bearable. He sighed to himself.

He dropped his paper balls for the twenty-fifth time. The phone rang. He left it. If it was important the person would leave a message anyhow. He continued with his twirling and juggling regime, now managing to reach ten juggles without dropping a thing. He knew it was sad, but he actually felt proud of what he had achieved that day; finally, something to get excited about.

Heleyna stuck to the promise she'd made herself and phoned Ted to drag him out for a coffee. It clicked into voicemail, so she wandered down to his office. She stuck her head round the door and watched him for a moment playing a childish game of juggling and chair twirling, a look of intense concentration on his face. 'Interesting priorities, Ted!'

'Hi there, how's it going?' Ted braked with his feet and his chair came to a standstill facing Heleyna, a grin spreading over his face.

'Fancy that coffee we talked about? I could do with a chat.'

Ted was on his feet and exiting his office before Heleyna had a chance to say anything further, his jacket swung over his shoulder. She followed him, his walk fast and purposeful.

'Will you slow down. Anyone would think you were in a race.'

He adjusted his pace. 'Sorry. I'm just bloody keen to get out of this place today. Shall we go to the usual?'

'It's so long since we went out for a coffee, I can't remember what "the usual" is,' she replied.

'Mono, you remember, the dingy joint round the corner. Make a wicked coffee that you can almost stand your spoon up in. Perks you up for the rest of the day.'

A couple of minutes later they'd ordered and were sat in the crusty armchairs in the non-smoking corner, facing each other across the equally crusty coffee table. Heleyna winked at the coffee-making guy behind the counter. She'd forgotten about him over the last few weeks. He responded with a half smile.

'Tell me how you're doing. How's the new job? How's Troy? How's Sam settling in? How are the art and hiking clubs? Come on, out with it. Give me the full briefing!'

Heleyna threw her head back, her deep infectious laugh filling the small coffee lounge. 'My, you are in need of company, aren't you?'

'Too bloody right I am. My job's pretty isolated these days. I still miss working with you – we were a good team.'

Heleyna had heard this before, and she was pleased to hear it again. She went in for the kill. 'I'm glad you should say that. Not because I want you to be miserable, of course. However, I do have a proposition for you.'

Coffee-making guy brought over their order, all the time staring at Heleyna as he plonked down the espresso and flat white. Heleyna didn't notice. She was too tied up in Ted and her little proposition.

'Sounds ominous. But go for it.' He began slurping his espresso.

'I'll give you a bit of background first, put it in context. Basically, and to cut a long and tedious story short, I think I've had enough of working for SPM. Not just SPM, but any other organisation. The thought of playing this game for the next thirty or so more years is unbearable. I want and need to do something I can put my heart into. However, I know what I'm good at, and I'm good at business. I also know that you too have a good business head on your shoulders, and that we're also a bloody good team together. So, on that basis, what do you reckon to going it alone? Us two together, in business, self-employed.'

Almost childlike, Ted was already jumping up and down in his seat with excitement. 'Fuck, that's the best thing I've heard this decade. When? It's a slight risk, of course, so I will need to pass it by Jacinta. But she should be absolutely fine with it. Oh my God, I haven't even asked – what kind of business were you thinking about?'

'Well, to be totally honest, I haven't come up with a fixed idea yet. But we're both bloody good project managers, so we have a real breadth of excellent transferable skills. I reckon the world's our oyster. How about we get the creative juices going when you and Jacinta come over to Troy's for dinner? A few glasses of wine should open up the gates!' The butterflies that come with excitement and anticipation were already flowing inside Heleyna's gut.

Ted appeared childlike in his enthusiasm, a strange sight for such a beefy bloke. 'Fucking brilliant, fucking brilliant. John will be bitterly disappointed, you know. But John's a friend out of work, too, so I'm sure I can have a good chat to him about this.'

'Don't rush ahead and do anything too soon. Let's get our ideas sorted, write a sound business plan, go to the bank manager, then speak to John.' Heleyna was, as always, the voice of reason when it came to plans and proposals.

'OK, you're on.'

Driving into the art-college car park Heleyna was singing along with Kylie at the top of her voice. She was in a mood so light she was floating, as if on a drug-induced high. She knew they were going to make it, Ted and her. This was going to be the best decision she'd ever made in her life. She switched off the engine. As she did, a very naughty-but-nice thought crept into her bad, bad mind: once she broke the ties with SPM she was free to do whatever she wanted and in whatever way, shape or form she desired with any employee of SPM. Sam would soon be on her shagging menu. It was a thought that put the final layer of icing on the already well-coated cake.

June and Fred, the older couple, pulled up next to her. They were mouthing incomprehensible words in her direction and pointing excitedly towards the back seat of their car, clearly wanting her to go and see something. She exited her own car and made her way over to them as they grabbed their art gear.

June looked up, her pale eyes bright and obvious against her delicate skin and whitest-of-white hair. 'You should see what Fred and I've brought in for class – to show you all.'

Heleyna peered at the not-so-abstract painting in June's hands – she didn't like what they were so keen for her to admire. It was a watercolour with no style, no texture, no perspective. In fact, Heleyna though it stank, but she was ever the politician, and so feigned enthusiasm. 'That's wonderful. Well done, you two. I hope Ben's remembered my, sorry, our piece.'

'What is yours? Come on, you can tell us.'

'It's definitely a surprise. Very different style from your work, though, that's for sure.'

The three of them strolled into class, chatting all the way, June making her usual mischievous comments about Bernadette.

Bet was buzzing round the room in her typically brusque manner, giving the students orders on where to exhibit their pieces. She was dressed in a particularly hideous beige smock that resembled an old-fashioned grain sack, all finished off with a green sash. Ben and Jemma sat there giggling away secretly. Annoyed at their childishness, Heleyna looked away from them and over at the two pieces Ben had brought. Her piece was actually pretty impressive: even though red was the only colour to appear on the canvas, the texture and patterns were impressive, bringing back some horny memories. She even thought she could make out a bum imprint, which made her giggle. The pink, with its splash of purple, was considerably more refined. Heleyna imagined a quick fuck in the missionary position had created that composition.

Bet spoke to them all. 'Thank you all for bringing in your work, and what a real variety we have, too. What we're going to do this evening is introduce our own compositions, giving a description of the process behind the work, your own feelings on the subject matter and what motivated you to paint this particular piece. Then I would like the rest of the class to pass comment on one thing they like and one thing they don't like about the work. Please remember that likes and dislikes are purely subjective, so there is no need to be upset by the comments. Heleyna, are you happy to go first?'

Heleyna was still feeling incredibly happy, in an I-don't-give-a-damn kind of a mood. Also feeling particularly naughty and irritated by Ben, she decided that embarrassing him might just put him back in the place where he should be. 'Absolutely, Bet. Firstly I would like to say that this composition was not produced by me on my own. Ben and I undertook this as a joint effort, didn't we Ben?'

A very sheepish Ben answered. 'Yup.'

Heleyna could see the terror growing in his eyes. She winked at him and continued. 'We haven't named it yet, but I rather think the name *Naughty but Nice* would suit it. What motivated me? Well, actually, it was sexual gratification that motivated both of us. This piece here is a product of a three-on-a-canvas romp with a pot of red paint. Ben, one of his college buddies and me. Very interesting and rewarding process.'

There was silence for a second. Unexpectedly June started clapping, followed by the timid accountant, Todd.

'I love this work, Heleyna. You're a very bad woman. Was it good fun?' June was more interested than Heleyna could have imagined.

'Very.' She grinned at the other students.

Ben and Jemma were silent, gobsmacked by her revelation. Bet, for once, didn't pass comment. Heleyna knew she'd shocked some of them, but she loved every minute of it. She was returning to her old and much happier self.

10

With a deadline looming Heleyna worked late for the first time in a long while. She conned Phoebe into helping her, and, for once, Phoebe agreed to stay on until 6.30 p.m. Heleyna had thanked her with a couple of cinema tickets – she was still very much aware of the need to stay on good terms with Phoebe.

Much to her relief Sam was still on his induction and unable yet to give Heleyna the assistance she required. The following week he was finally being brought into the project team and their working relationship would be forced into an uncomfortable closeness. She'd seen him sporadically over the last few days, with each occasion progressing her excitement for him. She was intensely and blissfully aware that before too long she would be able to respond to his advances. Containing her lust for this very, very arrogant bastard of a man was going to require some particularly fine acting skills.

It was already seven o'clock at night and she was eating a takeaway sushi, her taste buds teased to exploding point as she shovelled each piece whole into her mouth; she was ravenous. Her sushi-eating brought back the recent memories of an excellent weekend with Troy when they'd stopped for lunch at a local sushi bar. She could still smell his aftershave when she closed her eyes; even the thought of his scent was enough to provoke the luxurious swelling of her lips and nipples. She luxuriated in fancying that man.

Her mind wandered as it always did when her grey

matter began to tire; the antics of the Huxley Club were always the first in the queue when she couldn't be bothered to think about work any longer. Although Phoebe was back at work from sick leave Heleyna had maintained the access to her email. Much to her disappointment, nothing of any interest had come through since the provocative email from John. Knowing she'd hit a dead end with her detective work, she spoke aloud to herself. 'How the hell am I going to get more info on this bloody club ... I know what I'll try.' She jumped to her feet and worked her way from her office to the terrain of the IT nerds. Some of them worked late. Perhaps she could con one of them into giving her access to the emails of other employees?

The light was still on in Phil's office. He'd been so helpful last time with Phoebe's email, she hoped he was in the same cordial frame of mind this evening. She hesitated outside the door and composed herself. She was willing to give anything needed to achieve this little baby.

About to wish him a friendly good evening as she pushed open the door to his office, she was stopped in her tracks with her mouth wide open in astonishment: she'd caught him with his pants down, quite literally. He was sat slumped back in his chair, his pants round his ankles and hand firmly round the smallest prick she'd ever seen in her life. On his monitor she could just make out some cheesy porn: two bleach-blonde skinny birds in a 69 pose giving each other a supposed good time. The audio was turned up to just about audible: the tinny but inescapable grunts and groans could be heard at close range.

Though shocked by this behaviour from a guy she'd previously thought dead from the waist down, Heleyna couldn't help creasing up with laughter. Then she took control of the situation. She would definitely get her own way with him now! 'Well, well. What do we have going on here?' she bellowed.

'Oh shit! Shit, shit, shit!' Phil had turned his back on her and was quickly retrieving his trousers in the hope of recovering any ounce of dignity that may have been available to him.

She walked towards his PC monitor, enjoying the power trip the moment gave her. 'Well, this is very interesting, isn't it, Phil? Accessing porn at work – dismissable offence number one. Flashing at a female colleague – dismissable offence number two, I'd say. I'd better go and phone John and give him a statement before he commences disciplinary proceedings. How do I start? "I phoned Phil to ask his advice and he called me to his office. I walked in and there he was mastur-bating in front of me with porn on . . ."'

'Don't, please don't tell him. I won't do it again,' he pleaded. 'Please, I can't afford to lose my job.'

'Well then, perhaps we could arrange a little bargain,' she said, knowing herself that she was being as oily as any boss in her position would be. 'How does that sound?'

'Anything, anything. Just please don't report me.' He was pleading desperately, his tiny dick now tucked away in a pair of very unflattering boxers with the words 'suck here' plastered across the front.

A wave of hilarity hit her at the thought of fulfilling the request. She reeled herself in and back to a position of control. 'All right, I won't say anything,' she said, still giggling. 'But that's dependent upon you doing some-thing for me. I want to have access to everyone's email every evening for the next week. I need you to be here to guard the door whilst I do some serious reading. What do you reckon?'

'Absolutely. No problem. I can do that.'

'How about we start right now. Firstly, give me access to Ted Jones's account.'

Phil, his hands still shaking, began tapping away at the keyboard. Within a couple of minutes he was in. He whined at her, 'Please can I just go to the bathroom?'

'OK, but be quick.'

He rushed out of the room and Heleyna began scrolling through the hundreds of emails in Ted's inbox. She couldn't believe her good fortune. It was bloody lucky Phil was such a little wanker – literally, she giggled to herself.

The majority of the emails were work-related, but she noticed a few from Jacinta's home account. She decided to begin with that, then progress on to the ones from John, followed by Phoebe. As she opened the first one Phil returned to the office. He was still visibly shaking and his body language was subservient. He sat on the spare chair away from Heleyna for the next two hours and didn't move or utter a word whilst Heleyna read.

The first couple of emails were pretty mundane, but surprisingly flirtatious. Heleyna was overjoyed when she opened the next one. At least there was mention of Huxley, even if it was only to finalise the date for the next meeting. She began to feel more hopeful of finding some gossip. The fifth and final email was interesting and had only been sent that day, but it was still more guarded than Heleyna would have liked. She wanted facts and a clear indication, not more cryptic messages and comments to further tease her.

Hi Sexy
Hope the day's going well. I've been doing my usual wifely duties. Question/update on Huxley follows – can you answer today as I'm out tonight with the girls. I think we need a bit more of a theme for this one – any ideas? Do you think we should make any changes to

the basement? Did the third room work well last time or do we need more choice of devices? I've drafted the invite for Heleyna and Troy, so we're all go for that one when we're over at Troy's for dinner with them next week. Hope they enjoy themselves! I hope they're as open-minded as we think they are. Is there anything else I should be organising?

Sorry to bombard you at work, but sometimes we're like ships that pass in the night! I miss you when I don't see as much of you. Hope you've remembered Thursday night or you'll be in big trouble – can't wait to see that gorgeous arse of yours.

Love you

J x

Heleyna checked the sent emails for his reply, but Ted hadn't been either filing them or even keeping the unimportant ones.

John's emails to Ted were next. Heleyna became impatient at the tedious content. 'Boring, boring, boring.'

Phil looked round at her briefly. She ignored him and continued her scrolling. Glad that Ted wasn't as efficient at deleting his inbox as his sent items, she opened up an email from John from five months before with the interesting heading of 'Phoebe'.

Ted

Re: Huxley

Have met the most incredible filly. Hoping to bring her into SPM soon. She's damn hot. Very much a free spirit when it comes to the bedroom department, if you get my drift.

Anyhow, want to recommend that she be invited to the next Huxley meeting. Please advise ASAP.

Regards

John

Heleyna was now convinced that Troy was wrong – there must be more to Huxley than meets the eye, she thought. Printing off both the emails she granted Phil a filthy look, and spoke, 'OK, there, are you? Bored, by any chance? Bet you wonder what the hell I'm doing, don't you?'

He didn't respond to her patronising questions. He answered by a simple shake of a very downcast head.

Her next task was the emails to Ted from Phoebe. There were only two and both had the heading 'Thanks!' She opened them quickly and keenly.

Hiya Ted!
Thanks tons for the invite. I'm so excited! John's told me as much as he can – excellent! What's the dress code? – want to make sure I blend in.
   See ya Saturday!
   Phoebes ☺

The next one was written only a few days later. Heleyna worked out the date from the earlier email and established that the second was written after the Saturday night meeting.

Hi there Ted!
Excellent night! Can't wait for the next one! I hope that guy – Chris I think his name was – is there again. He was awesome...! By the way, I enjoyed J's company!!!!!!!
   See ya soon!?
   Phoebes ;-)

Although fascinated by the reading, she couldn't help but feel a sense of irritation at how immature Phoebe was. Each exclamation mark grated, making her hackles rise. She looked at her watch and couldn't believe it was almost nine-thirty. She stood up and began exiting the office. 'Oh well, time to go home, I suppose, heh, Phil?

I'll be here about seven o'clock tomorrow night. Remember the consequences if you don't turn up, you dirty, dirty little boy.' As she mouthed the last words she bent close to his head and hissed into his ear.

He flinched and blushed. Heleyna turned in the haughtiest way she knew how, and marched out of the office. She felt powerful, she felt authoritative, she felt strong – she loved every single minute of it.

The following evening Phil gave her access to John's account. He was still quiet, skipping around her nervously as they set up the PC. Tonight he had a comic and a plunger filled with coffee to keep him company. He sat in the same seat as the night before and began leafing through his comic. Heleyna glanced at his reading material before settling down to her mission. 'Reading comics, still, are we? Nothing pornographic in there, I hope!'

No response was forthcoming: he didn't dare in case he dropped himself in it even deeper than he was now.

John's inbox was huge, with no organisation. She sorted the emails, clumping together those from the same person. She began researching. There were tens of emails from Phoebe. Many had the same subject heading so Heleyna wisely picked the latest one received. That way she could read all the history, including responses. This one was an interesting read, giving her lots of details about their sexual exploits. She actually began to feel rather sick at the thought of Phoebe mounting an overweight John, her pussy planted on his mouth, his dick inside her. Imagining his dick to be short, fat and rather pasty, with two saggy, flabby balls planted underneath, she was reduced to sending a loud 'Yeuch!' around Phil's office.

Finally finding an email related to Huxley, she read rapidly, soaking up the details, her brain an ever-ready sponge. It frustrated her; unable to glean anything new from the email, she continued her search. Every one she found was hopeless; even those from other people she knew were involved. It was late again. She needed to find a more efficient way of getting the interesting emails. Perplexed and tired, she spoke to Phil. 'Is there any way of scanning emails for key words?'

'Yeah, that's . . . that's easy.' His words were still coy.

'OK then, I've got a job for you. Over the next week I want you to scan the inbox of every employee and search for the key word "Huxley". Then print off those that contain that word.'

'Every employee?' He sounded truly pissed off at the prospect.

'Yes, that's right, every employee. Any complaints?'

'Oh, no, no, of course not. I'll get on to it.'

'Of course you will.' She walked out of the office as she spoke her last words, her stride purposeful and cocky.

Heleyna left Phil alone with his task for the next few days and allowed herself to get on with her life until the information was ready and available. She loved having a gopher, especially one as ameneable as Phil.

She was gagging for some action, though. She wasn't getting as much as she usually liked, mainly because she was avoiding Troy's house, anxious at being trapped in the same kind of unbearably disconcerting situation Sam and he had inflicted upon her before. She phoned Troy from her mobile on the way home on the train and whispered naughty things to him; he always liked the intimate comments Heleyna made about what she would like to do to him. He agreed to come over that evening. Handsome man walked past her seat on the train as he searched out his own. She smiled and winked. He reciprocated.

She popped into the local supermarket on her walk

from the station and stocked up on provisions for a romantic meal for two: fresh king prawns, scallops, salad, lemon, garlic, crusty french bread and a couple of bottles of creamy, buttery Chardonnay. She wanted something quick and easy to prepare, but also quietly decadent.

She rushed home, dumped the food and jumped into the shower. Wanting to look and feel seductive for her ever-sexy man, she dressed in her favourite feeling-naughty outfit: the compulsory hold-ups, short-yet-slinky black dress with never-ending split and her highest shoes. No panties, of course. She put on black eye make-up and deep rich red lipstick. Her luscious tresses were left unrestricted across her shoulders and back. As she walked towards the kitchen to prepare dinner she wandered through the hall and past her full-length mirror. She stood in front for a moment and admired herself. She liked what she saw. She knew she looked great, like a woman wanting and needing sex – pure sex and nothing more.

She decided to take a few minutes out – dinner was easy to prepare anyhow. Plonking herself down on her functional sofa, she flicked through the TV channels until she came across the sure-to-find-shagging scene between some perfectly made-up couple. She slipped off her shoes and sat cross-legged, revealing lacy-topped hold-ups. The display in the film aroused her, the way it demonstrated the act without showing too much. The frustration of wanting to see more revved her up. Her no-holds-barred fingers attacked her pussy before she realised it. She began to lose herself, eyes closed, crossed legs forcing themselves open, fingers stroking and caressing, dick caressing her lips.

Shock forced her eyes open wide and she considered the scene. Standing in front of her – trousers and boxers round his ankles, long dick trying to find its way into her mouth – was her favourite man. This was exactly what she needed.

'You dirty bitch,' he growled. 'You deserve a good spanking, my girl.'

He dragged her to her feet, pulled up her dress, bent her over his bare leg and smacked her bottom. By the time he'd finished administering his punishment she was shaking with sexual hunger.

'Please do it to me,' she whined. 'Do it to me here and now and hard.'

He disobeyed her, pushed her back on the sofa and thrust his impatient penis into her mouth, pushed and shoved with the full force of a grown man. When given the chance, mock protest seeped out from her throat. She was in her own little heaven on earth.

He wasn't entirely selfish. After losing himself in her more than willing mouth for a glorious few moments, he withdrew. Lust-filled eyes looked down at her ready, willing and desperate pussy, quickly followed by his hot moist mouth and tongue. Fucking, prodding, entering and nibbling ensued. With her pulse up to one hundred and fifty she was paralysed. Why the hell would she want to move with that going on? His delicious touches brought her close to the place where she now wanted to stay: teetering on the edge of orgasm.

Pushing him away, her eyes scanned the room for a suitable shagging surface. He willingly followed her to the glass-topped table, pushed her down onto her back, and with one swift move he was in her. Her legs clasped recklessly around his waist. With one hand on her waist for support and one on her clit for pleasure, he rammed her, her bosoms jiggling with each attack.

She erupted around him, her body convulsing in erotic bliss. Her pulsating hole worked like a milking machine on his dick, shaping his orgasm, sucking the life out of him.

Bent over her, his heaving breath evident in her left ear, he spoke. 'I want more where that came from. I've missed fucking you, you gorgeous beast. God, you feel good.'

They lay in their intimate position for some time, enjoying the feel of each other's hot body relaxing around them.

When they finally moved, Troy suggested they skip dinner until later. He was in the mood for one of their favourite pastimes – impulse buying at the local sex shop. He was keen to purchase a few more toys for their ever-increasing collection.

'Why not give Chloe a ring and ask her to meet us there? She's always great fun for these occasions!' He asked.

Heleyna agreed. The last thing on her mind was food.

The sex shop was cliché sleazy: swing doors and blacked-out windows; old men reading porn mags that lined fifty per cent of the wall space; a door leading to wank cubicles that no doubt surrounded some poor, stoned woman.

'Can I help you?' The anorak behind the counter approached them as they faced the shelf of impressive strap-ons.

'We're looking for a ten-inch strap-on.' Heleyna looked him straight in the eye.

'Let me show you our selection.' He handed her double- and single-pronged devices, some vibrating, some static.

Chloe entered the shop, and found a position in between Heleyna and Troy.

'I would just love this one.' Heleyna was looking starry-eyed at the ultimate double-pronged vibrating strap-on with dual controls and pleasure zones for the female wearer.

'Expensive, that one,' the anorak said, eyeing Heleyna's voluptuous feminine body.

'How expensive?'

'One hundred and twenty pounds.' He spoke in a monotone.

'What do you reckon, Chloe?' Heleyna looked over at the beauty she'd savoured on more than one occasion.

'Looks bloody marvellous to me!'

'Any chance of a discount?' Heleyna addressed the anorak, never shy at coming forward.

Anorak looked like he was about to tell her to get lost, but, as he opened his mouth to speak, he perused the room, noticing the number of punters in his shop. 'Er, depends what you're willing to do for a discount. How about you two have a trial run with your new toy out the back?' He was pointing at Heleyna and Chloe.

They both knew what this meant, and all three were happy with the suggestion.

'That will mean a one hundred per cent discount.' Heleyna was one step ahead of him, as she normally was.

Anorak totted up the numbers of men around them and quickly agreed. Troy smiled at Heleyna, at her entrepreneurial approach.

It took two zips and four buttons to undo each other's dresses in the dimly lit room. As they undressed each other, eager for the first play with their new toy, they heard screens sliding open around them. Chloe looked up at Heleyna excitedly, then they disappeared into their own world, a world solely focused on pleasing each other, completely oblivious to the wanking mob, which included a more than happy Troy, surrounding them.

Chloe's face felt warm to Heleyna's fingertips, the

blonde hair which framed it silky to her touch. Heleyna allowed her hand to drop slowly down over her delicate jaw and slender neck, and over her subtle collarbone. She had the most amazing breasts – small and pert with milk-chocolate coloured nipples pointing up to the skies – that were more than obvious through her black lacy bra. There was a sharp intake of breath as Heleyna undid the front fastening clasp. Chloe's breasts tumbled out in front of her; they still pleased her after all this time.

Chloe was in no mood for gentle caresses: the look in her eye begged Heleyna to fuck her senseless, and Heleyna was more than willing to oblige. In desperation they ripped off the remainder of their clothes and Heleyna attached the strap-on to herself. It looked huge on her female frame, almost comical. These thoughts soon disappeared when Chloe took hold of the controls. Amazing, tantalising flutters emanated out of the base, and infiltrated Heleyna's groin, orbiting her clit, reaching subterranean zones. Afraid of coming too soon, she pushed Chloe forcibly onto the bed in the centre of the room and took hold of the controls. Chloe spread her legs instantly.

'Enter me now. Don't wait.' She looked pitiful, no, beautifully submissive: her moist, swollen, red pussy open wide for all to see.

Heleyna dropped down onto her, entering her with the full force of her body behind her, and began the alien thrusting, tweaking up the vibrations slowly, allowing them both time to adjust. Heleyna felt masculine and strong, for the first time gaining some understanding of what it's like to be a man: a petite frame beneath you looking powerless, all flushed face and desperate hands pulling you down to ram into their cunt, wanting it hard, fast and mean.

They both groaned compulsively, their breasts clashing together with each penetration. Heleyna watched her closely, wanted to gauge her hurtling orgasm to time herself with Chloe, who dug her fingers into her jiggling breasts. Vibrations, thrusting, heat, stimulation, soft bodies: lost in their lust, they looked amazing.

Strap-on at full throttle, Heleyna thrusting like an accelerating steam train, they came in glorious unison, both bodies convulsing, both bodies rigid with the full force of the female orgasm. Heleyna loved to watch Chloe's face as she came: her eyes closed, petite face turned to one side, lust seeping through her skin, whimpering noises escaping from her open, moistened, swollen lips. She watched her until her final spasm, before collapsing breathless and exhausted, wishing at that point that she had the muscle mass of a man in her arms and back.

That wasn't the last time they displayed themselves at that little peep show. In fact the two of them, sometimes with Troy in tow, sometimes not, were a regular feature. Before too long they had quite a collection of freebies hidden away in the bedroom closet.

11

'Good morning, gorgeous.' Heleyna was addressing a tired-looking Troy who was still cuddled up under her snug duvet.

'Hmmm ... morning.'

'I'm off now. You'd better get up or you'll be late for work.' She bent over and kissed him, the smell of last night's alcohol still evident on his breath. Not that she cared – hers had been worse before she'd attacked her teeth with her toothbrush.

'What time is it?' He pushed his hands through his scruffy hair in an attempt to tame it.

'Seven-thirty already.'

'OK, I'm up.' He crawled out from under the duvet and sat on the side of the bed, his head in his hands, his hair tousled and cute.

Heleyna admired his naked physique, all the while trying to prevent her pussy from obscuring her getting-to-work thoughts. 'See you soon,' she said. 'By the way, which night are we off to Ted and Jacinta's?'

He was concentrating on his thoughts, which were dulled by alcohol and sleep deprivation. 'Umm ... tomorrow ... yes, that's right, tomorrow night. Bye, sexy. You're looking hot today.'

Dressing and attempting to put her badly pickled brain into use had not come easily. She was looking a little less conservative than she normally would have: a tight shirt and shorter-than-usual skirt displaying her feminine charms. She simply hadn't realised.

* * *

It was the first morning that Sam was available to join the Proclaim project and Heleyna had organised a meeting for her small immediate team: herself, Sam and Phoebe. She was suffering from a hangover, a result of yet another evening with Troy at her Horsforth flat; one bottle of wine had turned into three too easily and she was now paying the consequences.

They never discussed the Sam situation any more. Heleyna knew it was a matter of ignoring what they both understood as the truth: that Sam and Troy were in lust; that Sam and Heleyna were in lust, but that Heleyna was being undeniably uptight about the situation; that Heleyna and Troy were still in lust, although now they also had something a bit more substantial to their relationship.

The meeting was informal. She arranged for it to take place in her office, around the coffee table, and had asked Phoebe to bring tea, coffee and muffins as a bit of a sweetener. She was going to tell them the good news: that they were all going to have to commit to some long hours over the next few months in order to meet the demands of high workload. She was going to have to get better at leading a team if they were to respond to her requests; lots of reward, recognition and the occasional yet simple thank you needed to be forthcoming.

Sam arrived first and wished her a smiley good morning, all the time examining her closely, pushing her into submission. He closed the door behind him. Heleyna turned a delicate shade of pink as he penetrated her office, and began rummaging around on her desk for non-existent papers.

'Sam, good to see you. How's everything going?' Words were flying round her head: I must not lose control, I must not lose control.

'Great. Looking forward to working closer with you, though.'

Heleyna tried hard to ignore his remark. 'It will be good to have you on our small team. We have a lot to achieve and we need your expertise, advice and energy to help make this happen for SPM.'

Sam finally sat in one of the stylish comfy seats. He faced her and maintained his eye contact with her body. She didn't look up at him, instead clicking through her emails pretending to do some urgent last-minute work, but in reality just ignoring him until Phoebe came in and saved her from this – from tension so thick that you could cut it with a very blunt knife.

He spoke to her again. 'You are a very fine-looking woman, Heleyna Lane. Your tits look superb in that shirt. Just look at the way they force your buttons open ever so slightly in the middle, giving me a peek at your lacy bra.'

'Sam, this truly is not appropriate. Firstly I am your boss, and secondly this is a work environment and I could have you reprimanded for comments such as that.'

The truth was, her lust had already crossed her self-imposed NO ENTRY barrier and was hurtling down that naughty-yet-delectable path; an indisputable dampness had appeared between her curvaceous legs.

To her horror Sam stood again and walked towards her, mentally removing her clothes with each step. Heleyna watched him from the corner of her eye as she stood over her keyboard, intent on looking like she was working. She remembered his delectable body and glorious dick and shuddered gently, her eyelids flickering uncontrollably for a split second. Sam registered the movement and responded accordingly, moving in closer.

She was still bent over her keyboard – caught, para-lysed, wet.

Sam stood behind her and spoke to her again. 'Your arse is just fucking perfect.' He placed a hand upon one of her rounded cheeks, cupping it firmly; the other touched her inner thigh.

Barely able to contain herself, her reaction was to stay put in the same rigid position. Turmoil filled her mind; the same turmoil she'd experienced before with this man. Every man she wanted to fuck she fucked – it was unbearably hard to change the habit of a lifetime, especially with one as tempting as Sam Molloy.

Sam's hand moved up between her thighs, his skin rough from a year of working outdoors in the North York Moors National Park. She could hear it catching on her silky tights. She was still rigid. He reached as high as her thighs would allow. She remained still, uncer-tainty dominating her thoughts. He removed his hand, took hold of her thighs and moved them apart, ever so gently. She allowed him to manoeuvre her. His hand returned to her inner thighs and this time he worked his way up to the summit. She was so wet he could feel her desire for him. He stroked her. She whimpered.

Sam spoke quietly. 'I told you that you wanted me, you dirty little tart. See how wet you are? You certainly can't deny it now. What you need – boss – is a damn good shag.' Sam removed his hand. 'But until you look me straight in the eye and ask me, no, beg me, to give you what you want, I am not going to.'

Lust was replaced by anger more quickly than Heleyna thought possible. She turned to face him. 'You arrogant, arrogant little shit. Get out of my office now. Go on – out!'

As Sam turned and began his journey towards her office door, a conceited grin across his unfeasibly hand-some face, there was a knock and the door opened.

'Hello, you guys. Sorry I'm so late – just don't know where the time went to this morning.' Phoebe looked from one to the other, picking up the unusual vibes.

Unable to hide her feelings, Heleyna replied aggressively. 'Come on in, please, and next time make sure you arrive on time. Nothing more unprofessional than people wasting their colleagues' time. Time is money you know, Phoebe.'

The meeting went ahead, but not as Heleyna had envisaged. She'd done nothing to motivate the two people she was going to have to rely on the most over the coming months, or, at least until she and Ted had got themselves into gear with setting up their own business.

Heleyna was now keener than ever to escape from SPM. The environment had become claustrophobic: both her boredom with the work itself and the stifling effect of Sam contributed to the feeling of being penned in. She wasn't trapped, though. The next stage, the escape from this, was in her court.

Heleyna rushed around Troy's stainless steel kitchen throwing orders at him. They were desperately trying to prepare a meal as sumptuous as the one Jacinta had prepared for them.

'I wish we had a bloody wife sometimes.' Heleyna talked to Troy in between rinsing the ready-prepared salad, which, in her absent-minded state she had forgotten didn't actually need washing.

'Yep, I know what you mean. Thank God for ready food – made especially for the workaholics or lazy gits of this world.'

'I live on this stuff, you know, along with microwaveable gourmet dishes.'

'You should come and live with me. I would look after you. My work's not half as important to me as yours is to you.' Troy was now opening a pre-prepared meal he'd bought on the way from the local deli. He'd picked up chicken breasts stuffed with fresh herbs, Brie, toasted pine nuts and vine-grown tomatoes – all ready to pop straight into a preheated oven.

'Actually, I think I would like that. You just need to encourage your lodger to find his own place, then I might just do that. Talking about your lodger, I hope you've told him not to come back early. Bloody hell, I didn't need to wash that. What am I playing at?' Heleyna had realised her error with the salad.

'No worries. That's sorted. He's off out with some mates. Shouldn't be back until around midnight. Anyhow, I like him living here. We have a good time together. Perhaps you'll come round to him eventually.' Troy didn't dare mention the Heleyna-fancying-Sam part. He was more than aware that doing so would create another eruption, and he much preferred it when they got along together.

'No chance, Troy. Not even an inkling of a chance.' The knife she was chopping the salad with was now held at head height and she was jabbing it pointedly in Troy's direction.

'OK, I've got the message. Now put that knife down and go and get yourself ready. They're due to arrive in forty minutes. I'll finish this.'

As Heleyna turned to walk out of the kitchen, Troy placed a crisp spank on her butt cheek. She passed him a cheeky glance over her shoulder in response to his flirting.

'I'll get you back for that.' She was grinning.

Jacinta and Ted arrived on time and by taxi, three bottles of wine between them clasped beneath their arms. They already seemed a little intoxicated when Heleyna opened the door. Heleyna had heard the giggling from Jacinta before she even heard the rap on Troy's front door.

'Come in, come in. Good to see you both.'

Ted hugged Heleyna, and Jacinta kissed her on both cheeks, her lips brushing Heleyna's skin. Heleyna liked that – she hated those false air kisses used by the Lords and Ladies of this world. Heleyna showed them into the lounge, where they both flopped into the three-seater down-filled sofa.

'Right then, who wants what to drink?'

Troy wandered out of the kitchen in his usual relaxed manner, a tea towel stuffed into the front pocket of his blue-and-white-striped apron. He welcomed them both then returned to the kitchen to put the dinner into the oven, giving them a good forty minutes or so to get some quality drinking in.

The evening began relatively politely. Once the second bottle of wine was nearly consumed, Jacinta recommenced the giggling Heleyna had heard as they walked up Troy's garden path. Heleyna couldn't help thinking how different Jacinta was from the woman she'd first thought she was.

'Oh, Ted, you're so funny.' She hit his arm playfully in reply to his tasteless joke.

'OK, OK, here's the next one. You'll love this, Troy. What do a pizza delivery boy and a gynaecologist have in common?'

'I don't know, what do a pizza delivery boy and a gynaecologist have in common?' Heleyna was being facetious.

'They can both smell it, but they can't eat it!'

As he gave the punch line Jacinta just about spat her drink all over Troy's trendy sofa. Heleyna was definitely seeing a side of Jacinta she hadn't thought existed. She was no longer simply the prim little housewife who gave her time to charity. There was something more there, something cheeky and mischievous and fun.

Troy jumped up when the timer sounded on his oven. 'Time for dinner. Come through to the dining room.'

Heleyna was relieved she didn't have to hear another of Ted's jokes. Time to move the conversation on to business propositions, she thought, and get those creative juices flowing.

The dining room was set with soft lighting, and Troy had strewn candles in every possible space. They sat round the large dining table, and Troy served.

'Get stuck in. There's dessert too, so leave a bit of room.'

'This looks wonderful. Thanks, Troy.' Jacinta seemed impressed at the quality of the food.

'Troy's a great cook, aren't you, Troy?' Heleyna winked at him as she spoke, knowing full well that this meal was about as home-made as a burger and fries from the local takeaway. She poured them all yet another glass of the divinely peppery Pinot Noir.

Heleyna moved the conversation towards where she wanted it to go. 'Ted, any more ideas on this partnership idea?'

'Oh yes, yes. J and I have had a good chat about it and she's fully supportive of me having a go, aren't you, darling?'

'Absolutely. It's not too much of a risk. I mean, if it doesn't work out, then you're both highly employable. Go for it!'

'Excellent. Good news to hear you're so supportive. So then, what the hell are we going to do?'

Ted was still unsure. 'You know what, there are many, many options but so many of them have been done before. We need to pick something we both have a passion for, then add a different angle – do it slightly differently or more professionally than anyone else in the market.'

Troy added his thoughts. 'It's going to be difficult to find something you're both totally passionate about. All Heleyna seems to do is work, eat, drink and, more recently, paint and hike. How about you, Ted, any hobbies?'

'Actually we're a pretty boring lot, aren't we? All I do when I'm not at work is spend money, watch TV and play the occasional game of rugby. Oh, I suppose we also put a lot of energy into Huxley.'

'Oh, yes, the ominous Huxley. When are you going to give us some more details on that, Ted?' By now Heleyna's words were slurred, the word 'ominous' barely audible, and escaping as an 'onimous'.

Jacinta jumped up. 'I've got the invite in my bag. I'll just go and get it.'

She wandered out of the dining room and retrieved her bag from the lounge.

'Come on, Ted, just give me one little morsel of information,' Heleyna asked.

Jacinta returned to the room waving a flash-looking envelope in her long delicate fingers.

Ted replied. 'OK, just one little piece. A couple of colleagues are also members. Actually, let me ask you a question. Are you and Troy very open-minded, you know, in the adult desires department?' He winked and nudged thin air with his elbow in his attempt to get them to understand what he was saying without actually saying it.

Heleyna hesitated.

Troy didn't. 'Yes, we are. No question there.'

Heleyna blushed, but no one could tell in the candle-light. Ted smiled and looked over at Jacinta, who winked at him and placed her hand on his large thigh under the table.

'I thought you might be, just thought you might be.' Ted nodded as he spoke.

'What makes you think I might be open-minded in that arena? Troy and I have been together for some time and we are very happy together.' Heleyna was defensive. She didn't like the fact that yet another work colleague was discovering her secret self. However, alcohol had reduced her to a less inhibited state.

'Let's just say I believe that you, Heleyna, have enjoyed yourself at my expense before today.'

Jacinta squeezed his leg painfully under the table.

Troy laughed raucously, filling the small dining room. 'And you thought you'd got away with it. Brilliant! Quite brilliant!'

In her more-than-tipsy state, Heleyna had forgotten her embarrassment for a moment and ran with the comment, as though talking with old and intimate friends. 'Oh shit, I've been caught! Bloody well thought I'd got away with that one. Damn!'

'Hope you enjoyed yourself. J and I certainly did.' Ted was being his usual brazen self.

Heleyna's face took on a look of shock and disbelief. 'Jacinta was there as well ... I just thought it was you and that man ... I was concerned Jacinta didn't know.'

'I was most definitely there, in the corner, watching them *and* watching you.' She pinched Ted's leg as hard as her nails would allow.

Ted interrupted. 'Oh yes, and, by the way, "that man" was one of your colleagues and a member of Huxley.'

'Come on, out with it. Who the hell was it?' Heleyna was nearly shouting at Ted in her excitement.

'It was Roger from Marketing.'

'Roger? Not quiet Roger? Oh, my God, there's no way. He's as timid as a mouse. You're winding me up?' Heleyna was still shouting.

'I'm not, you know. Not everything is as it seems, as

you demonstrated to me the night I saw you watching me. It must be said you do try and come across as a bit of a career-only woman at work. Now we know differently, don't we, love?' He turned and directed his comment at Jacinta. 'And we're both very excited by the discovery, very excited.'

Jacinta stroked the spot on Ted's thigh where she'd inflicted a considerable amount of pain. 'Absolutely, and for that reason we think you'll just love the Huxley Club. There's nothing more we can tell you on the subject. Just turn up on the night as per the invite with your open mind in place and you'll have one of the best evenings in a long time.'

Jacinta was the most animated Heleyna had ever seen her, now that she was talking about Huxley.

Troy looked over excitedly at Heleyna. 'Looks like we're in for a great night if you're saying what I think you're saying. Fantastic, right up our street. Just need to do a bit of work on Heleyna. She's a bit funny about the work/pleasure thing. I'll give her a few G&Ts before we come out. That should do the trick!'

'Whatever it takes, my good man, whatever it takes. Either that, or perhaps we may have made a move towards leaving SPM by then anyhow – you know, our business. Then she won't need to worry at all.'

'Hey! Stop talking about me as though I'm not here. I am capable of talking and thinking for myself, thank you very much.' Heleyna attempted to move the conversation on to something other than her sexual hangups. She felt like a politician trying to steer things away from the uncomfortable and on to a subject she wanted, except that her approach was a little more unsubtle, in the usual Heleyna way. 'So then, have we got any further with this business idea, which, clearly, as far as you're all concerned, we now need to move ahead with at some haste?'

Jacinta, who had been quiet for a short time, interjected. 'I have a storming idea. Seeing as you both have one obvious passion in common, why not make that the theme? Something like running adult theme parties. Or how about extending the Huxley Club across a wider area of Yorkshire and beyond, but make it more of a profit-making thing? Charge decent prices. What do you reckon?'

Heleyna looked over at Ted, who was nodding his head in the slow way people do when they agree but are still thinking through the options. She felt the same way that he looked: she liked the sound of it, but just needed to play around with the idea a bit more, analyse the market, establish if there really was a need, and if money could be made out of something as risky as this. She knew they also had to consider the fact that it might have to be run as a respectable business offering the full range of parties, and the more adventurous kind would have to trickle through by word of mouth. Her mind was racing now, her thoughts flowing, and she poured them all a glass of wine from the fourth bottle of the evening. Troy began gathering up the plates.

Heleyna broke the momentary silence. 'How about setup costs? You know, toys and so on.'

Jacinta replied, 'To be honest, we have so many already for Huxley that it might just be a matter of adding to an already full collection.'

'And Heleyna has discovered a very interesting way to get freebies out of the local Horsforth sex shop, too.'

'Shut up, Troy. Not now, OK?' Heleyna passed Troy a very meaningful glance which said more than the thoughts she verbalised.

Realising they still had some work to do on Heleyna, Ted brought the conversation back to the business proposition. 'Right then. That's our starting point. Heleyna, we need to do our research, find out what the customer needs are out there and see if there's any real competition, and so on. You know the ropes when it comes to these types of things. We'll get together every lunchtime and for an hour after work and start planning together. Sound good?'

There was still coyness evident in her tone of voice and body language. 'Sounds excellent and all pretty exciting. Imagine – making a business out of something so pleasurable. I think I could really enjoy this.'

'Just one thing. We're on holiday for a week from this weekend, so we'll have to kick-start this after that. Give us a week to put some objective thought into the task at hand, anyhow. The cooling-down period might do us some good.'

'Going anywhere nice?'

'Of course, of course. We're off to Greece. Do the bigger, more adventurous holiday later on in the year.'

Lying in bed that night, snuggled up behind a very asleep but wonderfully naked Troy, Heleyna thought about the future. Her eyes were wide open and focused on a mole on Troy's broad back – every time she closed them serious alcohol-related head spins would kick in. She was full to the brim with butterflies – excitement at the prospect of branching out. She actually felt pretty damn happy about the prospect of work, and getting away from a lifestyle that always had the words 'fucking' or 'bloody' or 'shit' spattered within her comments whenever she thought or spoke about it. She liked it, liked it very much indeed.

Ted and Jacinta sat up for an hour or so in their kitchen drinking strong coffee and a glass or two of water, and both took a vitamin C tablet. They were committed to preventing a hangover, a habit they'd got into as they'd reached their mid-thirties; neither was capable of consuming the large amounts of alcohol they had managed in their early twenties. They were chatting like old friends; they were drunk and perched on the kitchen barstools. They had a good marriage; it was just not the conventional type.

'I think we're on to a winner with that idea of yours. You're a bloody star, J. I mean, why shouldn't it work? We could fill parties here at ours every month, and that's just with people from the immediate area and from work. Imagine what we could do if we branched out into other parts of the county. We could easily charge double the price we do now, if not more, and make a handsome profit. Could probably have parties running once or twice a week if we played our cards right, with corporate functions on top of that.'

Jacinta didn't look quite the upright housewife that evening. She was sat slumped on the barstool, black make-up smudged round her eyes. She'd been rubbing them, forgetting they were heavily made up with her favourite liquid liner. Her French-plaited hair was now half-hanging around her shoulders and sections of her rich bronze lipstick were missing, probably around the wine glass she'd held close to her mouth for most of the evening.

'Ted, do we have to talk about this now? My head hurts and I can't concentrate. It is past midnight and I have just consumed well over a bottle of Pinot!'

'What do you think about Heleyna now, then?'

'Well, let's just say I'm very pleased. Can't wait to get a taste of her. Let's just hope she turns up, and that we haven't frightened her off!' Jacinta's gaze was focused in the distance: she was imagining Heleyna naked, her head between Heleyna's legs.

Ted laughed as he spoke. 'You dirty little bitch. She might not be into women anyhow. And, if that's the case, then she'll be all mine. I already know I do it for her.'

'I bet she does like women. And even if she doesn't yet know, I will convince her, don't you worry about that.'

'Oh, we are cocky tonight!'

'How could she resist the beautiful Jacinta?'

'Hmmm, not so beautiful tonight my dear.'

'Oi, leave me alone. You're not looking too hot your-self, you know. Anyhow, I'm knackered.' Jacinta plonked her head down on the work surface.

'Come on, then, I'll carry you to bed.'

Ted lifted Jacinta up and over his shoulder. She giggled as Ted walked her up the stairs. As they neared the top her giggling ceased, and Ted heard a very different sound.

'Blimey, J! Snoring already.'

Ted dropped Jacinta onto the bed and undressed her before removing his own clothes. Jacinta roused briefly but then promptly fell asleep, her head lolling on her shoulder. The two of them spent the night sprawled across their ample bed, snoring loudly in a dreamless sleep.

12

It had been a stormer of a week. Heleyna's head had been completely occupied with the business idea and with Sam. In fact, Sam had dominated her thoughts more than she cared to imagine. Knowing that he wasn't too far away and that soon she would be able to get her dirty little mitts on him, was enough to drive her into a sex-crazed state. She could almost smell her desire for him; he knew, he could sense her lust, and he played up to it, teasing her terribly whenever the opportunity arose. She feigned her usual response, but he didn't seem to tire. It pleased her: she knew that when she finally had him it would be incredibly and powerfully explosive.

At the next hiking club meet that weekend Heleyna spotted Mandy in the distance and they jogged towards each other and hugged like old friends. Mandy looked more homely than the last time they'd met, with her make-up removed and dressed in her outdoor gear, but she was still beautiful. They jumped onto the bus and began gassing away. Heleyna was looking forward to the weekend in Wales, to walking off some of her momentous frustration and off-loading her proposed life changes in Mandy's very good ear.

Meg hadn't changed since the last trip. 'Good evening, campers! Sit back, relax and enjoy. Next stop Betws-y-Coed. The walks this weekend are Snowdon and then, for the more adventurous on Sunday, Tryfan. If you're not wanting that on Sunday then there are two other options: tea rooms and craft shops or a valley walk. Any questions?'

Everyone kept their mouth closed in an attempt to stop her rambling. Heleyna and Mandy didn't look at each other; if they had, then mass hysteria would have ensued.

'Your driver this evening is Linton. Let's be off, Linton!'

Mandy took a peek at Linton. 'Hmmm, he's a bit tasty.'

Heleyna craned her neck. 'I can't see him. What's he like? Come on, give me the juicy details.'

'Looks about thirty to me. Black hair just touching his shoulders. Can't see his full face, but he's got about an inch of stubble, long eyelashes, nice-looking lips. Yummy. Sometimes I wish I were single!'

'Doesn't stop me.'

'Eh?'

'Let's just say Troy and I have a very open relationship. We're best mates, you know – it's not dysfunctional. We both just love shagging.'

Mandy leant closer to Heleyna and lowered her voice further. 'You mean you shag other people and he doesn't mind?'

'Actually, he gets off on the details.'

Mandy's mouth was now virtually in Heleyna's ear. She was giggling. 'No way! You're unbelievable. More's the point, you're now going to have to tell me all about it. How exciting!'

'Mind how close you get, Mands – I don't just stop at men, you know!'

Mandy began laughing uncontrollably, her hands on her stomach and tears streaming down her face. Her voice had quickly become very loud. 'You're not joking, are you? Oh, my God! You are a scream, Heleyna.'

There was something about this woman that

Heleyna just couldn't help opening up to. She didn't fancy her at all, and not because she wasn't an attractive woman. Heleyna understood that Mandy was a committed wife and mother and she would never even begin to try to penetrate something so genuine and strong. Subconsciously she'd switched off from viewing Mandy as anything more than a friend, which was incredibly powerful for Heleyna. She'd found someone who would truly be a friend, and somebody who was not about to judge her.

The rest of the journey disappeared, with Heleyna describing to Mandy her change in direction, even daring to tell her what the business proposition was. Mandy was so incredibly supportive that Heleyna realised, should it go horribly wrong, there would be someone there to help her through. She even disclosed her feelings for Sam, which reduced Mandy to a hysterical mess once more.

They were both knackered by the time they arrived at the YHA, but the ever-sexual Heleyna made sure she had a quick peek at Linton through her sleepy eyes as she jumped off the bus. Linton made Sam look squeaky clean: he was a true moody-looking Heathcliff.

Heleyna spoke excitedly to Mandy as they retrieved their rucksacks. 'Wow, he is pretty sexy. He's not going to be interested in me though, looking like this, and smelling like I'm going to after a day up Snowdon.'

'Heleyna, you are dreadful.' Mandy hit her playfully.

They disappeared into their hostel, to be herded by Meg into their rooms for a night of restful sleep, ready for an early start and plenty of fresh air the following day.

They woke to perfect weather, which evolved into a superb day despite the hundreds of people gathered at the top of Snowdon – tourists who'd made their lazy way to the summit courtesy of the train. Heleyna felt slightly cheated, but also very proud of her achievement: she'd earned the view from the summit through sheer hard work and determination.

On the way down, the two women spoke incessantly about exactly what meal they were going to order at the local pub that night, as if they had been starved of food for days on end. Neither had got to know any other club members: they were too engrossed in their building friendship. Both meals were going to be large and involve huge quantities of red meat accompanied by a pint or two of strong beer. They were pleasantly and deservedly famished.

That evening, showered and fresh-faced, they entered the pub. As usual, they'd chosen not to socialise with the other hikers, preferring the time they spent on their own together. Linton was at the bar, holding it up in the way that men do. One look and Heleyna knew she had no option but to try and have her wicked way with this divinely rugged and sullen man. She pre-warned Mandy.

'Look, Mands, I simply cannot resist such a stunner. Do you mind?'

'Absolutely not. But as long as you give me all the details afterwards. It's going to be the only way I get any excitement into my life these days – from the stories my friends tell me. I'm not complaining, though. I love it this way.' She smiled her cheeky grin. Her freckled face came alive with expression.

'Excellent. I'll have a pint and some food first, though.'

They ordered and took their seat in full view of Linton, who had already acknowledged their presence with a temperamental nod. Heleyna began her gentle look-at-me flirting: laughing and flicking her hair and catching his eye at any opportunity. He remained moody, and this only fuelled Heleyna's interest. There was no bloody way another man was going to get the better of her. She had a very definite point to prove.

'Where the hell do you get your energy from?' Mandy questioned Heleyna. 'I could think of nothing worse than sex this evening. All I want is food, beer and a good night's sleep!'

Heleyna didn't answer. Linton was leaving the pub.

'Wait here. I'm going to follow him.' Heleyna jumped from her seat and walked out of the bar, leaving Mandy to drink alone.

Mandy giggled to herself, still in awe of Heleyna's enterprising sex drive, and took another swig of her warm, flat, hoppy beer.

Heleyna followed Linton from the pub and along the street. He disappeared down a side alley. She waited a second then followed, her trainers quiet on the pavement. Taking the obligatory look at his arse, she noted how splendidly it was plonked inside a pair of old and worn jeans. He was a very big man. She liked what she saw, and she wanted it.

She met the end of the alley, which opened up into a playground and small park surrounded by lush bushes and well-kept gardens. Poking her head around the corner she realised she'd lost Linton, and so waited for a moment on the off chance that he would reappear or she might see some indication of the path he had taken from the park. Nothing was forthcoming. She had no option but to search him out. Heleyna was enjoying herself.

For no reason other than that she had to make a decision, she turned left, following the small, neat path towards the empty play area. The trail continued past the slide and swings in the direction of a small building. She continued towards it, a sense of excitement growing inside her. What happened if he knew she'd followed him and was waiting there for her? She secretly hoped that if he was waiting he had done a Troy – already removed his clothes to save her the bother. She wanted to walk in and see his hefty, strong body in all its glory and, hopefully, a proportionate dick.

Heleyna tried the door. No joy. She wandered round to the side of the building and towards the window. It was open and, much to her delighted curiosity, she heard muffled sounds coming from inside the small dark building. Now she had to find a way to break in. Her body was aching at the thought of what she might find inside.

The open window was too small to even begin to try and crawl through, so she continued round the building, now walking on tiptoe. There was another door to the rear. She tried the handle. It opened. She entered, giving herself a second for her eyes to adjust to the gloomy light.

She was standing in what looked like the park keeper's workshop. The room she was in was empty of people, so she followed the noise to the second, and only other, room. She imagined Linton standing there naked, his prick large and solid, his hand grasped round it, explicitly demonstrating his lust for her. Her panties were already wet with anticipation

Shocked joy hit her when she nudged her head round the corner; she'd walked in on Linton with another very keen woman. Heleyna watched his nakedness as he thrust into this woman from behind. She inspected his broad back and mobile bottom, the only view she had from the doorway. Feeling no fear, only lust, she took a step through the entrance.

The woman was laid face down on the worktop with her bottom high in the air, raised up by a small box. Her legs hung down towards the floor. Heleyna noticed how very fine this woman's muscular body was, her breasts small, no body fat in sight. She begged Linton to fuck her harder and Heleyna immediately recognised the voice: it was a very hot and excited Meg.

This didn't put Heleyna off. The vision of Linton was enough to encourage her to stay and see what she could get out of this situation for herself. She'd not yet been noticed. She made the ten steps it took to reach Linton. Heleyna was not afraid or concerned: she was confident in her sexual expertise and desirability as a woman.

She was now within centimetres of Linton's hot, sweaty body and, unable to contain herself any longer, her hand made its move towards his arse and between his slightly parted thighs. Heleyna grasped his huge jiggling balls in her right hand. Linton jumped, but continued his ferocious thrusting. He looked over his shoulder and stared Heleyna straight in the eye. She just made out a grin beneath his stubble-covered cheeks and smiled in return. She was on to a winner. Not a word passed between them. Meg was unaware of Heleyna's presence. They were in for a very, very naughty time.

Linton moved Heleyna's grasp away from his balls and to his side. He indicated for her to remove her clothes. She willingly obeyed as he maintained his aggressive thrusting into the ever-grateful Meg, who whimpered and wailed pathetically each time he reached her depths. Heleyna truly hoped she didn't sound as pathetic as Mrs Jollyhockeysticks when she was in the throes of passion; thinking back to some particularly lewd video footage of her and what's-his-name, she remembered her tone was relatively subdued, but definitely the sound of a woman enjoying herself.

Three naked tingling bodies in a confined space, with one of them unaware that there were three; this was a new yet gratifying experience for Heleyna. Linton grasped her hand as he removed himself from an unrelenting Meg – a Meg who cried out for him to retain his position. He ignored her cries and pushed Heleyna's hand in the direction of Meg's undeniably pink swollen pussy. Heleyna didn't hesitate. She knew exactly which spot would have Meg writhing and wanting more than this man could ever give her with his rigid penis.

Linton spoke. 'How does that feel, naughty Meg? Are my fingers delicate and soft against your hot cunt?'

'Oh yes, that's good. Please, give me more.' Meg lifted her butt cheeks up even higher as she spoke, displaying herself in her entirety.

Heleyna watched Meg's muscular arse in awe; there wasn't an ounce of cellulite in sight.

'How would you like me to touch you?' Linton lowered himself to his knees as he questioned Meg, his rugged face now in line with Heleyna's hand, which was still firmly planted on Meg.

'Just touch me ... anywhere. Just don't stop ... don't stop.'

Heleyna caressed every inch of Meg's pussy, stroking her gently, allowing her fingertips to reach her puckered paradise with each sweep of her hand. Heleyna could feel Linton's breath against her hand, then he turned and buried his face deep in her own cunt, nearly causing her to lose her balance and cry out with desire. She had no alternative but to remain silent if their game was to continue.

Heleyna could feel his stubble against her inner thighs, which she'd now parted in her eagerness to give him access to her. His warm tongue found its way through her hair and between her oily lips. Linton had one hand on her waist, keeping her close to him; the other found its way to her inviting breasts. Heleyna attempted to maintain focus, her fingers dipping in and out of Meg in between the delicate flick of her middle fingertip over Meg's soaking clit.

'Oh, my God, I'm going to come!' Meg was screaming.

Heleyna quickly removed her hand: she didn't want this venture to be over just yet, especially when she had yet to have the full satisfaction of the sullen sultry Linton.

Meg screamed again: 'Please fill me up again. I want to feel you inside of me.'

Heleyna looked avidly around the room. She was seeking a sizeable phallus to pleasure this woman with. Linton, who understood her intentions, grew increasingly excited – an excitement that he took out on the more-than-happy Heleyna. Heleyna spotted the object she wanted – the smooth round end of a large hammer. She reached and grabbed it and eased it inside Meg with one swift and very pointed move. Meg bucked and moaned in response as Linton buried himself still deeper into Heleyna's ever-sensitive zone.

Heleyna became aware that Linton would soon be seeking some pleasure for himself, beyond the erotic act of giving and watching. Remaining silent, she drew him to his feet with her left hand, whilst her right maintained its actions in and out of the ravenous Meg. He towered over her in height and breadth. Up until now she'd been willing to share him with the irritating Meg, but seeing this mysterious man facing her encouraged her selfish streak to kick in.

Heleyna's hand left the hammer, and it fell from Meg and onto the floor with an almighty clatter. Meg jumped. Heleyna ignored her response and grasped the shoulders of this enormous man, pulling him to her. He answered her physical plea by lifting her up and plonking her down on top of the worktop next to Meg.

Meg was startled for the second time. 'What the fuck . . . what the fuck is going on?'

Linton rammed into Heleyna with full force, his huge frame only just fitting between her legs and within her grasp. Neither replied to Meg, and Meg didn't question them again. Instead, Meg remained next to the horny Heleyna, playing with her wanton cunt as she enjoyed the show, occasionally reaching out to touch either of them, with a particular fascination for Linton's very rounded bottom and Heleyna's wobbling full breasts.

Linton shoved his hand between himself and Heleyna, finding her hungry clit, all the while shoving into her with the full force of a prop forward. Heleyna came first, letting out her first truly audible sound. Meg followed suit, the reaction intense and physical. Linton watched the two women in the throes of their orgasms and relented, almost squashing Heleyna as the force of his own orgasm was released.

Heleyna returned to the pub. She'd been gone nearly a full hour. Her face was flushed and her hair no longer in a ponytail. Mandy was talking to Julie, a fellow hiking-club member, an empty dinner plate in front of her. Heleyna saw her own dinner next to Mandy's plate and she remembered how very hungry she was. She went to order another pie and chips, realising that her previous order was lukewarm. Whilst she was at the bar, she bought both herself and Mandy another pint of beer: Heleyna was thirsty from her very active day.

Mandy saw her as she approached the table, took one look at her flushed face and grinned from ear to ear. She spoke to Julie. 'Do you mind if I talk to Heleyna for a bit? I'd promised her a bit of time to talk some things through this evening.'

'Oh, of course. No problem. Lovely to talk with you,

Mandy. Catch up with you later.' Julie nodded to Heleyna as she left the table and returned to her other friends.

Mandy was keen for the gossip. 'Come on then, girl. Tell me all about it. I can tell by the look on your face that you got exactly what you went out looking for!'

Heleyna sat and passed Mandy her beer. 'Not exactly, but almost.'

Heleyna gave an attentive Mandy all the gory details, including those about Meg.

'Now I feel really boring. Imagine someone like Meg getting into this kind of stuff. Then there's me, committed to one man for God knows how many years. I've never even entertained the idea of a threesome in my life. God, I'm boring!'

Heleyna attempted to convince Mandy that being married and committed was not boring. That, in fact, it was more fulfilling than the fleeting pleasure of any sexual exploit. Mandy was not convinced, her response sparking thoughts in Heleyna about Huxley, about introducing Mandy and her husband once she'd ascertained for herself exactly what it was all about – that it was what she envisioned it to be.

Conversation progressed to Heleyna and her ongoing trauma with work and Sam. Mandy advised that if Heleyna could not mix work with pleasure, then she had no alternative but to leave, especially since having the scrumptious Sam appeared to be top of her agenda.

'That way, you can have your naughty way with him and start working for yourself at the same time. Sounds like you'll be getting the best of everything, having your cake and eating it.'

Heleyna was now absolutely convinced she was doing the right thing. Being self-employed had to be the way to go. It was a way that would also give her the opportunity to consume the delectable Sam and perhaps, then, move in with her favourite man, Troy.

13

'I fucking hate work!' Heleyna was sitting at her desk, having just slammed down the phone. She'd been having a conversation with a very irate supplier, which had done nothing more than heighten her already appalling mood. Another volatile day was on the cards.

Sam had teased her. He'd been an absolute wanker, in Heleyna's opinion. Today he'd taken his lust for her a step further and rammed his very appealing hard-on into her thigh. She'd just about peed herself with delight at the closeness of his body and his more than obvious attraction to her. Playing her usual role whenever Sam came in for the kill, she'd ordered him out of her office and he'd left her, laughing arrogantly. He'd even had the balls to tell her, his boss, that she was playing a futile game. 'Before too long your pussy will rule the day,' were the words he'd used. She'd responded with an intellectual 'fuck off', a response which irritated her further – why could she never think of an intelligent comment when she so desperately needed one?

Having had enough, and concerned that her emotions would reduce her to a quivering, pathetic mess, Heleyna decided that for the first time in her working life she was going to swing a sickie. There was no way on earth she could be seen to lose her cool at work, to end up in tears and become the emotional woman all the junior male managers wished her to be.

She picked up the phone and called John. 'Hi, John.

I'm feeling absolutely terrible today – think I've got a fever coming. I'm off home – any problems?'

'That's not good at all, Heleyna, and not at all like you to be sick. Get yourself home and into bed. Wrap up, drink lots of water and watch a good video or something.'

'Thanks, John. Hopefully be in tomorrow.' Heleyna knew damn well that she wouldn't be in tomorrow. This was her opportunity to take some well-earned time off work and start the ball rolling with the business idea.

On the way out she popped in to see Phoebe, to warn her that she was out for the day. Heleyna had redirected her calls through to Phoebe – give her something to do for a change, she thought, as she walked up to her, feigning a smile.

After dumping on Phoebe, and about to exit the front door, Heleyna heard someone calling her. It was an obedient Phil. If he'd been a dog, his tail would've been well between his legs, his ears flat against the side of his head, his body subservient, low to the ground. He ran towards her with the short strides and knock-knee of a true computer geek, mumbled something inaudible, then flung a wallet full of papers into her hands. Heleyna undid her briefcase and hid the wallet hurriedly, not wanting to be caught up to no good. He was gone before she had even had time to dismiss him in the humiliating manner she had adopted since his embarrassment.

Heleyna jumped into her car and put her favourite contemplative music in the CD player. Her car was parked close to work; the train was getting less and less use as her apathy for work increased. It was an expensive option, but a necessary one if she was ever going to turn up for work each day.

Making her way up the Kirkstall Road towards Horsforth, Mozart's *Clarinet Concerto* filling every corner of her Beetle, Heleyna's mind began to take the first steps towards creativity. By the time she arrived home Mozart had given her the inspiration she needed for a successful brainstorm.

The next few hours were spent sitting at her glass-topped table, pieces of flipchart paper strewn across the top or scrunched up on the floor. Those that were visible were scattered with mood maps, writing sprawling across them in a huge array of colours, and arrows galore. Heleyna glanced at her watch. It was already three o'clock and she'd forgotten to eat lunch. Heleyna never forgot to eat. It amazed her just how excited she was about the prospect of being her own boss, and in an industry that suited her down to the ground.

She took a break and wandered to the fridge. It was pretty empty, as usual, but she managed to scrape together some cheese on toast, topped with some very old-looking chutney, then returned to her table and her plans. As she munched on her snack, Heleyna's mind wandered to Huxley. Sitting cross-legged on the large chair at the head of the table, she thought long and hard about the club and how testing it was for her to finalise her business plans without having even attended the club herself. She took a bite into the white toast and a string of cheese rested on her chin. Absent-mindedly, she left it there for a second before picking it up with her polished nails, detaching it from the toast and plonking it firmly in her mouth.

Determining that she had no alternative but to demand the gory details from Ted and Jacinta, she entered the hall and picked up the phone, looking at herself half-heartedly in the full-length mirror. She still looked gorgeous, despite the cargo pants, baggy sweatshirt and hair scraped up off her face. She liked what she saw, and knew she was bloody lucky to have such fine looks.

It was only once she got their answer machine that she remembered they were on holiday, and for a whole week at that. She needed another plan of attack if she was going to get anywhere this week with the skive off work she had planned.

Only then did Heleyna remember the A4 wallet given to her by Phil. She bent down and picked up her briefcase, which was in its usual spot under her rail of coats in the hall, directly opposite her full-length mirror.

She returned to her table. It was still covered. Reading the piece of paper on the top of the pile, with its multicoloured arrows and comments filling every available space, she laughed out loud at the two words she'd written in the centre of the page: *Sexual Strategy*. She liked it, the title for their business plan – though not the copy that would go to the bank, of course.

Dumping the wallet on top of the reams of paper, she refocused her mind and began reading the pile of emails in front of her. The first job, and the most interesting, was seeing which names were listed in the 'from' and 'to' headings. Heleyna was soon to be amazed.

Over the next four hours Heleyna read solidly, only taking a brief break for a cup of strong Yorkshire Gold tea. Alcohol didn't seem appropriate somehow; she needed to concentrate and for once she was interested.

Her reading proved a real eye-opener. Not only were about 25 people from SPM included in the email conversations, but many spoke quite candidly about some of the fun they'd had at the last meeting of the Huxley Club, and usually with each other. Heleyna did some statistics, and by her reckoning that accounted for about ten per cent of SPM fucking their colleagues, and on a regular and frighteningly open basis. Heleyna knew she loved sex and, more often than not, more than anything else in the world. But to be quite free to take part in this, and with people you need to be taken seriously by, still baffled her.

Still shocked that the lovely Jacinta could possibly run a party with such incredible goings-on, Heleyna thought excitedly about the next meeting, which was to take place in less than a month's time. First, though, she had to leave SPM or her excitement would be brought to a crashing halt. In her role within the business there was no way she could do the two, whatever the MD thought was acceptable behaviour. Dirty little sod, she thought.

Keen to share her findings with Troy and gloat still further about the fact that she'd been right from the start, she phoned him. He picked up quickly.

'Hi, sexy. How're you doing? When am I going to see you again?'

'Um, well, probably not till Thursday, because of art class, unless you could skive off in the daytime for an hour or two. I'm skiving off work this week – fake flu,' Heleyna replied.

'I could possibly come by in my lunch break on Wednesday. What do you reckon? Anyhow, what are you doing at home?'

'Brainstorming. Getting my ideas together on the business proposition before Ted gets back from hols. Can't be arsed with work big time. Anyway, I've got some interesting information to tell you about the dear old Huxley Club and, as usual, I was absolutely spot on. I don't know why you even question me sometimes!' She laughed as she teased him.

Heleyna spent the next quarter of an hour giving Troy the gory details and making sure she tormented him occasionally, rubbing his face in his lack of intuition. He was absolutely and completely delighted, as she'd expected. Lots of people and sex mixed with plenty of toys – just his cup of tea.

Heleyna feigned shock. 'Troy you're such a naughty, naughty boy. Sometimes you make me feel like the innocent virgin bride, the way you go on.'

'And you mean to tell me you're not excited, too? Pull the other one, girl. From that list you've given me, at least fifty per cent of your colleagues would go down on your personal list of fuckables, if you ask me.' Troy was laughing as he spoke.

Standing on one foot, the other rested on top of her briefcase, she responded with a giggle. 'I've just had a very naughty thought. I could break into Troy and Jacinta's whilst they're away and see what I can find hidden in that epitome of urban perfection. That way we would know exactly what we were letting ourselves in for and be well and truly prepared. What do you reckon?' The toes on her briefcase wiggled up and down with anticipation.

'Heleyna Lane, don't you bloody dare. Do you hear me? They've probably got it heavily alarmed and linked to the police station with the amount of gear in that house.'

Heleyna had stopped listening before he'd even begun his order. She'd already planned her activity for that night. She was enjoying this little game very much. Before she put down the phone she had each stage planned, the goal clear in her mind: discovering the final facts about Huxley – witnessing the full dirty details with her own eyes.

Heleyna pulled up her car half a mile from Ted's house and jumped out. She was still dressed in her cargo pants and sweatshirt, but now she had her rucksack on her back, filled with implements she thought might come in useful, including the obligatory torch.

The evening was still, but cold and crisp. A lovely early summer evening. It was truly dark, the streetlights showing her the way. She walked quickly in an attempt to keep warm, all the time cursing herself for not bringing her jacket, at least. Within ten minutes she hit the wall surrounding the house.

Arriving at the front gates, she pushed them. They were locked. She had no alternative but to climb either the wall or the gates. She chose the gates because, although more open to view, they didn't require any rock-climbing skills – skills she didn't possess.

Though her legs were still stiff from the previous weekend of walking, Heleyna climbed quickly. Once on the other side she was surrounded in darkness, the glow from the streetlights not quite making it over to Ted's front garden. Heleyna was not afraid – she very rarely let fear infiltrate her confident attitude. She stopped and pulled out her pencil torch, then made her way to the front of the house and began scouring its walls in search of an entry. But there wasn't going to be the easy access she'd hoped for – everything was locked and closed, every curtain or blind pulled to.

Arriving at a small window with frosted glass, which she assumed was the toilet, she stopped again and removed her rucksack. This time she removed a small hammer and cloth and broke the glass cleanly through the cloth – a trick she'd seen on movies that reduced the chance of the sound of her misdemeanour reaching the surrounding neighbours.

Her small hand found its way through the window and round to the latch; she felt both surprised and excited at the ease with which she was breaking into a house – and a smart house at that. As Troy had warned, she'd assumed security lights and alarms would have been rife in a house full to the brim with antiques and expensive gadgets. As a friend of Ted's she made a mental note to talk to him on his return about the importance of good security, especially in the city.

She continued.

After squirming her way through the small window and avoiding the broken glass, she indeed found herself in the small downstairs toilet. She opened the door and began walking through the house for signs of Huxley. The beam from her small torch was limited and made the going slow.

Heleyna wasn't interested in reading yet more documents; now she was desperate to see the real thing – to see the rooms or evidence of the parties. Suddenly aware of a warm dampness between her legs, she realised her body was already responding, anticipating a night of sexual contact with more beautiful people then she'd ever encountered in her life. I'm such a dirty little bitch, she thought happily.

By now Heleyna was in the dining room. So far she'd found absolutely nothing of interest – just the suburban house of a wealthy couple. Back to the corridor she went, and on to the next door – the cupboard under the stairs – and shone her torch into the darkness. It was not the cupboard she'd expected: steps led down into what had to be a cellar.

Heleyna strode confidently into the darkness, her torch just making out each step as she descended. On reaching the bottom she searched for a light switch – she'd already ascertained that neighbours wouldn't see lights in the basement. Not immediately finding the switch, she took the final tread, all the time watching her step, the first sight of carpet visible in the glow of her torch – a lush deep-pile deep-red carpet – not very cellar-like, she thought. She knew she was getting closer to something.

Finding a switch, finally, just two feet along the wall to her right, she felt a surge of exhilaration. Her pulse rate increased dramatically as her hand reached sideways and made the downward action needed to fill the room with light. She was in business. 'Oh, my God. This is absolutely incredible!' She walked quickly into the lit room, which was filled by a large dining table, her feet sinking with each step. She spoke out loud again, 'Fucking hell, carpeted bloody walls. Unbelievable!'

The room was set out with deep-red carpet across the floor and walls. In the centre of the room was an oak table large enough to seat well over a dozen people. Filling the wall at the end of the room were eight large TV screens with the Huxley slogan in large purple letters slung across the top: 'Chastity, the most unnatural of all the sexual perversions'. The table wasn't set, but there were three large silver candlesticks evenly spaced down the centre, each filled with six long green candles. Surrounding the table were heavy doors. She stood and counted them, her chest visibly heaving through her baggy sweatshirt as she surveyed the scene. There were eight.

Heleyna approached the first door to her left. Above the door was a beautifully hand-painted and illustrated sign which said simply 'Women Only'. Before entering she chose to walk round the room and read the signs hung above each of the doors. She read them aloud as she walked. 'Voyeurism, Men Only, Humiliation, Pain, Time Out, Jacinta's Parlour, Freedom. Un-bloody-believable. Can't wait to have a look at this lot.' By now her nipples had followed the pleasure that already penetrated her wanton, naughty pussy.

Feeling particularly hot, she removed her rucksack

and sweatshirt, revealing a petite shoestring vest top. Leaving them on the head dining chair she walked back to the 'Women Only' door and turned the handle. The room was in darkness. She stretched her arm round the corner and found the switch. The room took on a dim red glow. Another switch next to the first tempted her. She pressed it. The room filled with classical music; she guessed it was Vivaldi.

To the left of her was an Edwardian sideboard. Before looking any further, her curiosity pulled her towards its closed doors. She knelt, took the delicate handle in her hand and pulled the door quickly. A small gasp left her lips. Much to her delight, inside was a vast array of vibrators, strap-ons, clit clips, nipple rings and more.

Still kneeling, she pulled everything out haphazardly until a vast array of toys larger and more varied then her own covered the polished wooden floor all round her. Lifting them up, one at a time, she held each piece lovingly in her petite hands, turning each toy, examining it as if it were a beautiful piece of pottery or delicate ornament, and returned each piece to its position once she'd satisfied her curiosity.

Heleyna had been deep in a world of her own for well over fifteen minutes before she raised her head and took in the rest of the room. One corner was filled with two king-sized mattresses, and the walls were painted in rich red, matching the lighting. Paintings adorned three of the walls – copies of classical pieces by Rubens, beautifully curvaceous women dominating every single composition. The fourth wall was covered from top to toe in the largest gilt-edged mirror she'd ever seen. Two large empty candlesticks on top of lace coasters were placed on the sideboard, and more wall-mounted brass candle holders filled the spaces between the randomly placed paintings. The room felt warm and cosy yet sophisticated. She imagined women strewn across the bed, covering crisp white sheets, watching themselves and each other in the mirror-clad wall, and she smiled to herself as the twinges of desire took hold of her.

Whilst reflecting on her now deepening lust, Heleyna heard a noise. She sat still for a moment and cocked her head to one side; she heard nothing more, so ignored what she'd heard – she was prone to an overactive imagination. She then stood and took a step to leave the room. As she stepped she saw, in the corner above the door, a video camera focused in on the mattresses. She turned, searching for more, finding four in all, one in each corner focused on the principal peeking places, ready and waiting for action. Putting two and two together she guessed these were for the pleasure of those sat outside at the table and that there would be similar cameras elsewhere. One screen for each room, she thought. Marvellous.

Exiting, she switched off the lights and music, then turned and closed the door. It was so important to leave each room as she'd found it. As she pushed the door to, her back to the central room, she suddenly became very aware of a presence close behind her; she could feel the warmth of another body, though no sound was present. She froze, and, for the first time, felt fear.

Her senses were functioning well.

Something solid was shoved into the curve of her lower back and a very real person spoke.

'Put your arms in the air, young lady, and spread your legs.' The voice was almost robotic. It was a man.

He pushed her roughly against the wall as she obeyed his command and he frisked her forcefully. Heleyna felt cold metal around her wrists: she was being handcuffed, something she'd only ever experienced before as fun and pleasure. Now she was worried. Surprisingly for Heleyna she remained silent, anxiety making her speechless. She felt hopeless, caught like a rat which found itself in a trap purely from its own greed. Only, the thing that had tempted her was her overt and very frisky sexual curiosity.

The man spoke again. 'Turn around, slowly now. No sudden moves or I will have no alternative but to use force.'

Heleyna turned as slowly as her body would allow and faced the man for the first time. He was wearing a black outfit, the badge emblazoned on his jumper indicating quite obviously that he was a security guard. In his hand he held a large wooden baton, which he continued to point aggressively towards Heleyna in his attempt to retain her subservience. Heleyna had no intention of being anything but. She was in a very deep hole, and now she had to find herself a way out of it, and quickly.

The beast stared at her blankly. 'Walk to the table and sit. Don't try anything funny, all right. No games. I have a button here in my hand – if I press it, police backup will arrive in a matter of minutes.'

Heleyna responded to his request, watching him carefully with each step, afraid that he might just use the baton against her if she made even the vaguest move he didn't like. The guy was young, probably 25, with mousy-brown long hair held back in a low pony-tail. His eyes were dark and vacant – lifeless. He was huge, probably a good eighteen stone, and not all muscle. She would not want to get on the wrong side of this beast of a man.

Once she sat down, he walked up behind her, undid and redid the handcuffs. Heleyna rattled her wrists: she was now attached to the back of the high-backed wooden chair. He took another chair and sat down in it opposite her, easily filling its frame, and pulled a notebook out from his pocket.

'Name?'

'Heleyna Lane.' Heleyna's voice was quiet in response, a slight oscillation evident as she mouthed each word as if they were the first few words of an unaccustomed public speaker. Her eyes were downcast.

'Address?'

'Flat 4b, The Lane, Horsforth.'

'Date of birth?'

The questions continued for some time, and Heleyna gave the man the facts he wanted. He finished his questioning and returned the pen to the top pocket of his shirt, which was hidden by his tasteless wool jumper. Heleyna looked up at him from under her eyelashes. She caught him eyeing her generous cleavage, which peeped seductively out of her tiny vest top. He moved his gaze quickly, reached round to his back pocket and pulled out a mobile phone.

At that moment her mind began to wander on to thoughts which, in her fear, she had not yet contemplated – of getting herself out of this whopping great hole. 'By the way, I'm not an intruder. I do know Ted and Jacinta.'

His response was dismissive in tone, as if he'd been there many times before. 'If that's the case, then why did you break in through the downstairs toilet window? Do you think I'm stupid?'

'Well, umm . . .'

'If you'd stop making excuses and shut up, then perhaps I could make the phone call to the property owner and ask what action he would like me to take.' His expression didn't falter. His voice remained monotonous.

'Oh, please don't, please don't. I wasn't doing any harm. I do know them. I was just being nosy. Please . . .' She whined pitifully.

His face moved to within a few centimetres of hers

and he raised his voice one tone louder. 'Will you shut up and stop bloody whingeing. Let me get on with my job.'

Heleyna turned her head as he spat each insistent word. Heleyna obliged him once more, her thoughts swirling round in circles, desperate for a solution to this enormous problem. What frightened her more than anything was the thought that she may have destroyed any hope of setting up in business with Ted.

The guard dialled. Heleyna prayed for voicemail. Her prayers were answered. He switched off his phone.

'Looks like there's no answer at the moment. I'll try a couple more times before calling the police. Give it fifteen minutes.' He eyed Heleyna again, this time more obviously, and this time his gaze reached the curve of her thigh as well as her tits.

Heleyna watched him watching her and her demeanour changed within a split second – she knew exactly how to play this one. She sat upright, her shoulders back, and crossed her legs. Smiling she spoke sweetly to him. 'I'm really thirsty, any chance of a glass of water?'

Despite his gruff unemotional manner, he agreed easily and returned from upstairs carrying the water she claimed she needed. He put it down on the table next to her then sat down again. Pulling out his mobile phone yet again, he began dialling.

Heleyna interrupted. 'I don't mean to be funny, but I can't drink the water because my hands are behind my back. Any chance you could undo them?' She knew he wouldn't agree, but her plan had allowed for that.

'No chance. What do you take me for?' He still spat each word.

Heleyna smiled sweetly again. 'Perhaps you could feed me a couple of mouthfuls, then? I would truly appreciate it, my mouth is so terribly dry.'

'Oh, OK then. But no funny business. Remember what I said, all right.'

'By the way, what's your name?'

'Me? I'm Stu White. Mr White to you.' He stared through her as he spoke.

Stu put down his phone and picked up the glass – it appeared doll-sized in his enormous hand. He held it to her lips. His cheap aftershave hit her nose and it took her every effort not to pull away from him. As he held it there Heleyna allowed her warm moist tongue to leave her mouth for a second and pass over her plump lips, then she took delicate sips from the glass. He returned it to the table.

'Mr White, please could I have a couple more sips?'

He retrieved the glass again and put it to her lips. She looked up at him from under her lush eyelashes and licked her lips for a second time, before taking the glass that he presented to her. As he removed it from her mouth she spoke to him softly, still eyeing him with her most seductive of gazes.

'Your aftershave is very nice, Mr White. You smell divine.'

He grunted at her, but she saw his face soften slightly at her words and so she continued, her approach becoming increasingly unsubtle.

'What make is it? I would love my partner to wear that especially for me.'

'Dunno, just something I got for Christmas.'

'It's gorgeous. Do you have a girlfriend?'

'Yes.'

'I bet it does wonders for your love life. It's almost, well, irresistible. If it makes me feel so horny, imagine what it must do for her.'

By now, Stu was sitting back on his chair, facing her. His face had lost the blank look he had perfected for his job and now began to take on a softer, slightly embarrassed tone. Heleyna's plan appeared to be working.

'She does like it, yes.'

'How much?'

'Well, you know, enough for her to buy it for me.' By now Stu was looking almost human, his body language more relaxed, his eyes beginning to smile.

Heleyna suddenly realised how tired she was. Her face took on the contorted expression of a person hiding a yawn – with her hands taut behind her back, she had no way of disguising her weariness. Stu, who was now watching her intently after her gentle flirting, picked up his mobile one more time.

'This is fucking hopeless. These clients give you an emergency contact number, and then they never answer the f-ing phone. You know, it makes me so frigging mad.' Stu was now pacing the floor next to Heleyna. 'How the hell am I meant to do my job properly? Stupid posh arses. All this fucking money and not two brain cells to rub together.'

He redialled Ted. No answer. Stu chucked the phone onto the table in anger and it spun across, stopping just short of the opposite side. 'I have no other option, Heleyna. I have to call the police.' Stu looked almost sorry for her.

Heleyna was now frantic. Her eyes flitted rapidly as thoughts filled her normally rational brain. The flirting has been working, she thought. Maybe, just maybe, I could seduce this man – convince him to wait at least until the morning before doing anything further. She now knew that she might even have to take her flirting one step further and fuck this man to get what she wanted. And what she wanted was for him to let her go and report only a broken window to Ted and Jacinta. 'Tell me about your girlfriend, Stu.'

'I told you, I'm Mr White to you.'

'Sorry, sorry. Tell me about your girlfriend, Mr White.' Heleyna wanted to break down barriers, try and find some level ground with her captor.

Stu sat himself down opposite Heleyna, forgetting quickly that he was in the process of contacting the police. 'She's blonde, blue eyes, big knockers.'

Very intelligent man, Heleyna thought sarcastically. She still maintained her light smile and flirtatious glance. 'What's her name, and how did you meet her?'

'Local pub – the Chained Dog – about two years ago. Called Suz.'

'Wow, that's a long-term relationship. Serious is it?'

He shrugged his shoulders. 'I suppose.'

'I hope you don't find this question too open, but do you still have the sexual buzz in your relationship? You know, still want to fuck each other's brains out?'

Stu was not at all concerned by the nature of her question. 'Sometimes, sometimes. Haven't had much for a while, though – always seems to have a headache or be too tired.'

'I'm surprised. You're a very handsome man. If you were mine, I would want to fuck you all the time.'

'Really?' Stu's gaze left Heleyna and dropped to the floor.

'I've got a great idea, Mr White. Perhaps we could come to some kind of a deal. You know, do something to help each other out.'

'Like what exactly?'

'Well, I find you incredibly attractive, and, forgive me if I'm being presumptuous, you find me attractive. Perhaps we could wander into one of these rooms here and have a bit of fun together. In fact, more than that. I really think we, you and me, could have something going. Can you feel the sexual tension?' Heleyna was planning to fuck this man then get the hell out of there.

Stu shook his head. 'I could lose my job.'

He didn't say no, though, thought Heleyna, and so, using her negotiating skills, she replied, making no reference to his negative comment, 'I'm so pleased you find me attractive too. In fact, I'm flattered. All my boyfriends have been ordinary men, but you – you're quite something. You're a real man – strong, big, masculine.' And stupid, she thought. As she spoke she eyed his body, her gaze sweeping over every part of his frame. She paid particular attention to his groin as the word 'masculine' left her lips. Finishing the last word, she licked her lips provocatively and looked him in the eye.

Stu stood. 'I couldn't give a toss what you think of me. I think we can come to another little bargain. You do anything that I ask of you and you will walk free.' He didn't wait for an answer.

Heleyna noticed the bulge in his trousers as he walked past and behind her. She heard keys rattling. He bent down close behind her and found the lock. As he worked he lowered his face to her neck and kissed her bare shoulder. Heleyna feigned a shudder and groan in response. Stu continued some more, the touch of his lips at first disgusting her. She could smell sour body odour that penetrated the stench of his cheap aftershave. She couldn't let on she was faking. She had a purpose that she had to maintain focused on if she was ever to be free of a situation that could ruin her exciting and much-needed plans for the future.

Stu was now in front of her and he removed the band from her hair, pulling it roughly in his attempt to see her locks resting sexily across her bare skin. He buried his head into her ample cleavage, the depths of which just poked out from her tiny top. He was almost dribbling with desire. Heleyna, her hands now free, massaged his immense back – his position and large frame would not allow her movement to extend any further, whether she'd wanted to or not. Stu was now sweating and breathless for her. He ripped down her top, breaking both straps and revealing her breasts. He sucked hungrily on her large nipples. Much to Heleyna's surprise they perked in response to his sucking. She was beginning to feel a little fruity. Perhaps I could enjoy this after all, she thought, surprising herself.

Stu removed his jumper, then shirt, his actions quick and slick and deliberate. He didn't look Heleyna in the face as he worked, preferring the gorgeous roundness of her very appealing breasts. Heleyna realised she'd been so incredibly wrong about this man. He was not obese: he had the largest chest she'd ever encountered in her life before – a chest that was one hundred and ten per cent bodybuilding muscle.

Letting herself drift into sexual oblivion, Heleyna stroked Stu's monstrous chest, his pecs almost too large for her hands. Her caress drifted south, finding his belt. Before too long he was naked. He had the most solid arse she'd ever clapped her eyes upon – great for spanking she thought, wickedly. Heleyna tried to take control but he wouldn't allow her: he was keen to continue the roles they'd been in since first meeting – captor and captive.

'Right, young lady, you're coming with me.'

Stu dragged Heleyna with her arms behind her back, her breasts bouncing with each step, and led her to the 'Women Only' room.

'Mr White, you can't go in there. Look what it says over the door.' She played the subservient role, her voice light and girly.

'I'll do whatever the bloody hell I like,' he growled. 'You will go in there and put on a show for me. No arguments. If you don't do as I say, it's simple – I call the cops and you're in trouble.'

'OK, Mr White.'

Stu opened the door and pushed her violently into the darkened room. He did not come with her, but closed the door behind her, leaving her in pitch darkness. Heleyna heard a chair being dragged towards the door to her room – probably being put beneath the handle to stop her running, she imagined. Having been in there before, Heleyna groped her way to where she knew the light switch was. She pressed the wrong one at first, and Vivaldi filled the room. Wondering where the hell he was, she switched on the dim red light.

Heleyna was buzzing with excitement. Something she'd expected to be the most revolting sexual encounter of her life was turning into a game she'd never played before. However much she wanted to be in control, this time the ball was firmly out of her court – he had her as his little plaything, and he knew that all too well.

Wondering exactly what he expected of her, Heleyna wandered towards the sideboard, pulled out a few toys, then jumped onto the first mattress. At that point it hit her – the glass of the mirror had to be two-way, the room between the men's and women's a room for perving. 'Fucking awesome,' she whispered under her breath.

Heleyna had been an actress before, but always with a partner at the local sex shop. Still, she knew what to do. Leaving her ripped top in place, she walked over towards the mirror then turned and bent over, her arse facing it. Her heavy bosoms hung, her nipples still rigid with desire. Slowly and cleanly she pulled down her baggy trousers over the roundness of her cheeks, revealing precisely nothing beneath. They fell to her ankles. She stepped out of them then returned to her bent position, this time with her legs apart so he could see the first glances of her pussy.

Taking the clit clip that had been hidden in her tight

fist, she slipped it into place. She was already swollen and sensitive. The clip took her breath away and she dropped to her knees. With her face now on the polished floorboards, she spread her legs even wider and pushed her bottom as far to the sky as her back would allow. Now he would have a full view of her naughty, naughty pussy, her clit protruding heavily from the small metal clip – an object of wonder.

Heleyna's hand found its way and she marvelled at the largeness of her excited clit. Using the tip of her middle finger she touched it, gently at first, and in between each thrust of her buttocks – a subconscious action which grew in both speed and potency with each sweep of her fingertip.

Suddenly remembering she was acting for him and not simply pleasuring herself, she crawled slowly towards the open sideboard and, with each forward action, tried to decide what to take out next. Remembering the double-pronged vibrator with the spinning ends filled with little coloured balls, she decided that tonight it would be her plaything.

She retrieved it along with some hefty-looking nipple clamps, then made her way to the edge of the unmade mattress. Sitting facing the glass, she spread her legs for her captor. Here she remained for a while, focusing on her breasts, wishing, for one brief moment, that there was someone there to suck the life out of her nipples, painfully exciting each one into a sense of numbness.

Her other choice, of course, was the clamp, with its frighteningly fierce-looking teeth. All the time watching herself, she touched both her nipples in unison, her squeeze progressing to a pinch and then on to a glorious nip. Now rock-solid and a rich red-brown colour, they looked ready for the delightful ferocity she was about to bestow upon them. Turning to her left, she collected the clamps, which were strung together with a heavy metal chain. They rattled as she lifted them towards her chest. With her hair seductively random and tousled, she watched her reflection closely and with interest as she attached each one to the pert solidity of her nipples. A sharp intake of breath left her lips as each was put into place.

More than aware of her captor, and returning to her favourite on-all-fours position, Heleyna made her way towards her reflection in the mirror. Her breasts swung from side to side with each movement, her rounded stomach was curved and soft, the chain between her breasts chinking rhythmically. Between her legs the clip played its part in enhancing the desire that now coated every part of her delicate skin.

She almost touched the glass with her face before turning and presenting her behind and pussy. Pushing up against the glass, she smeared its sparkling, clean surface with the juices of her desire. Here she remained for a few minutes, enjoying the coolness of the surface against the hotness between her legs.

Grasped firmly in her right hand was the vibrator that was to bring her over the edge, a wonderful end to a wonderful experience. Moving just a few inches from the mirror, she took the now-vibrating black device, with its twelve-inch prong and more delicate anal prong, and thrust it into her waiting holes. The prongs not only vibrated, but also twisted and turned at each end, the small balls contained in each massaging her ever-delicate internal skin. Her nipples ached. Vivaldi boomed out 'Winter' from the 'Four Seasons'.

She hardly moved, letting the toy do the work, her left cheek hard against the floor, her shiny hair fanned out on the polished wooden surface around her and framing her face. A small protrusion on the dildo touched the delicate end of her clip-encircled clit. She turned up the revs. She began thrusting. Her hand remained stable, holding her plaything in just the right place. She rocked and bucked and moaned and groaned. Filled to the brim with both object and desire she leapt over the edge and entered the world of ultimate ecstasy. Falling flat against the floor, her legs still apart for her possessor, she spasmed uncontrollably as her orgasm filled every aspect of her beautifully curvaceous body. The device left her body one inch at a time, and in sync with the reflex actions of her relaxing, buzzing sex.

Heleyna remained in this position for some time, waiting for Mr White to return and release her. Now she was free to go, her bad, bad actions allowing her the freedom she wanted and needed and craved.

Stu waltzed into the room, full of beans. He was wearing only his trousers. 'You dirty fucking little tart.'

Heleyna woke from her postorgasmic slumber with a start and scurried to her feet. He stood within inches of her, well within her personal space.

He spoke to her again, his words quick and tone animated. 'Where did you learn to do that? You should have seen the come exploding out of me as that ... that thing left your cunt. It flew for miles.' As he mouthed that potent word he pointed directly at her moist triangle of dark hair.

Though feeling slightly self-conscious in her near nakedness, and with ornamented nipples that stung terrifically, Heleyna smiled. She removed the painful clamps as she replied, 'Glad you enjoyed yourself, Mr White.' She scanned his monstrous chest and momentarily wished her encounter with this animal had been more intimate, more one-on-one. Never before had she fucked such a beast and now, it seemed, she never would – at least, not in the immediate future.

'I more than enjoyed myself. That was the best fucking wank I've had in a long, long time.'

Heleyna suddenly felt a touch of panic at his obvious pleasure, panic that was initiated by the joy that emanated from Mr White. She was now very aware that perhaps she shouldn't have been quite so good, got carried away quite so much. Mr White may now not want to let her go. She was right, of course.

Stu grabbed her and shoved his mammoth hand between her legs, feeling for the clit clip. 'I've never seen a clit so big before. This thing is excellent.' He dropped to his knees and pushed her legs apart.

She could feel his breath close to her cold dampness, the remnant of her earlier lust. He was examining the clip and fingering her roughly as he did. Heleyna shivered as the enormity of the hole she was in just got bigger. She tried to remain calm. Perhaps if she remained as confident as she'd been earlier she would be able to get herself out of this mess.

'Interesting, aren't they?' she asked.

'Uh-huh.' His fingers were still all over her pussy as he continued his examination.

'Thanks for a great time, Mr White. And thanks for agreeing to let this little issue of me breaking into my friends' house disappear. You're a very, very generous man.'

Stu removed the clip and stood once more. He sniffed it. 'Hmmm, smells like you now, like the smell I've just been savouring.'

Heleyna walked towards her trousers then picked them up as if she was about to depart. As she did, she looked at her watch – it was 2 a.m. Stu came to his senses as Heleyna began to dress herself.

'And where do you think you're going? Have I told you you can dress? I don't think so. I want more where that came from ... Heleyna, wasn't it?'

Heleyna knew she had no option but to obey. She also knew that to give this man more wouldn't be too painful. She was in a strange predicament. 'Oh, OK.' She stepped out of her trousers.

Stu walked towards her again and ordered her to put her arms in the air. She did, and he removed her ruined vest-top. She was now totally naked, totally exposed. He was a big, big man – not someone she would want to mess with. She could see he was already getting aroused, his cock bulging at the crotch of his uniform trousers.

'Fancy a drink?' he asked.

She did. 'Yes, please, Mr White.'

'Come with me then, tart.' He pushed her with her arms behind her back towards the central dining room and back into the same chair she'd been in before.

She heard the rattle and clunk followed by the cold metal of handcuffs against her wrists. She was trapped. He sat down opposite her again, this time with his truncheon in his right hand. He eyed her for a moment, as if trying to decide what to do next, then reached behind him and pulled out another pair of handcuffs. This time he attached them to her feet, which he dragged behind the front legs of the solid wooden chair. Now her pussy was on show for him.

The emotion she felt was a mixture of pleasure and panic. At this stage she was unsure which road to take.

He remained kneeling between her legs after attaching the cuffs, but reached back and retrieved his truncheon from the table next to his seat. Returning to face her, he spoke to her pussy, not to her. 'Nice cunt, Heleyna, nice cunt.' His head stooped and he shoved his face into her, taking a deep breath as he did. His nose disappeared into her. Unable to prevent what she felt, Heleyna began to disappear down the road to pleasure, the choice of pleasure or panic being taken out of her hands – pleasure it was, pleasure it had to be.

He withdrew and she looked down at his moist face.

He positioned his truncheon and began pushing it gently into her. It was enormous – it needed to be inserted with care. She watched both him and the weapon closely. It slid in inch by inch. She groaned.

He looked her in the face. 'You are the dirtiest little tart I've ever come across.'

A good ten inches of his tool was now within her. He licked his lips and his face disappeared. His tongue teased the tightened edge of her wanton hole, which held the club in its grasp. She writhed, wanting more – to be touched by his tongue on her very ready clit. He did not give her what she desired, but stood, leaving his truncheon in place.

'Right then, I'm off to get us both a drink. You wait there, you dirty, dirty bitch.'

Heleyna sat there in disgust as he walked out of the doorway, leaving her in limbo, and up the dark corridor of stairs, no doubt to the kitchen. She hoped he would return.

Looking down at herself, the image below maintained her growing desire: her breasts stood out and upright, helped by the angle of her arms that were taut behind her back; her nipples were still dark and hard from the clips she'd punished them with; between her legs was a huge piece of polished wood, lost within her, teasing her, making her want more from this man.

She was aware that he knew exactly what he was doing to her – making her so hot for him that by the time he returned she would be gagging with lust. Although she knew this, she felt a touch of relief when his footsteps hit the top step of the basement stairs. At least he's not going to leave me here, she thought, leave me here to be found by Ted in a few days' time.

Stu was carrying two bottles of lager, already opened, in his left hand. He had a bottle of vodka under his arm and two shot glasses in his right hand. She could see his penis thick and hard and ready for action, trying to push its way out of the top of his tight black trousers. She wanted to feel this man on top of her. For him to squash her body that was so small in comparison to his. For him to fuck her hard and fast and aggressively. She wanted to smell his cheap aftershave, his body odour, to feel like an ordinary and dirty whore.

He sat opposite her again and plonked down the glasses and bottles on the table, then picked up one of the lager bottles as if to feed her with the alcohol she wanted. He didn't. Instead he pushed it against her pussy, the icy coldness of the bottle taking her breath away. The truncheon remained deep inside her. He took the bottle to his mouth and licked the spot that had caressed her. He returned it to her once more, this time gently and rhythmically rubbing her clit. She was swollen now. She was more than ready for whatever he wanted from her.

Stu lifted the bottle and pushed it towards her mouth – but not for her to drink from it. 'Smell that, my little beauty. Smell your wetness.'

Heleyna sniffed. She wasn't coy. She enjoyed her own scent. She pushed out her tongue to taste it. He obliged, moving the bottle to her mouth. The sticky wetness reached her warm tongue. She tasted horny.

Stu suddenly stood and walked behind her. He undid her hands, knowing full well that her tethered ankles would keep her where he wanted her. 'Touch my cock,' he ordered, almost angrily.

Heleyna leant forwards as he stood. As she did, the truncheon left her and landed on the floor next to his feet. She giggled and undid his trousers. His hard cock sprung out. This was the first time she'd seen it at close range. Though small against his frame, it was large in Heleyna's estimation – after all, she'd seen enough dicks in her time to be a good judge.

She took the base in her left hand, touching the rim with her right using the gentlest of sweeps.

He groaned then said breathlessly, 'Suck it, bitch. Put it into your dirty mouth and taste me.'

Heleyna leaned in closer and opened her mouth. Her tongue flickered out and she touched his end with hers, lapping away the first bead of his juices. His appendage was deep red with desire. She breathed her warm breath onto it then nudged him ever so gently between her lips and into the depths of her mouth, all the while playing with his sensitive end with her rampant tongue.

Stu began thrusting into her, gagging her with each push. She encouraged him, grasping his hard-as-rock butt cheeks and pulling him towards her. She couldn't feel an inch of wobble – every bit was as solid as she'd imagined. They remained in their position for many minutes, both enjoying the sensations the action gave. He growled, his noise as masculine as his physique. His growl became louder and suddenly, without warning, he stopped and withdrew. Heleyna scanned her eyes over his cock: it was larger now, his veins stood out and were a deep blue-purple in colour, his balls solid and ready to release.

He poured two shots of vodka and pushed one towards her without a word, like a preoccupied barman. She knocked it back in one swift and practised action. He followed, then poured again. Wondering how long this was going to go on for, she eagerly drank the second, the harshness of the alcohol burning, warming, sending lively messages all over her body.

No more vodka came. Stu bent over and picked up both Heleyna and the chair, the weight of both apparently little effort for him. She watched his muscles contract with the lift. She liked what she saw. She also liked the look of where he was carrying her – to the room named 'Pain'.

He walked into the centre of the room, which was still in darkness. He put her down, then found the light switch. Fake candelabra lit up on each wall, the flickering orange glow giving the room an eerie feel. As her eyes adjusted to the light, he closed the door. The view of him from the rear was almost frightening, his huge legs causing him to waddle with each step as the gigantic inner thigh muscles rubbed together.

Heleyna realised quite suddenly that Stu seemed to know each room, what was where. Whether this was because he was a nosy security guard or a member of Huxley she could not make out. She was sure to find out soon.

Before she had a chance to inspect the room he had returned and unleashed her legs, picked her up and carried her towards one of the walls. Here he took her wrists one at a time and secured them tightly in shackles. He did the same with her ankles. Yet again, Heleyna was trapped and secured by her captor.

'I assume you get off on pain, judging by your response to those naughty little nipple clamps?'

Heleyna nodded in response, her eyes large in anticipation of what he was about to administer.

'You look stunning stood there, my voluptuous plaything attached to the wall. Quite comical really, but very fucking horny.' As he spoke he walked towards a narrow, tall wardrobe in the corner nearest Heleyna, his cock still solid and desiring of her.

Heleyna finally took the opportunity to explore the room he had taken her to. The walls were painted black, with gold borders. No mirror was to be seen. She noted the cameras dotted around the room, and shackles on three of the walls, including her own. Up against the fourth wall was an interesting looking physio-style table, except this one had attachments you would be shocked to see at any chiropractor's. She noticed, too, that the bed itself was made of thin see-through material. For watching from below, she giggled to herself, remembering Mr Handsome and her own glass-topped dining-room-table experience. A foot pedal lay on the floor – suggestive and exciting.

Hearing the creak of the dark wooden wardrobe door, she strained her head to see inside. Hanging behind the door were more handcuffs. Inside, and standing to attention, were some ominous-looking paddles of differing lengths and with huge leather smacking flaps on the end of solid wooden handles. She shuddered in expectation and fear. She was trapped. This man could do anything to her. There was more in the darkness of the cupboard, but what exactly she was unable to determine. Stu pushed the door to and, in his burly hand, held a dangerous-looking shorter-length paddle, flat on one side and with a raised symmetrical pattern on the other.

He rested the contraption against the physio table and moved towards her, all the time demonstrating how horny he was by the excessive swollenness of his veiny dick. The muscles in his legs and torso popped out with each swagger of his imposing body. He opened her shackles and lifted her over his shoulder with incredible ease. She didn't wiggle or try to escape his grasp. Why the hell would she?

He laid her on the table, her face perched on the hole made especially for face-down action, tied her arms to it with the rope fastenings, then bent below the counter and pulled out an attachment. Retrieving a huge dildo he slotted it onto the clear tabletop in its fastening high up between her legs. His movements brushed her gently, teased her, made her desperate for more. She was swollen, she was hot, she was ready.

'Push down onto that, my beauty.'

Heleyna pushed, enjoying the sensation of cold metal within her that caused her to cry out with the gentlest of whimpers.

Stu, a man with a mission, shackled her legs as far apart as the narrow surface would allow, took a remote control in his hands and pressed a few buttons. He knows exactly what he's doing, Heleyna thought. The table began moving, pivoting on a central point, lifting Heleyna's arse up and down, moving her up and down the cold metal shaft which was nestled deep inside and between her legs. She groaned. It was good, but still sedate. She was a dirty, dirty little bitch who would stop at nothing when it came to satisfying her physical desires.

'Get ready for some pain, young lady, for some spanking which will bring tears to your large pretty eyes.' As he spoke he lifted the paddle above his head, pattern side down.

Heleyna's body was already prepared. As her bottom was lifted by the action of the table, he brought down the paddle in one swift action. The sound echoed round the small room like the aftershock of a small explosion. She whimpered. Her bottom stung. Her pussy enjoyed every inch of the agony. The spanking could easily have been instigated even harder against her round arse, an arse that had enjoyed such pleasures on more than one occasion before and no doubt would do again in the future.

'You have been a very, very naughty and dirty young lady. And, for that, I am going to make sure you are well and truly punished. Do you want more?'

'Yes.'

'Yes, what?'

'Yes, please, Mr White, sir.'

He lifted the paddle and this time attacked her left cheek as her bottom reached the uppermost point in the withdrawal from the metal stem, and before the shaft disappeared back inside her wanton hole. This time he administered his punishment more severely, and she shouted in response.

'Shut up, bitch. No more noise.' Stu bent and pulled out a gag from under the table. He wrenched back her head and shoved the gag in her mouth, then dropped her head without thought.

Now Heleyna was unable to make little noise other than a rather comical gurgle. The gag was firm, tied tightly round the back of her head, some strands of hair caught in the knot and pulling sharply.

'This obviously isn't hard enough for a woman such as you.'

Heleyna heard him walking away from her, and the creak of the wardrobe door followed. She was unable to look, her head stuck in position staring down at the floor. The door creaked again and his footsteps returned. She braced herself for whatever he was about to do to her.

Heleyna knew it was a cane before the appliance hit her bare bottom – the thwack note of it flying through the air on the way to her gave the game away. Now this will hurt, she thought, as the cane neared her peachy behind. She was right. She gurgled profusely – her pussy enjoyed the cold metal, her cheeks were insanely sore. She'd reached that point of delicious confusion that pain and pleasure brought.

Stu dispensed a dozen more canings before stopping quite suddenly and unexpectedly. Heleyna didn't know whether she should be crying out with the pleasure or crying from the pain – the intense, hot stinging that radiated from her arse was so pleasurably sore. Her eyes were full of tears, her pussy full of desire. She knew she wouldn't be able to sit for a week after this little episode – a constant reminder to her of her lewd, rude habits.

So far removed from the real world, Heleyna had not realised that Stu now had her firmly over his shoulder until he began walking. Her view was of his cock, her mouth now released from its gag. Reaching the wall at the opposite side to the table, he turned and placed his back up against the wall, as if for support, then took Heleyna by the legs and dangled her upside down in front of him, his cock only millimetres away from her face. The man was a machine, his strength almost superhuman.

'Suck on that, and enjoy.'

Heleyna took him hungrily into her mouth and sucked him hard, Stu assisting her action with his strong, muscular arms and back. Her head filled with blood. She kept sucking. He wanted it hard and aggressive. She felt faint. She drew on him, energetically. Then she felt dizzy and signalled to be let down.

The next Heleyna knew she was flat on her back on the dining room table. Stu, on seeing her eyes focused again, jumped straight on top of her and gave her what she'd been craving – a good hard fuck – smothering and squashing her with the full weight of a giant man. By the time he had reached his own roaring climax they'd travelled from one end of the long wooden table to the other, Heleyna's bottom, which was raw and inflamed, suffering favourably with each angry thrust.

Heleyna needed satisfying now and he was more than keen to give her that final release. She bucked towards his mouth as if drawn by a magnetic force, and he disappeared between her legs with the truncheon firmly in his grasp. This time it entered her with incredible ease, and he rammed her with it in between each surprisingly delicate tickle to her clit with his hot tongue.

Heleyna shuddered and shook and quivered and screamed as her orgasm hit her, the truncheon almost catapulted out of her with the intensity of the squeezing action, only kept in place by the force of Stu's incredible and delectable muscle power.

When Heleyna awoke Stu was nowhere in sight and she was still naked. Her captor had not shackled her. She looked at her watch and was surprised to see it was 9 a.m. – the lack of daylight made estimating the time confusing. She stood and, believing that she was free to leave, went to find her clothes for a second time.

She pulled on her trousers gingerly, the waistband catching her throbbing bottom. It felt like she'd spent a night on a bed of nails. Curious to know the state it was in, she wandered into the 'Women Only' room, her trousers around her ankles, and presented her bottom to the mirror. She could not quite believe the rich red stripes that crisscrossed it – she counted thirteen in all. Having seen her punishment, she was not at all surprised at the pain she felt this morning.

With all her belongings gathered up she wearily ascended the stairs. She was relieved to be finally out of the mess she'd found herself in, a mess that was purely self-inflicted and a result of her arrogant curiosity. She couldn't wait to get home, and down to formalising some of her business ideas before Ted returned from his jet-setting. She was also insanely hungry.

She turned the handle. No response. She tried again, thinking that perhaps it was just a little awkward. Still no response. She tried a few more times, each attempt bringing with it the realisation that she was locked in there, unable to escape. Her joy quickly diminished to distress and fear that she was locked in there until Ted and Jacinta or the police arrived on the doorstep. Silent tears leaked onto her cheeks, tears of tiredness and tears of concern.

'What do you think you're doing?' Stu's voice came through clearly from the other side of the door. 'Thought it was time to leave, did you? No bloody chance, my dear. I'm having fun, and fun is something I want more of. Get your pretty little self back down those stairs and make sure you're naked by the time I arrive with breakfast.'

Heleyna turned. She was despondent, exhausted and, quite frankly, had had enough of this man's games. She knew she'd no one else to blame but herself, and this very thought intensified her morose response to her situation.

The next 24 hours were a mixture of phenomenal indulgence and anger at her stupidity. The only belief keeping her going was the knowledge that this beast could not keep her locked up for more than a few days, with Ted and Jacinta due to return the following weekend.

Heleyna felt she had no choice but to pleasure Mr White in the hope that he would honour his promise and release her without a word to a soul. Bizarrely, and despite her belief that she was pleasuring him, she was having a wildly erotic time in the company of this animal. In some ways she wished the scenario could continue, this fantasy which had now become a deeply pleasurable reality that could never be replayed in the comfort of her own home – here she was held against her will, a true prisoner. At home it would never be more than role-play; how could play-acting ever compare to the genuine article?

She awoke on Wednesday after many, many hours back in the pain room. Stu had pleaded to be the recipient, but would not allow her to lock him in place for fear she might escape his clutches. His desire for the cane was verging on the obsessional – or any other spanking device she could find, for that matter: the paddle, the leather strap, the horsewhip, the lasso. The man was insatiable when it came to being walloped and lashed and smacked and spanked, and the welts across his back and bottom were the evidence of his desire. At one stage he even pleaded for Heleyna to take the strap to his throbbing cock, a request she could not bring herself to obey despite her joy at playing the persecutor. In his anger with her, he'd jumped up and pinned her against the wall and fucked her there and then, without one flutter of a thought for her needs or wants. She was in ecstasy.

Sitting up on the mattress in the 'Women Only' room, her arms felt stiff from the hours of beating as she supported herself in a cross-legged position. She was cold. He hadn't allowed her a blanket. His bedroom had been the room for voyeurs, and he wanted every possible opportunity to see her naked body, to wank over her from the other side of the glass mirror as the desire took him.

She heard voices. She stood quickly, not knowing what to do with herself, suddenly feeling frighteningly vulnerable in her nakedness, and with nowhere to hide. The voices continued. She put her ear up against the locked door and tried to listen. The voices became louder. It was two men, arguing, shouting. She couldn't tell whose the voices were or what they were saying, the thickness of the walls and door taking care of that. She was afraid it was Ted or the police.

The voices were now outside her door, or there-abouts. She rushed into the corner of the room and curled up in a ball, her head between her knees. The door flew open. She didn't dare look. A person, a man,

walked towards her. She felt his presence within millimetres of her.

He spoke. 'Come on, Heleyna, it's time to go home.'

Troy picked her up in his arms and carried her into
the dining room. She was shivering. He found her
clothes and her bag and her torch, then helped her with
her dressing.

'Some of the messes you get yourself into. What
would you do without me?' Troy was smiling at her as
he spoke, a genuine softness in his voice.

Heleyna could not find words to verbalise her relief.
She dressed in silence, let Troy walk her out of Ted's
home and to his car. Stu was nowhere in sight.

Heleyna took the remainder of the week off work as
she'd promised herself. She continued with her business
plans, putting them into a formal business case for the
bank manager – a draft for Ted to cast his eyes over on
his return. No longer able to sit, she had work laid out
on her sitting-room floor and she lay on her front as
she laboured – not the most comfortable of positions.
Her bottom wasn't going to be right for some time.

Troy had given Stu a huge cheque – a silencer which
also covered the broken window. He had accepted the
money willingly and was sworn to secrecy and to
tidying the house to look as though no one had ever
entered apart from himself on his rounds. If it hadn't
been for the vague plans Heleyna had made to see Troy
on Wednesday lunchtime she would probably still have
been imprisoned. She shuddered at the thought, but
was unable to verify whether this was a shudder of
delight or fear, finally deciding it was probably both.

Troy had also slept at Heleyna's each night for the
remainder of the week and spent the weekend at hers,
rubbing soothing unguent into her abused bottom. She

was fine, she was loved and secure. On more than one occasion she explained how wonderfully erotic the whole experience had been and he had listened, attentive and horny. But she let him play the man, take the protective role. She found it kind of cute.

14

Heleyna phoned Ted first thing Monday morning on her way into work, bold as brass, as if nothing had happened. She was like a child in a sweet shop with five pounds in her pocket, rushing round, unable to hold back her eagerness. His mobile clicked into the voice-message service – she left one as requested, her excitement about their joint venture showing with each and every word.

Within fifteen minutes Ted called her back. Her train was just pulling into Leeds station; she could already smell the putrid air that hung round the impossibly busy platforms on still summer days. The train was full, not one available seat in sight. But it was actually a relief to be standing, with her bottom still so sore, huge welts still raised across her scrumptious cheeks. A few restless nights meant she was dazed – a result of the pain she felt every time she rolled onto her back in her sleep. Adrenaline was the only thing keeping her going.

There'd been no sign of Mr Handsome that morning. She was disappointed: she fancied a flirt.

'Heleyna! How are you, darling?' Ted was even more outrageously happy than normal.

'I'm good. How was the holiday?' Heleyna tried to stabilise herself as the train came to a standstill.

'Warm. Plenty of drinking, eating and sun.'

Heleyna was a little cautious, generated by the fact that she'd never wanted to do anything more in her life before. 'You haven't changed your mind about our business venture have you?'

'Well, actually, I wanted to talk to you about that.'

'Ted. You can't drop out now.' Heleyna's heart sunk.

'Only teasing, Heleyna, only teasing. Of course I'm still up for it. So then, when are you free to meet today?'

'How about a long lunch?' she asked, her heart back where it should be.

'Sounds good.'

'Come by my office at eleven-thirty and we'll head out somewhere. I've already put a lot of thought in, Ted. I've got a draft business plan for you to look at.'

Ted was not at all surprised at how organised and efficient Heleyna had been. 'My, my, you have been busy. Look forward to it. See you later. Oh, before you go, remember Huxley meets a week on Saturday. Looking forward to seeing you there.'

'Don't you worry, Ted, I hadn't forgotten that one. Are you flirting with me, Ted?'

Ted's response was only just audible above his deep, loud laugh. 'Me, flirt with a colleague? Now I wouldn't do a thing like that.'

Walking into work, Heleyna felt overwhelmingly comforted. Ted hadn't mentioned anything about intruders. Despite the fact she'd 'endured' two days of captivity, she'd got away with her little fact-finding adventure. Now her and Troy were ready, willing and able. Huxley was going to be just their cup of tea.

Heleyna was going to have to face Sam today, and she knew this only too well. As she walked into her plush office she decided that as of now she was committed to keeping her cool around this arrogant, testosterone-ridden man. He was not going to throw her off her normally professional stride – no bloody way he's getting the better of me, she thought. No bloody way at all.

Sam appeared earlier than she anticipated, like an animal on the prowl circling his target before going in for the kill.

She looked him directly in the eye without a waver. 'Morning, Sam. How are you?'

'Good, thanks. So, today I've got some proper work to do, have I?' He looked straight at her chest as he spoke.

She ignored his glances. 'Absolutely. How about we meet, say, in ten minutes? Just get a cup of coffee, check my emails and post, then we can get started?'

More naughty glances from Sam. 'Excellent. I'll grab you a cuppa if you like. Black, no sugar, isn't it?'

She was proud of herself. 'Yes, please, Sam, that would be very kind.'

'And, by the way, you're looking particularly sexy today. Like that top. It shows off your tits terrifically.'

Wilting inside, she didn't bat an eyelid. 'That will be all, Sam. Thank you. See you in ten minutes.'

Sam walked out of the room, silent for once. She'd won her first battle, albeit an easy one – at least this time he hadn't pushed her hand onto his hot, hot prick. Now, that would be hard to resist, she thought, as she watched his butt disappearing from the room.

Her meeting with Sam had sapped all her mental energy. His effort to flirt had proved futile and he hadn't attempted his usual less-than-subtle physical approach. So, by the time she met Ted, she was pretty shattered, hungry and ready for some time out.

They wandered into Papillon, a small French restaurant in The Calls, Heleyna with her briefcase under her arm. She meant business today, but first she wanted time to catch up with Ted and recharge her batteries after a morning of Sam. She surprised herself at how relaxed she felt with Ted, how much she was looking forward to seeing him at Huxley. Perhaps it's the thought of leaving the work environment, she pondered.

'How are the plans going for the next Huxley meet? I'm looking forward to it, Ted – to getting a true feel of what exactly I'm entering into with you on this partnership.'

'Are you sure your excitement is only to do with business, young Heleyna?'

Heleyna giggled. Still slightly uneasy about mixing work and pleasure, she replied, 'Umm, probably a bit of both.' She hung her head and looked at her menu as she spoke, not quite able to look Ted in the eye.

'Come on, Heleyna, no need to be shy with me. I know what you like.' He bent forwards and whispered, 'Remember, J told me all about your little masturbation over me – every detail. She's looking forward to seeing you at Huxley as much as me.'

Heleyna forced herself to be herself. She was going to have to be that way with Ted and Jacinta anyhow if their plans were going to come to fruition. 'OK, I know. I've got some work to do on myself. Never been very good at the work/pleasure-mix thing. Something to do with my Church of England upbringing – normally keep the two very separate. But with you, and this new enterprise, I've got to be myself. I will get there, just give me time.'

'In that case, if you're ever going to enjøy Huxley, we have only one option. We need to finalise this business plan and get to the bank manager this week, then next week you can hand in your notice. You'll be surprised at the number of colleagues you'll come ... umm ... face to face with. Don't want it to ruin your evening. Nothing for you to worry about, though – we've all been doing this for some time now. At work we treat each other as any other professional colleagues would.

professional with anyone?'

'No, actually, I haven't. But how can you take people seriously after ... well ... fucking their brains out or giving them head?' There was a touch of anguish in Heleyna's tone.

Ted's response was matter of fact. 'You just do it because you have to and because you enjoy both. Separate the two in your mind. It's easy. I bet you've wanted me since you realised who you were watching, haven't you?'

Heleyna forced an honest answer. 'Actually, I have looked at you kind of differently since then. I've noticed things I'd not noticed before. But I just blanked it from my mind.'

'Well, stop blanking it and go with your feelings. Sex is just that – sex. What's there to be worried about? I mean, it's not as if you're a chaste being, is it. From what I can gather you love a bit of the naughty stuff as much as the next person, if not more. Just get over it and let yourself go a little. Stop being so uptight.'

Heleyna began laughing. It was the understatement of the year. 'It's bizarre, really. To think I've been such a prudish businesswoman at work, when at home I'm such a tart. And now I'm hoping to go into business, mixing the two quite spectacularly. Oh, by the way – I haven't put any of that in the business plan. I've talked about corporate functions, wedding receptions, parties and so on. With the fiscal assistance we're going to need we need the bank firmly on our side over the first twelve to eighteen months.'

Ted sat back in his chair and sipped at his glass of Cabernet Sauvignon. 'Well then, now we've dealt with you and your little hang-ups, let's get on to this draft proposal of yours, which, no doubt, is perfectly suitable for the bank manager in its current form if you're working at your normal excellent level. Mind if I read it now?'

'No, no problem. Oh, and by the way, to us this is our *Sexual Strategy* – a title I'll obviously remove for the bank manager.'

'I love it, love it,' he replied.

Heleyna relaxed into her chair and let Ted read whilst she ate her simple meal of steak so rare it could almost have walked out of the restaurant, salad in a divine dressing and a piece of crusty French bread – simple yet delicious. While she sat there she vowed to get out and do some clothes shopping: change her work wardrobe; stop being so bloody uptight about her straight lines and long skirts; make herself glamorous for her new business challenge with tight-tailored suits that gave a subtle hint of what hid beneath. A new and more refreshing her to go with her new and more refreshing life.

That night, slumped in the bath with a cold beer in her hand, she contemplated where her life was heading. Ted's approval of the draft had resulted in a quick call to the bank manager, who agreed to see them later that week. Things were rolling, and rolling quickly. Ted had plenty of collateral to help them along their way. Heleyna had some – a small inheritance that she'd been sitting on for a rainy day.

They'd agreed that they would both hand in their notices at the same time – sit down with John together and tell him the news. They both needed plans to help John out – perhaps to suggest a successor to their respective roles. Heleyna's would be easy. Sam was proving to be intelligent, knowledgeable and well qualified. She knew from the start that he would move on quickly if he didn't achieve an internal promotion. Ted's was a little harder to deal with, but Ted was a good networker – he knew plenty of good people out there who were looking for a job with a firm such as SPM. He'd committed himself to making a few tentative phone calls that week to test the waters before breaking the news to John.

Sam continued to tease Heleyna, his actions becoming increasingly painful to handle. By Thursday that week she'd had enough – she'd won many battles with him that week, but now she just had to sit down and tell this gorgeous specimen her plans, put them both out of their misery. The pretence, the playing, was sapping all her energy, and she needed all her reserves for her new venture.

She returned from the bank in excellent spirits, Ted and her deciding to have a champagne dinner with partners that evening. Everything was go. Now it was time to talk to Sam, to let him know what she wanted from him and when she planned to have it. As soon as she wasn't his boss any more she was going to rip his clothes off and eat every bit of him up.

Sam's office was next to hers, so she popped her head into his room, which was almost identical to her own. Although she hadn't yet been clothes shopping, she was dressed as glamorously as her wardrobe would allow – stylish with a hint of tart.

Sat on his desk was a brightly attired Phoebe, skirt up to her armpits giggling at his every word. Heleyna wanted to nip that relationship in the bud.

'Thank you, Phoebe. Please leave now. I want some time with Sam – alone.'

A startled Phoebe jumped to her feet and scuttled out of the room, cowering as she passed within a few feet of her boss and looking very much like a guilty child who knows very well they've been caught doing something wholly inappropriate.

Heleyna walked in and closed the door, for the first time feeling one hundred per cent comfortable in the presence of this man she'd been craving for so long. He remained seated behind his desk, watching her every move as she approached him. He was not the kind of man to stand as a woman approached him – an example of the arrogance that many women find hard to resist.

His tie was pulled loosely from around his neck, his top button undone, and he was sat well back in his chair, legs apart, showing his wares. Heleyna sat on the corner of his desk, the spot where Phoebe had been only seconds earlier. She noticed that his look faltered ever so slightly in response to her confidence, then resumed its normal haughtiness, his nostrils flared in pre-sex hunger.

'We need to talk, Sam.'

'Indeed we do, boss.'

She detected an element of unease in him and felt good and strong and confident. 'I need to let you in on a little secret, a secret which I don't expect you to share with anyone until I say so.'

'Fire away.' He swivelled his chair and faced her directly.

'I'm leaving SPM. I've been looking for other opportunities for a while now and have decided to go it alone. I think it will suit me better. Just got approval from the bank today.'

'Well done.'

'I haven't finished yet. So, that's why I need to talk to you. I've lusted after you since the moment I set my eyes on you back at the Bear Inn, as you well know. Back then you didn't respond to my advances, and now I know why – Troy was your preference out of the two of us. Since you've had him, you've made every effort to seduce me, your boss – not an ideal situation, you must agree. But now ... well ... now I will respond to your advances. At least, once I am no longer your boss I will respond. Actually, to be honest, I won't wait for you to make a move, I will initiate the moment I know I'm free to. I will eat you alive, savour every little last bit of you.'

Heleyna didn't wait for him to respond. She stood, turned and walked quickly out of his office, closing his door firmly and purposefully behind her. Once in the privacy of her own office she giggled away to herself, wondering what the hell was going through Sam's mind at that moment in time. He hadn't run after her, or tried to talk as she left his company. She had finally rendered him speechless. Now she was in control of the situation, and she liked it.

15

The taxi pulled up outside Troy's. Heleyna didn't want to walk tonight: her shoes were far too ridiculously high for anything more than socialising in. As she pulled her pashmina tightly round her shoulders before walking out into the cool night air, Troy leaned forward and kissed her neck.

'You look absolutely divine, my little beast. Irresistible. Good enough to eat.'

She turned to him and gave him the once over. 'You don't look bad yourself.' She reached round and gave his butt one almighty pinch, a sign of her appreciation.

Heleyna took one last swig of her G&T, her third one of the evening before opening the door. Her stomach was filled to the brim with butterflies. Troy had admitted the same syndrome was attacking him. The buildup to the Huxley Club over the last few weeks had increased their anticipation, the feeling of excitement shaken together with a touch of fear, like the moment before a roller coaster begins its first stomach-churning descent.

Five minutes later they were pulling up outside Ted and Jacinta's. Cars that reeked of huge salaries littered the driveway and the roads around their property. Ted had warned her that it would be a full night after so long between parties, and he was right.

Heleyna rang the front-door bell. Troy stood just behind her, protecting her from the chill which hung like a cloud in the summer evening air. Jacinta came to the door.

'Hello, darlings, so good to see you. Come in, make yourself at home. Everything's set up downstairs – just follow the lights and music. Help yourself to a drink. I'll be down shortly to show you around, give you a bit of background info, then leave you to enjoy the evening.' She was breathless with excitement.

'Any chance of using the bathroom?' Heleyna asked.

'Why, of course, Heleyna. No problem. You know where the upstairs one is. Go right ahead.' Jacinta sensed Heleyna's nerves and added, 'Don't you worry yourself. I'll take you both downstairs if you like, as soon as you've freshened up. And, by the way, Heleyna, you look absolutely gorgeous.' Jacinta winked at Heleyna then turned and hurried towards the kitchen as her mobile rang.

Heleyna left Troy in the hallway and made her way to the bathroom, marvelling at how intoxicatingly beautiful Jacinta looked this evening. Her long, lean frame was coated in the most revealing outfit Heleyna had ever seen in real life – the kind she marvelled over in magazines, which was normally only worn by Hollywood stars. It was see-through: a long sheen of a dress, beneath which peeped out two petite bosoms topped with small brown nipples, and a matching cream G-string. Her hair rolled over her shoulders, her jewellery and make-up simple; the dress was the masterpiece and she obviously didn't want anything else to dominate that.

Heleyna didn't need the toilet. She needed time to compose herself. For something to do, she washed her hands then looked at herself in the mirror. She did look as good as Troy had described. The dress she'd bought for the occasion enveloped her curves perfectly, showing the world her tiny waist and rounded curved hips and bottom. The shop assistant had described it as medieval in style. The bustier pushed her breasts out as high as they could go without spilling over the edge; they bounced beautifully with each step she took. Her shoes peeped out from beneath – they were strappy, non-existent, fuck-me shoes of the highest order. The split up the front of her red-green shot-silk gown flashed a glimpse of shimmering silk panties with each stride. The bikini wax she'd put herself through had been worth every ounce of pain, her muff now displaying only the tiniest of mohicans – but that wouldn't be seen, at least not until later.

Seeing how damn hot she looked boosted her confidence, and she marched out of the bathroom, almost bumping into Ted, who was checking messages on his mobile phone.

'Fuck me, Heleyna, you look ... absolutely bloody amazing! You're going to steal the show, you know – you and J. Everyone's going to want your company tonight.'

Heleyna smiled then changed the subject. 'Glad John took the news so well. Sam is pleased with the promotion too. Only three weeks to go and we're free! How good is that?'

'It's bloody good, Heleyna, bloody good. Now get yourself down those stairs and enjoy yourself. Troy is already down there relishing the shows on the screens with a glass of champagne in his hand. Make sure you watch, listen and learn – soon it will be us running these events and we need you to know as much as you can. By the way, J has agreed to remain maitre d' for all the parties. She's already planning to hand in her notice in a couple of months, once we get things up and running. We're going to make a bloody good team.'

Soul music filled her ears as she neared the bottom step of the stairs she hardly recognised; stairs that had been tastefully decorated in simple white lights, with an elaborate carpet covering each step. She felt slightly nauseous with excitement and nerves.

Jacinta called from the top step, 'I'm just coming, Heleyna. I'll show you around.'

Heleyna stopped for a second to allow Jacinta to catch her up and overtake her, to take the lead into the room that Troy was already enjoying. As she passed Heleyna, Jacinta rubbed up against her. It was a rub that Heleyna could not decipher – was it a come-on, or was it an accident?

The two deliciously gorgeous but very different women hit the central dining room together, Jacinta talking to Heleyna all the way. Heleyna hardly heard a word: she couldn't believe the transformation the room had undergone from the prison she'd been held captive in only a few days before.

The central room was filled with people, some she recognised, some she didn't. Many were standing up, others were sitting at the table, many were talking, others were just watching the screens at the end of the room. Heleyna noticed how many turned and looked and stared and almost dribbled with desire at both herself and Jacinta.

The screens caught her eye and Heleyna turned and looked. A small appreciative gasp left her lips. Only one room had people playing – it was early in the evening, after all. It was most definitely the pain room, a room Heleyna now knew well. The couple clearly loved every minute of their fun. The man, a middle-aged guy, was strapped to the table face down, an anal probe shoved deep into his arse. The woman was whipping him senseless with the paddle Mr White had inflicted upon Heleyna. She was a petite thing with a long black wig and wearing a skin-tight all-in-one leather outfit with

G-string only, revealing a small yet very peachy bottom. Little rounded breasts hung out of the front of this leave-nothing-to-the-imagination outfit.

'Anyone I know?' Heleyna leaned over and whispered into Jacinta's ear.

'Actually, yes. It's John and Phoebe. Great, aren't they?' The twinkle in Jacinta's eye was more than evident.

Heleyna was confused. 'Fuck me! Not Phoebe my assistant? From behind I would hardly recognise her. The outfit, the wig ... I mean ... fuck me!'

'I take it you're shocked then?'

'Well, yes, I suppose I am. I can't quite believe it's the same person.'

'Let's get you a drink to calm you down then,' Jacinta teased.

Jacinta collected a glass of bubbling champagne for her from the large table, which was covered in lit candles, tapas-style food and an extensive choice of alcohol. Heleyna took a sip and waved discreetly at Troy, who was sitting next to a man she didn't know and chatting in between watching the action.

Jacinta grabbed her arm. 'Come with me. Let me show you around each of these rooms.'

The door was already open to the 'Women Only' room. It was still empty.

'Later on we'll get plenty of action in here. We'll close the door and get the classical music going.'

Heleyna surveyed the room. The bed was coated in the crispy white cotton sheets she'd imagined, and purple, red and cream cushions covered the sheets in a random formation. The candles on the sideboard were lit, the cupboard doors were open, revealing the instruments of pleasure Heleyna had fingered, and more, not too long ago. Bowls were scattered haphazardly across the sideboard and around the bed. Heleyna couldn't make out their contents in the dim light, which forced her to screw up her pretty face in her attempt to look.

'What's in those, Jacinta?' Heleyna asked, pointing at the dishes with her red polished nails.

'Just a bit of food. You know, strawberries, cream, chocolate spread. In that larger one over there –' Jacinta pointed to a large dish close to the bed, '– there're some more interesting vegetables – courgettes, cucumbers and the odd carrot.'

Heleyna's eyes were large with delight. 'Bloody marvellous.'

'Come on. Let me show you the rest.' Jacinta spoke excitedly, thoroughly enjoying the pleasure she gained from Heleyna's delight.

As they turned, Ted appeared. 'You weren't planning your fun for later, were you?'

'You leave that to me, you naughty beast.' Jacinta slapped Ted's bum as they walked past and on to the other rooms.

They continued, Jacinta pointing out the intricacies of each room, intricacies that Heleyna was more than aware of in most cases. She didn't let on. Her feet sunk into the carpet with each step, and she stroked the walls. She just couldn't help herself.

Walking in on John and Phoebe had been an unusual yet liberating experience for Heleyna. Phoebe looked even more unsure of herself than Heleyna felt, but Heleyna took the experience in her stride, even asking for a go with the paddle on naughty John's backside. It was white, pasty and wobbly, but she'd still taken pleasure from it. The indulgence had not been sexual, more a freeing of her previous self – a self who was hung up about anything remotely connecting work with sexual pleasure.

Jacinta was particularly dynamic when discussing her own room, aptly named 'Jacinta's Parlour'. 'This is my room, my space, where anyone can come, with my permission of course, and ask for whatever treatment they desire. I love it. Love the control – very liberating after being the dutiful housewife.' She nudged Heleyna as she spoke, and winked for a second time.

Honesty seeped out from Heleyna's lips. 'You know, I wouldn't have put you down as anything other than a respectable middle-class woman until more recently. You're a very surprising woman, Jacinta.'

'And hopefully you will surprise us all tonight, Heleyna. You have always portrayed yourself as a strong, strait-laced businesswoman. I know now you're not, but would love to see some proof of that.' She touched Heleyna's arm as she spoke, a gentle but meaningful touch.

Jacinta's mobile rang. 'Sorry, Heleyna. Duty calls, see you later.'

Heleyna was left to her own devices. She took a deep breath and walked towards the crowd of people, which had grown significantly in number since she'd first set foot in the room only twenty minutes earlier. As she took her first few steps, her eyes were drawn through the crowd and towards the back of a person she knew only too well. She could just see the irresistible dimples and the stubble and the dark, dark hair. Her heart stopped momentarily. How could she not have known he would be there?

She walked towards him, grabbing her third glass of champagne on the way, and interrupted the conversation he was having with yet another of Heleyna's colleagues – Roger from Marketing, Ted's little piece of fun.

'Hello, Mr Molloy. Good to see you here.' Heleyna didn't betray her confusion.

'Hello, Heleyna.' He made his excuses to Roger, took Heleyna's arm and walked her to the side of the room, to the right of the screens where images of Phoebe astride John, who was now face up, fucking him wildly, were on display.

'So then, how come you're here?' She was trying to keep her cool.

'Troy, your ever-lovely Troy, got me an invite through Jacinta. Great, eh? Now we can have our first night of passion on display for the world to see, and captured on camera. How fantastic is that?'

'I'm still your boss, Sam. And, more to the point, if we ever do consummate our lust it will be very much on my terms. Enjoy your evening.' She turned and walked away towards the crowd.

A man she didn't know walked towards her, and they began the small-talk ritual. During the five-minute conversation she managed to knock back a couple more glasses of bubbly and was feeling delightfully squiffy. He was handsome and charming, but he bored her. She soon moved on and sat down. She wanted time to view the shows and take in the room, pick her person, then make her move.

The show had changed on the screen. John was now in the 'Humiliation' room, licking the floor with his hands tied behind his back, a tight blindfold in place, a very large woman kicking him with her stiletto shoes and shouting orders. Another face she knew, Mr Security Guard White, was slouched in a huge armchair in the 'Voyeurism' room, playing with himself energetically. Heleyna looked at the screen next to his to see what was giving him his pleasure. Phoebe had moved on to the 'Women Only' room now and was putting on a display almost, but not quite, as good as her own. She felt a tinge of jealousy, then let it slide. Well, no point being competitive. They were all here to enjoy themselves. The only goal was pleasure, however it was accessed, and whoever was indulging.

Before she knew what was happening, and undoubtedly alcohol-induced, she had stood and was walking towards the door of the room that Phoebe occupied. Despite the live-and-let-live opinions, Heleyna wasn't one hundred per cent comfortable at being pushed into second place as the Queen of Tarts by Phoebe. She would show her a thing or two.

Heleyna slinked into the room and made her way to the bed, where she removed her very high shoes and gorgeous dress. She watched the camera: if it had had eyes, she would have been looking directly into them. She wanted the people watching the show to think she was doing this for them, for each individual. There she lay, all curves and roundness and womanly assets, with tiny silk panties just covering her wet pussy – she could feel the dampness of the silk touching her inner thighs.

Tonight she'd decided to prolong the fun: start slowly and build up to the kind of display she normally gave. With her head and shoulders propped, giving her a view of the rest of the room, she lowered her hand down and over the gently sweeping curve of her stomach and onto and into her panties. She stroked her newly-created mohican, then slipped her finger delicately yet swiftly between her swollen lips. Her other hand, her left, satisfied the tingling in her nipples. With her eyes still focused on the camera, she teased herself and the crowd of people outside the room.

Phoebe crawled onto the bed and lay directly next to Heleyna. Heleyna looked over at her, all previous antagonisms now forgotten. Phoebe looked pumped with lust, ready for anything. Heleyna couldn't help noticing how sensuous Phoebe looked, like an erotic dancer with her long dark hair and all-in-one leather still in place, which was now zipped wide open at the crotch to reveal a clean-shaven pussy.

Phoebe placed her hand on top of Heleyna's and

guided it over her clit through the silken material. Heleyna didn't stop her.

'You keep doing that,' Phoebe whispered before reaching over the edge of the bed, leaning over and touching Heleyna suggestively in the process. She brought two bowls back with her that were piled high with refreshingly interesting fruit.

Phoebe spread her legs wide, took a large red strawberry and popped it directly into her waiting hole. Heleyna watched avidly.

'Watch this, Heleyna.' Phoebe straddled Heleyna, her pussy within centimetres of her face.

Heleyna observed, at the same time removing her panties. As they reached her ankles, the strawberry popped out of Phoebe, as if in slow motion, and landed on Heleyna's lips before rolling off her, down her neck and onto the white sheets. Heleyna licked her lips and savoured the first taste of Phoebe. Heleyna was surprising herself tonight beyond her wildest expectations.

Taking another strawberry, Heleyna inserted it into Phoebe. Then another, and then another, until ten filled her to the brim. Heleyna waited patiently for the show, all the while her right hand pleasuring her own pussy. Phoebe didn't let them go at first, instead dropping directly onto Heleyna's mouth, smothering her face with her juices. Heleyna lapped them up, and one by one the strawberries appeared in Heleyna's mouth. She ate every single one.

Still deep in Phoebe, Heleyna felt other hands touching her. Another woman had entered the room. Who it was, she didn't know and didn't really care – the hands were gentle and expert. They removed her own hand and she felt the heavenly and cold sensation of what she guessed was a cucumber entering her, filling her, pleasuring her, then the mouth surround her clit, sucking gently and rhythmically.

Phoebe changed position. Heleyna had relished all ten strawberries and now Phoebe wanted something different. She encouraged Heleyna onto her side, then pushed herself back into position against Heleyna's experienced mouth. Heleyna guessed very quickly what was happening. The three women had taken on a triangular arrangement, each one orally pleasuring another. She still didn't know who was eagerly lapping and sucking at her in such a practised and enchanting way. Whoever it was, they were pretty damn good.

Heleyna still felt that somehow the show was tame compared to what she was normally inclined towards. But it was a start, a sexy start to what was going to be a very interesting evening.

Phoebe came abruptly, her orgasm nearly knocking Heleyna sideways, her girlie ejaculation seeping onto Heleyna's tongue. The taste, the feel, the contractions were all it took to push Heleyna into her own little utopia. Her body bucked aggressively as her orgasm hit her, the cold cucumber grasped with each spasm, the woman between her legs teasing her until the last feelings of pleasure had completely subsided.

Two hours of drinking, eating, mingling and small-talk later, and Heleyna finally bumped into Troy. The music and general chitchat filling the room meant standing in close proximity to each other was paramount if conversation was ever going to take place.

'You, my dear, are a real performer. There were three of you in the room, but you were the one everyone was interested in. You should have heard the comments about "the new woman on the block". And to think you're *my* woman.' Troy put his arm round her shoulders and gave her a squeeze as he spoke.

Heleyna didn't respond to his comments. Although she was proud of the big step forwards she'd made that evening, she still felt a touch of embarrassment at the fact that her ex-boss's wife had given her a thrill and that she'd enjoyed every second of her delicious lips and tongue. It was an embarrassment numbed by the excellent and very moreish bubbly. She leaned into his neck and spoke directly into his ear. 'So then, handsome, more to the point, what have you been up to?'

'Me, mainly talking.' He glanced at the screens as he spoke. Two bleach-blondes were giving a man neither of them knew a time to remember in the 'Freedom' room: one on his cock, one planted firmly on his mouth.

She took in his handsome strong features and magnetic blue eyes as he looked at her with that fascinating and appealing concentration. Giving him a wry look, followed by a smile, she spoke. 'Come off it, I know your type – out with it.'

'Oh, OK then. Actually I've been giving a few of your soon to be ex-colleagues a bit of the pain treatment. That Roger from Marketing is a real little goer. And as for boring Bernard from accounts – well, he really is a man up for anything. Who would have thought, eh? Actually, I was talking to Jacinta just now and she said she'd like to see you in her parlour some time this evening. What do you reckon?'

By now Heleyna was well and truly drunk. It was a pleasant drunkenness where inhibitions go and joy is all around. 'Anything – sure, whatever. Where is J now, by the way? I'll go and find her and see what she expects!'

'You go, girl!' Troy patted her provocative, wiggling arse as she walked away to find the playful, surprising Jacinta.

Jacinta was already in her parlour. After five minutes of wandering, Heleyna looked up at the screens to see Jacinta dressed in thigh-length PVC boots and little else, a long black whip in her fine delicate hand. Much to

Heleyna's admiration, her long lean body didn't even utter a wobble as she walked: though tall and lean, she was muscular, obviously benefiting from her regular gym sessions. As Heleyna watched, Jacinta lifted her left foot and placed it on the lower back of yet another colleague who was positioned on all fours – Phil, the naughty IT man. She then proceeded to whip his skinny little bottom. Heleyna giggled to herself. However hard she looked she could not see his weeny pride and joy. She was surprised to see him there, though. Not one of the emails he'd given her mentioned his name – she would have to chastise him for that later.

Heleyna wandered into Jacinta's parlour and spoke to her as she continued her beating.

'Hi, J. Troy asked me to come and see you.'

'Having a good time, I hope, Heleyna?'

'Absolutely. Getting lots of ideas for rolling out Huxley to all and sundry, as well as, believe it or not, ideas for the more ordinary party!'

'Get up, Phil. I'm bored of you now.' Jacinta removed her foot from his back and kicked him.

Phil jumped up and scuttled out of the room, thanking her for her time as he went.

Jacinta spoke again. 'I was wondering if you fancied a bit of fun in here with me?'

'Like what exactly, you dark horse, you!' Heleyna eyed Jacinta's pert breasts and marvelled at how they could be so small yet so perfect.

'You'll just have to trust me, Heleyna. Trust me that it will be good, trust me that you will not regret leaving yourself in my very experienced hands.'

Heleyna's right hand gave a hasty flutter. 'OK, then – what have I got to lose?'

Jacinta switched into organisation mode. 'I'll just go grab Ted. Get your clothes off, girl!' Jacinta left the room as she spoke.

Ted and Jacinta returned within no time, just giving Heleyna the opportunity to strip down to her cream-silk panties.

Ted walked up behind her and grabbed her right butt cheek. 'Hmm, been wanting to do that for a long time. Magnificent arse, simply magnificent.' His hand disappeared temporarily between her legs. 'And as for that, I'll have a piece of that later.'

Heleyna didn't jump or scream or pull away from Ted. She let him touch her, let him stroke her, let him tease her.

Jacinta spoke. 'Right, Ted, we need this high bench between us. Bowl of condoms on the end of the bench. Then you need to shackle us together at the wrists. That way we can bend over, facing each other, and our bottoms will be perked up in the air. What do you reckon?'

'Sounds fantastic to me, my gorgeous hussy.' He moved the bench into position. 'Right then, you two stunning wenches! Get into position.'

Jacinta and Heleyna faced each other and bent over, their hands touching and faces only a small distance apart. Ted grabbed their wrists harshly and tied them firmly with thin, strong rope.

'Just to make sure you can't get away, I'm tying you two to the bench as well.' Ted pulled the rope round the base of the bench and the two women were firmly locked in position.

Heleyna marvelled at what was happening: at how easy it all was; at what exactly was going to happen to her next; at the amazing view of two stunning women bent over – hot, poised and ready for action, their heads lower than their high-as-the-sky arses, both of them naked apart from their incredibly high heels.

Jacinta gave the game away. 'Right then, big boy, let in the masses.' She gave Heleyna one of her now-infamous winks and mouthed the words 'enjoy, sweetie' before leaning forwards and giving Heleyna one of the tastiest snogs she'd had in a long time.

Their kiss was endless. As Heleyna enjoyed the tenderness of this woman against her, she heard footsteps entering the room, their sound muffled against the thick pile carpet, and her body began its journey down the exhilarating path of sexual anticipation. As she disappeared into one of her favourite utopian places, her legs were grasped, roughly, and pulled apart, and the tip of a prick nudged its way into her, filling her, tormenting her.

Their kiss came to an abrupt end as both women cried out in ecstasy. Between her groans, Heleyna turned to see who was behind her. The queue of people went out of the door, and for how long she didn't know. A real mixture of people, she noticed, and amongst them women with strap-ons already in place. Sam was third in line. Damn, she thought, now it isn't going to be on my terms, damn, damn, damn.

Every one of them was naked; every one of them wanted a part of either her or Jacinta. She twisted her neck further to find her first suitor – the sturdy Ted had helped himself to her. His rugby-player physique was appealing, very appealing.

'Enjoying yourself now, Heleyna? Am I as you imagined way back when you watched me, when you took pleasure in your own boss?' Ted's words were breathless, and a sheen of sweat appeared on his brow.

'Oh yes, Ted, I am. Please fuck me harder.'

'Watch Troy inside my wife, darling, then I'll fuck you harder.'

Up until that moment Heleyna had not taken notice of Jacinta's pleasurer. She turned her head from the sight of Ted and inhaled the scene of her very own strong bronzed brunette giving Jacinta a damn good ramming. Heleyna's squeal of delight gave Ted the signal he needed and he began his vicious pumping, his lower stomach battering her arse with each thrust, his balls in sync against her cunt. With her gaze firmly on her luxurious man, Heleyna felt the head of another person close to her face. The head spoke. It was Sam.

'On your terms, eh? In your dreams. You are the dirtiest little whore I've ever met and I'm going to give you a damn good fucking – the first of many more to come.' His voice was deep, low and hoarse, his stubble harsh against her smooth cheek. He laughed as he returned to his rightful place in the queue.

Ted came, violently. Jacinta cried out at her husband in ecstasy. Heleyna remained in her enforced position, hot, horny and ready for more – much more.

The woman she'd expected next, who was ready for Heleyna with strap-on in place, was not the next person she discovered inside her. The size of this very real-feeling prick and the thick, arrogant Yorkshire accent, which ordered her to remain still, meant it had to be Sam. She savoured every bit of him as he entered her and filled her to bursting. She was desperate to turn and feel every inch of his flesh, to have his hot, power-ful frame surround her as she'd imagined and day-dreamed about on more than one occasion. Next time, next time.

'You, get down on the floor between her legs.' Sam was authoritative in tone.

Heleyna didn't care what or who he was ordering. Her hungry pussy invariably made her obedient. Her eyes were closed now that Troy had relished Jacinta, leaving the scrawny Phil in his place. Small hands, which had to be a woman's, grasped her thighs and pulled apart her lips to reveal her rigid moist clit, and a delicate tongue began working its way over her as Sam fucked, using a slow strong rhythm that allowed her to savour every inch of his glorious dick. She was about to sample the second of many orgasms she would be blessed with that evening. She was glad to be a woman, with the power to enjoy so much fun so many times over.

The bench wobbled. Someone was mounting it. She opened her eyes to find Roger knelt close to them both. He was more than ready for action, and he eagerly thrust himself between them, grasped their heads and pushed them onto his dick – one on each side, their tongues unintentionally touching as they slid over, round and along the length of his rigidity.

Heleyna nearly bit him, the strength of her orgasm causing her jaw to clamp, and a loud, long groan left her wet lips. Sam hadn't finished yet – he was luxuriating in the sensation of her orgasm – and the woman lost between her legs seemed happy to remain there. She was already relishing the thought of a more intimate encounter with Mr Sex-on-Legs Molloy.

Heleyna and Jacinta kept their position for nearly two hours as the masses pleasured themselves, and, by default, gave both women a night to remember. Heleyna discovered the woman between her legs to be Phoebe. Phoebe remained there for the whole two hours, ensuring Heleyna came as often as her body would allow. For the second time in her life, Heleyna was delighted to be in the presence of Phoebe.

Both women had never been fucked, in succession, so many times in their lives before, nor had so many men shoved their cocks in their faces to be given the same treatment Roger had requested. They were both sore, they were both in paradise and neither wanted it to end.

Heleyna realised more than ever that evening how successful their business was going to be. The number of very respectable and successful people she'd seen who savoured all sorts of shenanigans once they walked out of the office door rubber-stamped their plans. If this was an informal club which had grown by default, she imagined what could take off if careful planning and good marketing came into play. They were onto a winner. She felt unbelievably lucky – she had the brains and the brawn to make this work, and she knew it.

16

Three months had passed since the orgiastic spree that had left Heleyna sore for a week, a throbbing that delighted her every time she thought about it. Dressed in a tight-tailored black suit and high strappy heels, she was sitting at her new desk in their new office with its sleek lines and sophisticated decor, looking out over the recently upgraded Leeds canal.

Her phone rang. 'Huxley. Heleyna Lane speaking. Yes, Madam, it's all booked in for seventy-five guests. Yes, fifty pounds per head. I know. As you say, it's worth every single penny. Glad you enjoyed the last one. How was Jacinta? Excellent. See you, then. Cheers.'

Ted looked up from his desk at the opposite end of the window. He was avidly putting together a proposal for running corporate functions for a director he played golf with, a proposal he already knew they were going to win thanks to a round of golf the day before. He spoke. 'Another satisfied customer?'

'Yup, second party for them in three months, too. We've almost got more business than we can handle already. Can you believe it? We've surpassed even our most optimistic forecasts. We'll pay that bank manager back in no time. Bloody marvellous.' Heleyna had never felt so content in her life.

Her phone rang again and Ted returned to his keyboard.

'Hi, Heleyna, Mands here. Hope your day's going well. By the way, I've booked us both in to that alpine instruction course in the French Alps this August. Looks great, but very scary – ice climbing, snow caving, cramponing. I don't even know what half these things are, but, bloody hell, we're going to have some fun.'

Heleyna still couldn't believe what she was letting herself in for. 'I can't fucking wait. It's almost as exciting as Linton was.'

'Heleyna!' Mandy nearly blew her eardrum away with her exclamation of shock.

'I know, I know. I'll never change. By the way, I'm taking my painting stuff with me too – hope to capture some of the beauty down there. I've got to pull together a portfolio for this fine-art degree I'm applying for. Did I tell you about that?'

'No. Come on, tell me all.' Mandy was sincere in her interest.

'I'm hoping to do it part time over the next six years or so at Bradford College of Art – take a bit of time out of here two afternoons and evenings a week. It's going to be a challenge with everything else, but who cares. I love it!'

'Bloody brilliant. Wow, you're a changed woman. Guess what?' Mandy's voice had lifted a tone and Heleyna sensed excitement in her voice.

'Come on, out with it.' Heleyna was keen to hear her news.

'I spoke to my darling hubby about Huxley and he agreed to come along.'

'Fucking brilliant, Mands. Your names are being added to the list as we speak.' Heleyna motioned to Ted who promptly added their names to the ever-growing register of people attending the next function at their home.

'Excellent. I still can't believe we're coming. We'll have to meet for lunch soon and you can give me all the details for a second time. I need a prep talk!'

They arranged to meet the next day for a bite to eat

at a local bistro, and, when Heleyna hung up, Ted looked up at her again.

He looked pensive and serious as he spoke. 'We really made the right decision, Heleyna, leaving SPM. We had it good there, but now we've got it sussed. We've both got the kind of lives that suit us down to the ground. Look at us, we're made for running our own business.'

Heleyna looked at her watch and began packing up her laptop. 'If things carry on like this, we're going to be so unbelievably rich. Thanks Ted, thanks for agreeing to do this. Without you none of this could have happened.' She put her palmtop and mobile into her briefcase.

'And without you perving at me all that time ago, none of this would have happened!' Ted laughed one of his loud deep belly laughs. 'In your case it's more a case of "curiosity made the cat"! You leaving early for once?'

'Yup. Got to get home by six tonight. The powers that be have ordered me to be in for a romantic meal.' Heleyna started to make her way out of the door.

'Talking about meals, you guys will have to come over to ours again. Perhaps next week? We could have some fun on our own, without the masses.' Ted gave her a 'Jacinta' wink.

'You know what, Ted, that sounds bloody great. Let me know when, and we'll be there. Must dash. Oh, got my phone diverted to my mobile so you won't be disturbed. See you tomorrow.'

'See you then, my naughty, but decidedly nice, business partner.'

Heleyna walked quickly to their private parking spaces beneath the office block. She was looking forward to having a night in. She jumped in her Beetle, an action she took more gingerly these days owing to the tightness of her little suit skirts, and switched on the CD player. Her favourite clarinet concerto filled her car.

She sat back, relaxed and began the rush-hour journey out to Alwoodley.

She pulled up outside Troy's and parked on the kerbside, the passenger-side wheels up on the pavement. There was never any room for her on the driveway with the number of vehicles they had between them. This was her house too; her own flat was now rented out to a single professional woman called Kate. Heleyna had agreed to Troy's continuous requests and moved in just over two months ago, but had only had time to move the week before. Her new business had been priority number one. This was to be their first meal at home together – their first cosy, homely meal.

The smell of cooking hit her as she opened the front door. Has to be a good old-fashioned roast dinner, she thought, one of my favourites. Troy came out to greet her from the kitchen, his stripy apron in place, a tea towel over his arm. He was carrying a glass of what could only have been the deep rich golden colour of a quality Chardonnay.

'Get this down you. Put your feet up and relax. Dinner will be served in approximately one hour.' He leaned over and kissed her on the neck before squeezing her bottom playfully.

'You're wonderful, do you know that?' Heleyna replied, reciprocating his squeeze with one of her own.

Troy returned to the kitchen and Heleyna found herself a spot on the sofa. Removing her shoes, she curled up, switched on the TV and grabbed a crap magazine from the wrought-iron rack.

There was a call from the kitchen. 'Give me a shout when you want a top-up with the wine.'

Heleyna grinned to herself and took a large swig. She loved that accent, that broad Yorkshire twang. She was the luckiest woman alive, there was no doubt about it. There she was, sat like Lady Muck, whilst her two favourite men in the world waited on her hand and foot. It was her little Alwoodley harem of pure testosterone, a newly formed unconventional family she could call her own. She was already beginning to look forward to the after-dinner games more than the meal itself. It looked like her Sexual Strategy had worked all right!

LOOK OUT FOR THE ALL-NEW BLACK LACE BOOKS – AVAILABLE NOW!

All books priced £6.99 in the UK. Please note publication dates apply to the UK only. For other territories, please contact your retailer.

ARTISTIC LICENCE
Vivienne La Fay
ISBN 0 352 33210 7

In Renaissance Italy, Carla is determined to find a new life for herself where she can put her artistic talents to good use. Dressed as boy – albeit a very pretty one – she travels to Florence and finds work as an apprentice to a master craftsman. All goes well until she is expected to perform licentious favours for her employer. In an atmosphere of repressed passion, it is only a matter of time before her secret is revealed. **Historical, gender-bending fun in this delightful romp.**

Coming in October

SOMETHING ABOUT WORKMEN
Alison Tyler
ISBN 0 352 33847 4

Cat Harrington works in script development at a large Hollywood studio. She and her engineer boyfriend enjoy glittering parties, film screenings and international travel. But Cat leads a double life that would shock her friends and her beau: she engages in a rough and ready sex with the head of a road crew, who knows how hard and dirty Cat likes her loving. What begins as a raucous fling turns far more complicated when Cat's boyfriend is put in charge of her lover and they begin to run into each other in the workplace. **Explores the appeal of hot and horny blue-collar guys!**

PALAZZO
Jan Smith
ISBN O 352 33156 9

When Claire and Cherry take a vacation in Venice they both succumb to the seductive charms of the city and the men who inhabit it. In the famous Harry's Bar, Claire meets a half-Italian, half-Scottish art dealer who introduces her to new facets of life, both cultural and sexual. Torn between the mysterious Stuart and her estranged husband Claire is faced with an impossible dilemma while Cherry is learning all about sexual indulgence. **Sophisticated and sexy.**

Coming in November

HARD BLUE MIDNIGHT
Alaine Hood
ISBN O 352 33851 2

Lori owns an antique clothes shop in a seaside town in New England, devoting all her energies to the business at the expense of her sex life. When she meets handsome Gavin MacLellan, a transformation begins. Gavin is writing a book about Lori's great-aunt, an erotic photographer who disappeared during World War II. Lori gets so wrapped up in solving the mystery that she accompanies Gavin to Paris to trace her ancestor's past. A growing fascination with bondage and discipline leads her into a world of secrecy and danger.

THE NAME OF AN ANGEL
Laura Thornton

ISBN 0 352 33205 0

Clarissa Cornwall is a respectable university lecturer who has little time for romance until she encounters the insolently sexy Nicholas St Clair in her class on erotic literature. Suddenly her position – and the age gap between them – no longer matters as she finds herself becoming obsessed with this provocative young man. She tries to fight her desire but soon finds herself involved in a secret affair with this dangerously charismatic student.

Black Lace Booklist

Information is correct at time of printing. To avoid disappointment check availability before ordering. Go to www.blacklace-books.co.uk. All books are priced £6.99 unless another price is given.

BLACK LACE BOOKS WITH A CONTEMPORARY SETTING

☐ IN THE FLESH Emma Holly	ISBN O 352 33498 3 £5.99
☐ SHAMELESS Stella Black	ISBN O 352 33485 1 £5.99
☐ INTENSE BLUE Lyn Wood	ISBN O 352 33496 7 £5.99
☐ THE NAKED TRUTH Natasha Rostova	ISBN O 352 33497 5 £5.99
☐ A SPORTING CHANCE Susie Raymond	ISBN O 352 33501 7 £5.99
☐ TAKING LIBERTIES Susie Raymond	ISBN O 352 33357 X £5.99
☐ A SCANDALOUS AFFAIR Holly Graham	ISBN O 352 33523 8 £5.99
☐ THE NAKED FLAME Crystalle Valentino	ISBN O 352 33528 9 £5.99
☐ ON THE EDGE Laura Hamilton	ISBN O 352 33534 3 £5.99
☐ LURED BY LUST Tania Picarda	ISBN O 352 33533 5 £5.99
☐ THE HOTTEST PLACE Tabitha Flyte	ISBN O 352 33536 X £5.99
☐ THE NINETY DAYS OF GENEVIEVE Lucinda Carrington	ISBN O 352 33070 8 £5.99
☐ DREAMING SPIRES Juliet Hastings	ISBN O 352 33584 X
☐ THE TRANSFORMATION Natasha Rostova	ISBN O 352 33311 1
☐ SIN.NET Helena Ravenscroft	ISBN O 352 33598 X
☐ TWO WEEKS IN TANGIER Annabel Lee	ISBN O 352 33599 8
☐ HIGHLAND FLING Jane Justine	ISBN O 352 33616 1
☐ PLAYING HARD Tina Troy	ISBN O 352 33617 X
☐ SYMPHONY X Jasmine Stone	ISBN O 352 33629 3
☐ SUMMER FEVER Anna Ricci	ISBN O 352 33625 0
☐ CONTINUUM Portia Da Costa	ISBN O 352 33120 8
☐ OPENING ACTS Suki Cunningham	ISBN O 352 33630 7
☐ FULL STEAM AHEAD Tabitha Flyte	ISBN O 352 33637 4
☐ A SECRET PLACE Ella Broussard	ISBN O 352 33307 3
☐ GAME FOR ANYTHING Lyn Wood	ISBN O 352 33639 0
☐ FORBIDDEN FRUIT Susie Raymond	ISBN O 352 33306 5
☐ CHEAP TRICK Astrid Fox	ISBN O 352 33640 4

To find out the latest information about Black Lace titles, check out the website: www.blacklace-books.co.uk or send for a booklist with complete synopses by writing to:

Black Lace Booklist, Virgin Books Ltd
Thames Wharf Studios
Rainville Road
London W6 9HA

Please include an SAE of decent size. Please note only British stamps are valid.

Our privacy policy
We will not disclose information you supply us to any other parties. We will not disclose any information which identifies you personally to any person without your express consent.

From time to time we may send out information about Black Lace books and special offers. Please tick here if you do not wish to receive Black Lace information. ❏

Please send me the books I have ticked above.

Name ....

Address ....

....

....

....

Post Code ....

Send to: Cash Sales, Black Lace Books, Thames Wharf Studios, Rainville Road, London W6 9HA.

US customers: for prices and details of how to order books for delivery by mail, call 1-800-343-4499.

Please enclose a cheque or postal order, made payable to Virgin Books Ltd, to the value of the books you have ordered plus postage and packing costs as follows:

UK and BFPO – £1.00 for the first book, 50p for each subsequent book.

Overseas (including Republic of Ireland) – £2.00 for the first book, £1.00 for each subsequent book.

If you would prefer to pay by VISA, ACCESS/MASTERCARD, DINERS CLUB, AMEX or SWITCH, please write your card number and expiry date here:

....

Signature ....

Please allow up to 28 days for delivery.